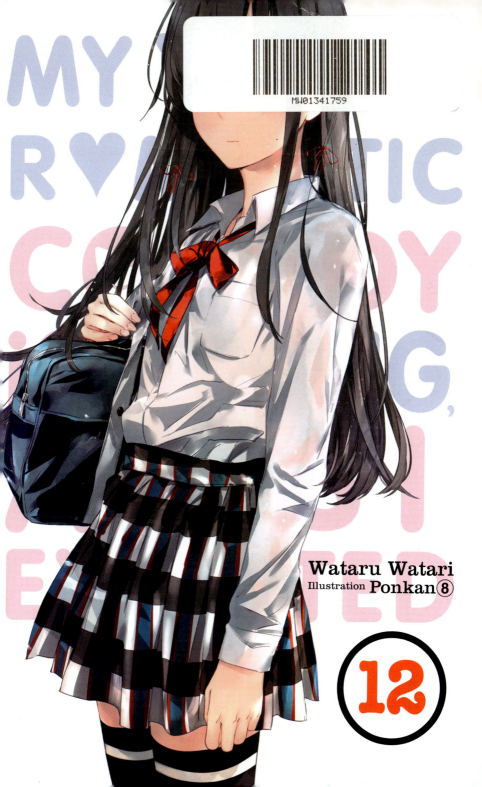

# Contents

**Interlude** — 003

**1** Eventually, **the seasons** change, and the **snow** melts away. — 005

**2** Despite appearances, **Haruno Yukinoshita** is not drunk. — 033

**Interlude** — 059

**3** **Komachi Hikigaya** takes him by surprise and gets formal. — 063

**4** Until today, he has never once touched that **key**. — 095

**5** Unsurprisingly, **Iroha Isshiki** is the most powerful of underclassmen. — 135

**6** ~~Yui Yuigahama's thoughts happen to turn to the future.~~ — ~~195~~

**7** Even knowing that he will regret the **decision**… — 231

**Interlude** — 239

Translation Notes — 241

Soubu High School Prom ★ The filming of the promotional dance video

Hachiman Hikigaya

Yui Yuigahama

# MY YOUTH R♥MANTIC C☻MEDY iS WR∅NG, AS I EXPECTED

Wataru Watari
Illustration Ponkan⑧

VOLUME 12

NEW YORK

**MY YOUTH ROMANTIC COMEDY IS WRONG, AS I EXPECTED** Vol. 12
WATARU WATARI
Illustration by Ponkan⑧

Translation by Jennifer Ward
Cover art by Ponkan⑧

This book is a work of fiction. Names, characters, places, and incidents are the product of the author's imagination or are used fictitiously. Any resemblance to actual events, locales, or persons, living or dead, is coincidental.

YAHARI ORE NO SEISHUN LOVE COME WA MACHIGATTEIRU.
Vol. 12 by Wataru WATARI
© 2011 Wataru WATARI
Illustration by PONKAN⑧
All rights reserved.
Original Japanese edition published by SHOGAKUKAN.
English translation rights in the United States of America, Canada, the United Kingdom, Ireland, Australia and New Zealand arranged with SHOGAKUKAN through Tuttle-Mori Agency, Inc.

English translation © 2021 by Yen Press, LLC

Yen Press, LLC supports the right to free expression and the value of copyright. The purpose of copyright is to encourage writers and artists to produce the creative works that enrich our culture.

The scanning, uploading, and distribution of this book without permission is a theft of the author's intellectual property. If you would like permission to use material from the book (other than for review purposes), please contact the publisher. Thank you for your support of the author's rights.

Yen On
150 West 30th Street, 19th Floor
New York, NY 10001

Visit us at yenpress.com
facebook.com/yenpress
twitter.com/yenpress
yenpress.tumblr.com
instagram.com/yenpress

First Yen On Edition: September 2021

Yen On is an imprint of Yen Press, LLC.
The Yen On name and logo are trademarks of Yen Press, LLC.

The publisher is not responsible for websites (or their content) that are not owned by the publisher.

Library of Congress Cataloging-in-Publication Data
Names: Watari, Wataru, author. | Ponkan 8, illustrator.
Title: My youth romantic comedy is wrong, as I expected / Wataru Watari ; illustration by Ponkan 8.
Other titles: Yahari ore no seishun love come wa machigatteiru. English
Description: New York : Yen On, 2016–
Identifiers: LCCN 2016005816 | ISBN 9780316312295 (v. 1 : pbk.) | ISBN 9780316396011 (v. 2 : pbk.) | ISBN 9780316318068 (v. 3 : pbk.) | ISBN 9780316318075 (v. 4 : pbk.) | ISBN 9780316318082 (v. 5 : pbk.) | ISBN 9780316411868 (v. 6 : pbk.) | ISBN 9781975384166 (v. 6.5 : pbk.) | ISBN 9781975384128 (v. 7 : pbk.) | ISBN 9781975384159 (v. 7.5 : pbk.) | ISBN 9781975384135 (v. 8 : pbk.) | ISBN 9781975384142 (v. 9 : pbk.) | ISBN 9781975384111 (v. 10 : pbk.) | ISBN 9781975384173 (v. 10.5 : pbk.) | ISBN 9781975324988 (v. 11 : pbk.) | ISBN 9781975324995 (v. 12 : pbk.)
Subjects: | CYAC: Optimism—Fiction. | School—Fiction.
Classification: LCC PZ7.1.W396 My 2016 | DDC [Fic]—dc23
LC record available at http://lccn.loc.gov/2016005816

ISBNs: 978-1-9753-2499-5 (paperback)
       978-1-9753-3364-5 (ebook)

10 9 8 7 6 5 4 3 2 1

LSC-C

Printed in the United States of America

# Cast of Characters

**Hachiman Hikigaya** ............ The main character. High school second-year. Twisted personality.

**Yukino Yukinoshita** ........... Captain of the Service Club. Perfectionist.

**Yui Yuigahama** .................. Hachiman's classmate. Tends to worry about what other people think.

**Saika Totsuka** .................... In tennis club. Very cute. A boy, though.

**Saki Kawasaki** ................... Hachiman's classmate. Sort of a delinquent type.

**Hayato Hayama** .................. Hachiman's classmate. Popular. In the soccer club.

**Kakeru Tobe** ...................... Hachiman's classmate. An excitable character and member of Hayama's clique.

**Yumiko Miura** .................... Hachiman's classmate. Reigns over the girls in class as queen bee.

**Hina Ebina** ......................... Hachiman's classmate. Part of Miura's clique, but a slash fangirl.

**Iroha Isshiki** ...................... Manager of the soccer club. First-year student who was elected student council president.

**Shizuka Hiratsuka** ............. Japanese teacher. Guidance counselor.

**Haruno Yukinoshita** .......... Yukino's older sister. In university.

**Komachi Hikigaya** ............. Hachiman's little sister. In her third year in middle school.

**Taishi Kawasaki** ................ Saki Kawasaki's little brother. In his third year in middle school.

# Interlude...

The silence was long.

Our feelings couldn't keep up with our passionate arguments, and our would-be logic was now nowhere to be found.

And words have to have a meaning behind them; otherwise, you might as well have said nothing at all.

Therefore, that time could technically be called a silence.

Before, the setting sun peeking out from between the clouds had painted the ocean crimson, but now its color had turned deep blue.

The snowflakes drifted down, disappearing into the long shadows stretching over the ground.

When the streetlamps eventually came on, it made those shadows spread in every direction, then gradually fade away until their original shapes could no longer be distinguished.

It seemed as if it would be a long talk.

One of us had said that. Perhaps it was me.

Though the conversation had come to an end at that point, the meaning of what came after was communicated without words. And none of us opposed it, the curtains drawn with a smile and a nod.

The truth is, I wanted to grit my teeth and say, *You're running away now?*

I wanted to say it to myself. I was the most relieved of all.

Even if we had had this brief time, that would not strengthen my faint hopes.

I just knew a clear answer would announce the end of a short-lived phenomenon. Which was why I should give voice to that answer.

I had to say it, or they wouldn't know. Even if I did, they still might not understand.

Which was why I should give it voice.

Even if I knew I would regret that choice.

—Because the truth is…

I don't want something real if it's just cold, cruel, and sad.

# 1

Eventually, **the seasons** change, and the **snow** melts away.

I'm used to the cold.

I've never lived far from this city, and it's been like this since I was a kid. Chiba winters were just like this, I'd assumed. I've never hated it, even though I've been irritated by the dryness, the wind that stabs at your cheeks, and the cold air that comes up from the ground to crawl along your back.

I'm used to it, actually. I'd just taken for granted that this was how things were.

At the end of the day, hot and cold just come down to a difference in degree—an issue of whether you've experienced a situation dramatically different from the current standard. In other words, if you've never known other winters, you won't have any basis of comparison.

So maybe you could say I'm unused to warmth because I have nothing to contrast it with.

Imagine different types of heat, like white breath blown to warm frozen fingers.

Or the sound of a scarf, tugged by gloves, sliding against a coat.

And knees sitting in a line on a bench, touching at odd moments.

The heat that was clearly there, in the people sitting beside me.

Contact with those sources of heat triggered an undefinable anxiety that made me squirm. I used the movement to inch a fist's worth of distance away from Yukinoshita and Yuigahama, who were sitting next to me.

The three of us were the only ones there that night in the park not far from the ocean. When I happened to look up, I could see the two towers of the high-rise apartment where Yukinoshita lived.

The seaside park area was a short walk from the commercial district around the station, and crossing the main road took you to a silent and deserted neighborhood of apartment buildings. Even here, the wind wasn't that chilly thanks to the trees—they were probably planted both for the scenery and to prevent erosion.

But I still felt a strong wintery vibe, probably because we were the only ones around, and there was a thin layer of snow on the ground.

Today was February 14, and midnight hadn't yet changed the date.

It was the day the world called Valentine's Day, or Dried Sardine Day, and it was also the day when my little sister Komachi was taking the entrance exams for the high school I go to.

It was also the day we'd gone to the aquarium.

Light snow had been falling from the afternoon through the evening. It didn't stick much on the ground, but there were still thin traces of it lying on the green and atop the hedges.

They say snow absorbs sound.

You wouldn't think such a small amount of snow would absorb anything, but it was a fact that none of us were talking, just listening to each other breathing as we gazed into the quiet night.

The sparse coating of snow reflected the moonlight and the glow of the streetlamps; there was more light than there should have been at this hour. If the bulbs had been the old-fashioned, pale fluorescent ones, it would have looked colder. But the light reflected on the snow had an orangish tinge that seemed a bit warm, even.

Still, if you touched it, it would vanish like dew. That warm glow seemed false, twinkling in the setting sun as it told us that the snow that had fallen over the ocean had been no illusion.

The snow had indeed fallen; the day we'd spent had clearly

happened. The proof of it was just a slight difference in temperature and time, and we knew that it could easily vanish. Touch it in jest, and it would melt away; sweep it aside for fun, and it would scatter into nothing. But even if you pretended you didn't see it at all, it would eventually disappear. Unless the cold stuck around forever—but that was a pointless thing to think.

I shook my head a little, disguising it with a shiver. The chances of an eternal winter had already been demonstrated with the snowmen I'd made when I was little.

In the same motion, I rose from the bench. In my field of vision was a red-and-blue vending machine right at the edge of the park. Before heading over, I turned to the other two. "…Want something to drink?" I asked.

They exchanged a momentary glance before immediately responding with little head shakes. I answered with a quick dip of my chin.

Walking to the vending machine, I pulled some change out of my wallet.

I chose my usual canned coffee. Then while I was at it, two black teas in plastic bottles, too. I squatted down and slid them into my coat pockets.

I touched the can last. The metal was obviously hot, but I felt a mysterious chill. If I kept holding on to it, it would burn me. I tossed it in the air casually a few times as I considered why it felt cold. By the time my icy hand got used to the temperature of the can, that confusion in my mind had melted away.

The temperature perceived on your skin is meaningless, nothing more than a number. You have to assign it meaning.

I knew a more significant warmth. Words hadn't told me the difference between a high temperature and warmth. I learned it from my experience. Although this was something I'd only just figured out, so it's not like I could brag about that.

The thirty-six degrees from touching that knee through cloth for just an instant was far hotter than the warmth you could buy with just a hundred yen.

As I strolled back to the bench where I'd been sitting before, I reflected upon not the heat in my hand, but the heat I'd touched then that still remained in my heart. I took my time, knowing deep down that I wouldn't feel that again, but I didn't ever stop, either.

No one was going to sit in the space I'd left when I'd gotten up, not now. And now that I'd noticed that heat, that had only become more true.

Even now, I still don't know what the right distance is.

*So it's okay to come this far; I'm allowed to take just one more step in*, I thought as I slowly walked onward.

Just like this whole past year.

I'd been fumbling along, constantly evaluating and reevaluating how many steps it was okay to take as we tried to meet each other halfway.

Back when I knew nothing, I'd barged forward without inhibition. Once I'd realized a thing or two, I was more timid. But when I realized I didn't understand anything, my legs couldn't take even a single step more.

*Just one more. Half a step, at least.*

When my thoughts reached that point, I came to a stop.

The streetlamp illuminated the bench like a spotlight. The shadows of the pair sitting there stretched in many directions, each one faint and kind of hazy.

While vacantly gazing at the sight, I offered them the plastic bottles from my pockets without a word. They seemed a bit bewildered as they thanked me, but they both reached for the drinks. I made sure our fingers wouldn't touch as I handed them over, then shoved my hands into my empty pockets.

As I did, I heard the rustle of a cellophane bag and felt something smooth against my fingers. I took a low-key peek in there to see whether the cookies I'd received were still inside. The number of those cookies wasn't going to shrink or grow. Patting my pocket wouldn't get me any more.

You don't get more happiness that easily. Somebody said that—Peter or Cheater or Carrousel or whoever.

What sucks is that they'll actually decrease or vanish, just like that.

I pulled the bag out slightly to make sure the cookies weren't broken or crumbling, but the pink paper had cushioned them well enough. Relieved, I was about to slide it back into my pocket when I heard a soft sigh.

Yukinoshita's gaze was focused on the cookies. "…That's very pretty," she murmured, watching them with something almost like yearning.

Yuigahama seemed momentarily surprised to hear her break the silence, but she immediately leaned forward with enthusiasm. "Oh, yeah! I really shopped around for that stuff, like the bag and the *maste*!"

"What? *Maste*? Is that an Indian greeting?" I said.

"That's *namaste*. She means *masking tape*," Yukinoshita said with exasperation, putting a hand to her temple. "What a pointless fact for you to know. You hardly ever have to greet anyone."

"Don't be stupid—even just saying hello makes it feel like you're having a conversation, right? Canned greetings are vital knowledge," I said.

Yukinoshita made a face, looking weary. "In your mind, greetings count as conversation, hmm…?"

"Yeah, so I avoid greeting anyone as much as possible, too."

"That's going pretty far to avoid talking to someone, Hikki!"

*Well, that's because I'm a Hikki, so there's nothing you can do about that. The power of a name, am I right? Man, I've really gotten used to Yuigahama's nickname, huh…?* Way back when, I used to go like, *I don't know anyone by such an embarrassing name…*, and deny it quietly as I cutely blushed and looked away. Wait, I don't remember ever doing that. I accepted my fate pretty much immediately, huh?!

*Maste… That's short for* masking tape, *then? Chii is learning. I don't really know what it's used for. Goodness, Miss Yukinoshita is ever so informed about youth culture nowadays…* With that thought, I glanced at her.

Yukinoshita seemed to sense what that look meant, a smile cracking on her face. "Masking tape was originally used for painting, but lately there are many elaborately decorated sorts."

"Yeah, yeah! The cute ones are in right now, and there's so many kinds! You can use 'em for decorating wrapping and notebooks and stuff…" As Yuigahama launched into an enthusiastic explanation, I looked at the wrapping again. It really had been fancied up, with a border and other details.

The ribbon wasn't too big and was made with golden thread, and the tape was patterned with puppy prints. The decorations were cute and pretty.

The sudden attention must have made Yuigahama anxious, as she started to fidget, gaze shifting this way and that. "I… I can't make any promises about the flavor. But…I did my best." At the end, she looked straight at me, speaking with clear intention.

I could never make fun of such an earnest gaze, and I gently stroked the bag of cookies in my hands. "…Yeah, I can really tell."

I really did think she'd done a good job. I hadn't eaten them yet, so I didn't know how they tasted, but this girl who was a bad cook had given her all. She'd put her heart into the gift for the sake of its recipient.

So I made an effort to reply to her as sincerely as possible, no more, no less. The price for honesty was a total lack of wit, but it seemed like she got what I was trying to say anyway.

"Right? I mean, you're the one who said that. You know, about a girl trying hard," Yuigahama said, wagging her finger and puffing out her chest with a smug chuckle.

"…You remembered?" I was a little surprised. She had an unexpectedly good memory… Well, in that case, so did I.

I hadn't been lying or anything when I'd said what I had, and I still sincerely believed it. Hearing her repeat that now would obviously be kinda embarrassing. Yep, it's me, the guy who often remembers things I said a long time ago that make me want to die.

But it seemed I wasn't the only one who was embarrassed.

"W-well, of course. I remember it. I mean, like, I couldn't forget, y'know… I was a little surprised, after all…" With an *ah-ha-ha*, Yuigahama gave a tiny shy smile as she twisted around in a fluster.

*Now that she's said that, I can't stay calm, either, though!* It made even me start awkwardly laughing…in an attempt to hide it.

When our eyes met, she jerked her gaze away. "…W-well, Hikki, you've always been kinda like that. But I'm used to it now!" she added jokingly at the end.

That brought a smile to Yukinoshita's face. "Yes, you're always so… nonstandard."

"Yeah, yeah." Yuigahama nodded in agreement.

*Hmm, I'd appreciate it if you held back your opinions for a moment…*, I thought, flicking a look of objection at Yukinoshita. "Um, I don't think that's just me, though? You are, too, aren't you, Miss Yukinonstandard?"

"What is that even supposed to mean…?" Eyebrows twitching downward, Miss Yukinonstandard glared at me out of the corner of her eye.

Yuigahama's eyebrows, on the other hand, were tilting in the opposite direction as if she were at a loss, until she finally said, "Ohhh…like with the animal therapy thing…"

"Yeah, yeah, like with that, I guess. Though I dunno if you'd call that nonstandard or just unexpected." I nodded in agreement. We hadn't been that close back then, so I hadn't really been able to challenge that—but looking back at it now, I was kinda like, *Where the heck did that idea come from…?*

Yuigahama must have felt the same, *hmm-hmm*ing pensively. "Hmm…I dunno, I thought that was a smart idea, but…"

*Whoa there, that's a contrastive conjunction.* Once you've said *but…*, then all that can follow is a refutation of that statement… She probably just wanted to play with a cat, huh…?

But it would be kinder not to say as much. If I pressed too hard,

I'd get a long-winded, rapid-fire counterargument. So I tucked that thought away in my breast.

It seemed, however, that Yuigahama couldn't do the same. Not much room in there for it, huh?

"W-well, but! You can be a bit airheaded sometimes, Yukinon!" Yuigahama sort of flung herself into that remark, probably with the intention of disguising her hesitation.

Yukinoshita shot her a cold glare. "Isn't that you?"

"N-no! Like that time we played Millionaire, you know, I was actually considering things…," Yuigahama argued, as if she'd just remembered the event, before trailing off with a groan.

I pulled up my hazy memories as well, thinking back to how that shady game against the UG Club had concluded. "I feel like you were just lucky, though…"

"Wh-whatever, luck is a part of talent, too! That day, um, it was my birthday, so of course I'd be lucky, and good stuff did actually happen, so I was happy…" Yuigahama rushed into her words at first, but as she approached the end of the sentence, her head sank down, and her voice got quieter and quieter.

*I'd really like it if you could stop muttering to yourself so I can kind of hear you. Remembering that gift even has me sort of embarrassed now!* I wound up looking down, too.

Then Yukinoshita murmured quietly, "Does luck have anything to do with birthdays…?" She tilted her head with a serious expression.

"Wh-whatever! It does! We won, so whatever! Geez!" Yuigahama said in a sulky tone.

Watching them, I couldn't help but grin. Yuigahama was right. Regardless of how we'd gotten there, the result was that we'd won the game. So it was fine. I'm sure that positivity of hers has always been a saving grace—for me and for Yukinoshita.

Yukinoshita must have understood that as well, as her face softened a bit. Then she swept the hair off her shoulders as she nodded with satisfaction. "…Well, that's true. It was good we won."

"There it is. You always hate to lose..." I could feel my smile going a bit crooked.

Yukinoshita shot me a dull look. "And you love to lose, don't you?"

"It's not like I enjoy it, you know... I do in fact intend to win every time, more or less," I said, but neither of them was listening.

Yuigahama voiced an *ahhh* of understanding. "Like when you were in that tennis game and the judo tournament and stuff, huh...?"

"...I suppose you would call that sort of thing a waste of effort." Yukinoshita let out a sigh that may have been either exasperated or exhausted.

I was a little indignant about that comment, too, and I had to correct her on this. "Hey, I made sure not to go through any real physical effort. The only great pains during that judo tournament were in my back," I said smugly.

Yukinoshita rubbed her temple. "I should have expected as much. If anyone's wasting their effort, it's me. And did you make sure to go to the doctor? When you get back pain habitually, it'll never heal. That can affect you later in life, you know?" Yukinoshita showered me with a string of interrogating accusations.

"You were actually worried?!" Yuigahama seemed startled at first, but then she casually jumped on the bandwagon and added, "I—I worried a bit, too, though!".

*Hmm, I would have preferred to receive your gracious words of advice and concern when they were actually relevant, though... But if they were worried about me, then I shall dutifully report the events of the time...*

"I did go. To an osteopath. Got a note that got me out of gym class," I said proudly.

"Sneaky! I was concerned for nothing!" Yuigahama said with mild horror.

*Uh, in that case, you weren't super worried, were you...?*

Instead of acknowledging my reproachful look, Yuigahama clapped her hands. "But those events were fun, huh? Even if they were kinda silly. Like, the ones we all did together."

"...You think?" I agreed with the "kinda silly" part, but as for whether doing them with everyone was fun or not...

When I expressed my doubts, Yuigahama swelled with confidence. "I do think. Hanging out with everyone, like Yumiko and Hina and Hayato and Sai-chan and Komachi-chan, was pretty fun, right? Like during summer vacation and stuff," she said, her gaze drifting far into the distance.

Yukinoshita nodded with a *hmm*. "You mean the camping trip. I don't know about *fun*, but it was certainly lively... But aren't we forgetting someone?" Yukinoshita tilted her head thoughtfully.

*Now that you mention it...* I counted off in my head, folding down a finger for each person who'd been there in Chiba Village, and it hit me. "Miss Hiratsuka...? She was supervising, so I guess you couldn't say we hung out together."

"...I believe she also enjoyed herself quite thoroughly, though." Yukinoshita frowned with a thoughtful noise.

Not that I couldn't understand the sentiment. Miss Hiratsuka generally always seems to be having a good time, after all...

Okay, Tobe had been there, too, but who cares about him. He's Tobe. I did actually remember him, so can we just let it rest? I'm the only one who has to remember that stuff—including that time I got all broody because I heard Tobe's weird questions to Hayama.

There had been many such things that summer...things that had left their mark on me and me alone.

The bitterness had hung heavy all this time, like sediment, leaving a bad aftertaste.

The reason I'd been unable to just leave that girl Rumi Tsurumi was because I'd seen someone else in a part of her. The hive mind exerts such pressure to conform to its nebulous existence—I think I'd been unwilling to let it crush her, or unforgiving of how it had always been crushing her.

I'm not going to say the outcome there was positive.

It's just...seeing her trying to reach out despite knowing it was all fake, I'd felt a kind of hope. Like a faint wish or a prayer. And that was another thing nobody had to remember but me.

But memories will be shared by those you spent that time with, whether you want them to or not. So she would bring up the things she thought she should remember, too.

"The fireworks were fun, too, huh?" Yuigahama muttered, looking up at the night sky.

I followed her gaze. The night sky was black with no blooms of light or rain of golden sand. "...Fireworks, huh?"

"So you do remember," Yuigahama teased.

I shrugged and shot back, rather self-deprecatingly, "Yeah, well, it's not like I was doing anything else. I do remember days when stuff happened."

And so, we carefully and quietly tucked away the memories we'd shared.

All that remained afterward were faint smiles, quiet sighs, and the specter of silence.

As if to fill up that space, Yukinoshita expelled an exaggerated sigh. "So you only remember a few days of a vacation that was nearly forty days long, hmm...?"

"That's just how it works. Before you know it, it's over, right...? And besides, we were ridiculously busy after that."

"We had a lot of events in the second semester, huh?" Yuigahama agreed.

"Yeah... And basically all of that was the chair's fault." That came out meaner than I'd intended because a certain someone happened to come to mind.

Yuigahama seemed uncomfortable; her lips barely opened as she replied, "Hmm...no comment."

*Aw, geez, Miss Yuigahama is so nice!* Usually, this would be a time for a trial in absentia, a super-impeachment—an instant death sentence, even!

As I was having such thoughts, Yukinoshita shrugged. It seemed she had her own response to my opinions, too! *Aw, geez! Is Miss Yukinoshita a nice girl, too?*

Or so I thought…

"Sagami wasn't the only one at fault."

"Ahhh, you said her name…"

"…Rather shameless of you to say, when you had absolutely no intention of avoiding it." Yukinoshita put a hand to her temple as if she had a headache, then brought her eyebrows together as she glanced at me. I gave her a lazy nod back as if to say, *I get it, I get it, my bad*, and Yukinoshita cleared her throat lightly and started over.

"There were many factors at the time that contributed to that situation, after all…," she muttered. She was speaking in very broad terms, but what other way could she put it? We knew what she was referring to.

There had been plenty of factors—inadvertently pressing your own ideals on another, or getting stubborn because you thought it was bad to rely on others so casually, or selfishly holding back while thinking you're being considerate.

But I think that after so many incidents like this, we'd come to know each other a little and had gained some limited answers.

Those answers were different for each of us, yet in the end, they were probably the same.

That was why Yukinoshita summed it up with something more out of left field: "Mostly, it was the overcrowded schedule."

Yuigahama and I nodded at that.

"Yeah. And we went on the field trip right after that, too," said Yuigahama.

"Uh-huh. We were running around like headless chickens." I let the rest slide by, making no move to press that further.

Yuigahama and Yukinoshita took over from there instead.

"We didn't really get that chill sightseeing experience, huh?" said Yuigahama. "Just Kiyomizu-dera Temple. And then some place that had tons of torii gates. And we didn't eat many local specialties… Oh, but the Toei Kyoto Studio Park was so much fun! And the haunted house, too!"

"...I believe that was when we were rushing around the most, though." Yukinoshita seemed less enthusiastic than Yuigahama. We were in different classes, so we hadn't been together then—but even if we had been, Yukinoshita probably would've passed on the haunted house. She can't really handle that sort of thing, after all! Neither can I, though, to be fair.

"And I thought we visited a fair number of sightseeing spots. Ryouan-ji Temple, Fushimi Inari Shrine, Toufuku-ji Temple, and Kitano Tenmangu Shrine...among others. And as for food, there was boiled tofu and *udon-suki* served at the *ryokan*, wasn't there? And we were able to stop by that café I wanted to see, too," Yukinoshita said, with a hint of pleasure.

*...Ahhh, so the café where she had that breakfast set was her pick after all. That place was fancy. Food was good, though, so I had no complaints...*

As my mind was turning back to those memories, Yukinoshita continued to mutter, "And then there was the ramen..."

"Ramen?" Yuigahama tilted her head with a question mark, and Yukinoshita's mouth immediately snapped shut.

To fill the pause, I started to speak. "Yeah. There's a lot of famous shops in Kyoto. Like around Kita-Shirakawa. And Ichijou-ji is a hot spot with intense competition. I wanted to go, too, but I didn't have the time... Takayasu, Tentenyuu, Yume wo Katare..."

"Huh? Uh, what?"

"It's fine—it's nothing. Those are just the names of shops I wanted to go to. Don't worry about it."

"O-okay..."

Yuigahama still looked like she had a question mark floating over her head, but I barreled on past that and continued on my merry way. "And it didn't really get better after that, did it? As soon as we were free from Sagami, Isshiki came in with a mountain of problems..."

"Ah-ha-ha... We had a tough time with the student council

election, too, huh?" Yuigahama smiled a bit nervously, while Yukinoshita's shoulders dropped just a bit.

Catching that in the corner of my eye, I let out a slightly exaggerated sigh. "Then right after the election was over, the Christmas event hit us immediately. That was hell. All that *innovative disruptive* yes-yes-yes-ing…"

"That whole thing was really incomprehensible, wasn't it…? Almost as incomprehensible as what you just said," Yukinoshita taunted with a giggle and a smile. The hunch in her shoulders had straightened back into a dignified posture.

Yuigahama bumped her shoulder against Yukinoshita's. "But we got to go to Destiny for free. That was fun, right? And you were able to buy lots of Grue-bear merch!" Yuigahama smiled at her with an *eh-heh*.

Yukinoshita turned her face away shyly. "…Well, that's true. It wasn't all bad."

Watching that exchange, even I started feeling good about it.

It was true. It hadn't all been bad.

I did think the things we did then were meaningful. I couldn't say for sure if I'd really managed to take responsibility for Iroha Isshiki, and I didn't know if the way things had gone with Rumi Tsurumi had been right, either. And I sure as hell didn't know the meaning of what she'd said to me.

But at the very least, I didn't think it had been meaningless.

Those feelings had made it possible for me to welcome the quiet New Year. And I don't think I was the only one who felt that warmth, either—those two sensed it, too.

That was why Yuigahama's tone was so gentle as she reminisced. "It all went by so fast, huh? I guess it was because so much happened last year…"

"It's been plenty busy in the New Year, too… Particularly at my house, since Komachi got serious about studying for her exams."

With the start of school, we'd been at the mercy of stupid rumors and all of that, and the whole time had passed in a blur of activity. The only time I'd been able to take it easy had been around the beginning of the year. Which made my thoughts turn entirely to earlier this year, which then stirred up my worries about Komachi's entrance exams.

"I hope that shrine visit does the trick for her," Yukinoshita said, attempting to cheer me up. Guess those anxieties had come out on my face.

"Hmm? Yeah. Seriously... Well, there's no point in getting worked up about this," I said, trying to get myself over it.

Yuigahama nodded back at me. "Uh-uh... Oh, then I know! Once it's all over, let's have a post-exam party!"

"Yeah, let's. Give her a big celebration for passing."

"...All right."

"Yep!"

There was an implicit assumption Komachi would pass, but neither of them commented on it, answering with smiles instead. That was truly something to be grateful for. I grinned broadly, too.

Suddenly, a shadow fell over Yuigahama's face. "Maybe we should be a bit more worried about ourselves, though..."

"Indeed. This time next year will be the period for university entrance exams. And once that's done..." Yukinoshita quietly lowered her eyes. She didn't have to say the rest.

After exams were over, graduation came next.

"A year goes by pretty fast, huh...?" I said out loud, and it felt way more real than I'd anticipated. This was just the weight of the time we'd been discussing. Having shared in that conversation themselves, the other two would understand that plenty.

"The year has passed more quickly than any other in my life," Yukinoshita said with a deep sigh.

Yuigahama clapped her hands. "I thought so, too! It's kinda, I dunno—adults say stuff about that, right? When you get older, a year feels shorter. Or something like that!"

"Well, we were pretty busy with stuff...," I said. "Waves of requests and consults and everything. Though we can blame all that on Miss Hiratsuka."

"The root of all evil, so to speak?" Yukinoshita said with a wry smile, and Yuigahama and I made similar sorts of expressions.

It was true. It had all begun with her words.

The start of it all was so damn trivial. Maybe it had just been a whim of hers.

And that would end soon, too.

Ultimately, nothing resembling a competition had ever been settled, and the results had only ever been vague, everything lost in the grove.

But I had decided to eliminate that vagueness, even if it was a mistake, even if things would be lost, to produce my answer. Our answers.

If you start looking back, you'll never stop. You could get as much conversation as you want, talking about this past year—and all of it nothing but happy, fun stories that would keep a smile on your face. You can talk about only what you want to talk about and leave out what you don't.

Without saying any of what you actually want to say.

And that's completely intentional. By avoiding those things, you understand very quickly they're what you're most worried about. I think all three of us were aware of that. That was exactly why the conversation trailed off.

The time we'd spent together filled less than a year. Of that time, there'd been lots we'd remembered, more we'd forgotten, and much we'd pretended to forget.

Even this sort of reminiscing would eventually run dry. Once you're done going over the past to the present, you'll always trail off.

Meaning what we should talk about now was the future.

Maybe that was why they both expelled breaths almost like sighs, then closed their mouths.

Invisible, unknowable, incomprehensible, and irreversible.

You're not going to see it. You're not going to know it. And despite all of that, once you've made your way forward, there's no more backing down.

In the silence born then, there was the soft rustle of a scarf being rewrapped.

"It's stopped snowing, huh?" Yuigahama said to no one in particular. The night sky seemed hazy, as if it were behind a veil of smoke.

Yukinoshita didn't answer with words. With a smile like the moonlight filtering through thin clouds, she gave a little nod and turned her gaze upward.

We were probably looking at the same moon.

And I'm sure we always had been.

Thanks to our proximity, we'd witnessed similar things and spent some time together. But I doubted that would lead us to the same answers. I could say with certainty that it was the one answer that would never change.

So to keep from saying so, we were bringing up different topics—like casually mentioning the weather or the most sickly-sweet coffee or the ordinary recollections of the past.

"I'm told it was snowing on the day I was born, too. So they called me Yukino… It's too simple, isn't it?" Yukinoshita said suddenly as the hushed time flowed by, a mildly self-deprecating smile on her face.

Yuigahama's response was gentle. "…But it's a lovely name."

I knew Yuigahama wasn't seeking agreement, but I automatically nodded along. "…Yeah, it's a nice name," I said only half consciously.

Yuigahama blinked at me like she was a little startled, and Yukinoshita's eyes widened in shock. If they were gonna react like that, I might get kind of really embarrassed. My gaze slid to the side.

To cover the awkward pause, I put my lips on my can of coffee and took a sip. I did actually think it was a good name, so I couldn't exactly take back what I said. The coffee was my only option.

The name Yukino did really suit her. It was pretty and ephemeral, with a sort of lonely ring to it. And weirdly enough, I didn't associate it with any words like *coldness* or *chill*.

"...Thank you," Yukinoshita murmured quietly, and when I looked back at her again, she was squeezing her fists tight over her skirt with her face tilted down. Her black hair flowed downward like a bamboo screen to cover her face, but the pink tinge on her cheeks could be glimpsed underneath. Yuigahama must have noticed that, too; her lips relaxed in a happy smile, and she let out a gentle breath.

Her faint giggle must have reached Yukinoshita's ears, as she cleared her throat in an unassuming manner and raised her chin before adjusting her posture. "I'm told my mother picked it. Though I only heard that secondhand from my sister…" She sounded composed at the beginning, but by the end, her voice melted away into the air, as if to disappear. Her eyes had lowered from the sky to the ground. A shadow had fallen over her expression, which had something of a grimace in it.

Yuigahama and I didn't know what to say for a moment.

Should I have found an appropriate reply, an opportunity to continue the conversation somehow? Like for example, I could have said my parents had put even less effort into picking the name Hachiman and that they'd decided on mine instantly before spending forever deciding Komachi's—that sort of stupid, attention-seeking clowning that I could pretend helped.

Or maybe I should have left it to Yuigahama and had her take over from there.

But both Yuigahama and I chose silence.

There were no words. Our only comments were sighs.

Yukinoshita, her mother, and Haruno.

I didn't know much about their relationship. Well, it wasn't like I knew anything at all about Yuigahama's relationship with her family, either, and they didn't know much about mine.

So this not knowing was something far more fundamental. I didn't know her; I didn't know them. And because of that, I didn't know the right way to answer.

If this had been back when I was completely ignorant, I would have had any number of justifications for that. I could have said, *I don't know her, so there's no point in saying something weird* or *I don't know her, so of course I'll misunderstand* or *I don't know her, so I shouldn't assume any interaction.* If you can smell trouble coming, then you can pretend you don't know someone—since you honestly don't.

But we knew each other enough that I couldn't feign ignorance. At this stage, it would be the height of shamelessness.

In the end, I didn't know the appropriate response based on what our relationship currently was. I think I could have superficially continued the conversation, with decently appropriate and convincing sympathy, by disclosing a similar experience of my own and then offering advice of some sort, but not so much that it came off as pushy. That would probably be the standard response. Everyone else manages natural exchanges like that just fine.

But it was my desire to eliminate the phoniness that had made us like this.

Unknowingly, my hand tightened around the can. The steel wasn't going to cave. My fingers trembled instead as the liquid made a slight sloshing sound.

We were quiet enough that the splash could be heard.

I slowly brought the can to my mouth, then lightly shook it to check what was left. Once I'd finished drinking this, I would talk.

Those little decisions of mine always forced me to act. That was how it had been all this time. Even if I'd been swept along, pulled in, dragged in, I'd ultimately made the final judgments myself.

That's just my nature. Nothing more than a habit, and definitely not the "decisiveness" people like to praise or brag about. Loners are generally by themselves, so they wind up doing everything on their own. They're like utility players, you might say, but it's not like they're omnipotent—they're generally bad at everything. About all they're good at is consoling themselves, accepting their lot, and giving up.

It was just that at that particular moment, I didn't feel like I could deceive myself with that kind of nonsense.

If I can speak candidly—the truth is, I think I've always avoided imagining what would come next.

It's not quite right to say I was running away. *Avoiding* is the best word for it. Or maybe *evading*.

I don't think it was an attempt at escape at all.

Because I actually did find it aggravating.

In the end, I wasn't seeking all the answers, resolutions, or conclusions. I'm sure I wished for things to be canceled out. For the question to be dissolved rather than resolved. I'd been waiting for an ambiguous ending, where the various problems, dilemmas, and predicaments before me would vanish before they could be defined.

I selfishly believed that all of us were probably unconsciously wishing for it all to just become like it had never happened. It was the height of arrogance to make conjectures about their feelings, but I still don't think I was that far off.

I mean, the time we'd been spending together had been like a slumber, dragged out slowly and tortuously, joy and sorrow mingled together.

But I knew we couldn't go back.

Yui Yuigahama had already posed the question to us.

Yukino Yukinoshita had indicated her intent to answer, too.

So what about Hachiman Hikigaya?

In the past, I would have scoffed at such a situation, calling this complacency. And in the future, a conclusion that didn't qualify as an answer wouldn't be enough. In the present, I still didn't know what "right" was, but I still felt keenly that this was wrong.

What I should probably do is make an effort to fix that wrong. That's the topic I should go for.

I took one last swallow of the now-cold canned coffee and opened my mouth.

All that came out at first was a sigh, then a sort of *hmm* sound as I chose my words. After that, finally, a sentence that was at least in the right ballpark. "...Yukinoshita. Can I ask about you?"

Even I wondered how a remark like that would express anything to her. I wasn't even sure what I was trying to ask.

But it seemed like that was enough for them. You couldn't find a single tiny leaf from the tree that was this issue, never mind getting down to the trunk or the root of it. But maybe there was a seed. We at least intended to talk, to push these relationships out of the deadlock we'd come to.

Yuigahama gulped quietly, then gave me a long look. I think she was asking if I was ready.

Yukinoshita, on the other hand, was frozen, her head tilted downward. "...Would you...mind listening?"

Her reticent tone hinted at her indecision. She weakly examined Yuigahama and me, and then she gave a hesitant sigh.

Yukinoshita's question—was it a question? I can't say whether her words had been directed at me. She'd muttered them more like a confirmation, and I responded with a look and a nod. Then her eyebrows turned down with some consternation, and she paused a moment.

She was probably thinking about how to put it, just like I had.

Yuigahama softly leaned close to her, as if to give her a gentle push. Inching up close on the bench where they sat side by side, she touched Yukinoshita's hand. "You know, I...I was always thinking that maybe it was best to wait. You've been telling me all sorts of stuff, even if it was bit by bit." She rested her head on Yukinoshita's shoulder. I don't know what lay behind her closed eyelids, but that puppylike cuddling was enough to generate some heat. Just like ice slowly melting, Yukinoshita's tension eased away. Her fists, clenched tight on top of her skirt, gradually opened, and she cautiously squeezed Yuigahama's hand back.

Hand in hand, feeling her heat, Yukinoshita slowly began to

speak. "Yuigahama. You asked me what I want to do… But I really don't know," she said, sounding almost mesmerized. She spoke like a lost child. I'm sure Yuigahama and I had the same expression. Because we *were* lost children.

Yuigahama sadly lowered her eyes.

Yukinoshita noticed and made an effort to show some cheer to encourage us. "But you know, there were actually things I wanted to do, before."

"Things you wanted to do?" Yuigahama parroted back at her, sounding puzzled.

Yukinoshita looked a little proud as she nodded. "My father's work," she said.

"Ohhh… But that's—," I said, tracing back in my memories. Then I figured it out. I remembered hearing that Yukinoshita's father was a member of the prefectural assembly and that he managed a construction company. Haruno had told me about that, too.

"Yes," Yukinoshita cut in, picking up where I'd left off. "But there's my sister…so I'm not the one to make that decision. My mother has always decided." Her tone had turned a little cold, and she seemed to be glaring at something far in the distance. We didn't interrupt.

She'd get this faraway look whenever she was talking about the past. She was staring up at the sky. That drew me to look up, too.

The winds had to be blowing up high, as thin, cotton-candy-like clouds were flowing like a river. Their fleecy, shifting shapes were clearly visible under the moonlight.

We wouldn't have to worry about the weather anymore. The snow clouds had already been whisked far away, and stars twinkled in the sky.

The light of the stars is from the distant past, dozens of light-years away. You can't say for sure if their light even exists in the present—maybe that's just why it's so lovely. The most beautiful things are the ones you've lost and the ones that are unattainable.

I knew that, and that's why I couldn't reach out to it. The moment I touched it, it would fade and rot away. It was beyond the reach of someone like me anyway.

Perhaps they both understood that, too—Yukinoshita, who had spoken of her own wishes in the past tense, and Yuigahama, who had listened.

"My mother has always been the one to decide everything, always tying my sister down and letting me do as I please. So I've only ever chased after my sister. I didn't know how to act...," Yukinoshita whispered with something like nostalgia or regret.

The eyes watching her profile contained a tinge of desolation, even contrition.

"...Even now, I still don't know... My sister's right," Yukinoshita muttered softly. Her gaze left the sky to shift to her toes, neatly aligned. They were evidence of her constant position, not one step away from her spot.

We were unable to say a word.

Yukinoshita must have realized herself how painfully quiet it was, as she jerked her head up and smiled bashfully to fill the silence. "This is the first anyone's ever listened to me talk about this."

Her smile elicited a breath from my dry lips that was close to a sigh of relief. Instead of making some vague listening noise, I asked, "You've never said this to anyone?"

"I think I've said as much indirectly to my parents, but..." A thoughtful gesture. It must have been long ago. She reflected and considered but then gave up with a little shake of her head. "But I don't remember them ever having taken me seriously. Every time, they told me I didn't have to worry about it... Though I'm sure that's because my sister will take over the family business."

"Have you told Haruno?" Yuigahama asked.

Yukinoshita laid a hand on her chin and tilted her head. "...I don't think I have." Then she smiled wryly. "You know what she's like."

"Ahhh, I see..."

From what I'd heard from the younger sister and the impression I'd gotten from Hayama, their childhood friend...Haruno Yukinoshita was not the kind of person you'd turn to for a supportive conversation about your future or matters of romance, hope, or dreams or anything like that.

With a stranger who had no connection to her, I'm sure she'd offer specific advice. She'd draw inspiration from mainstream views and stay cordial but definitely not go far enough to sound overbearing. Or maybe she'd just make skillful use of listening noises and meaningless remarks to give you a temporary sense of satisfaction and make you feel like there was a weight off your shoulders. She could pull that off with ease.

But with her family, she'd handle things completely differently. She'd laugh and tease and make fun, and even if your problem did get resolved, she'd dig it up again later to play with it and drag it out. It'd be her toy for your whole life. Hayato Hayama had said something like that once.

They all knew the base assumptions. Maybe that was why Yukinoshita had never spoken to Haruno about those things before.

Well, it's not like I'm going to go to the trouble of bringing up my career and future with my family, either. I don't know if this is good or bad, but I've never been forced to make any big choices that were beyond my ability to decide.

But it was true that because of that, her description of family interactions didn't quite click with me. If my family had some kind of hereditary business, maybe I could have sympathized, but unfortunately, I've grown up in a salaryman family. This stuff is way out of my purview.

Yuigahama must have felt similarly; her expression turned glum, her head dropping.

Heedless of our reactions, Yukinoshita let out a little sigh. "But maybe I should have said it. Even if I wouldn't get what I wanted… I think I was scared to come up with a proper answer, so I never made certain."

I sensed nostalgia in her tone—or maybe regret. Whichever it was, it was in the past and couldn't be taken back.

But her eyes were facing forward.

Ahead of that gaze was Yuigahama…and me.

"So I'm going to make certain of that, first... And this time, I will make the decision of my own will. I want to think about it myself and accept it on my own terms—not because someone else told me—and I want to give up on it."

A tiny sigh and a quiet smile.

Yukinoshita had said, clear and serene: *I want to give up on it.*

All this time, she must have carried resignation inside her. But since no decisions had ever been made, she'd held it and held it.

You won't know what's inside a box until you try opening it. The outcome is undecided until the contents are observed. But nevertheless, once the observer accepts that outcome, whether they want it or not, it will come to an end.

It will converge in a single result.

"...I have just one request... I want you two to watch how it plays out. That's enough." Yukinoshita touched her hand to the scarf around her neck and closed her eyes. I didn't think she was doing it against the cold, but as if she were adjusting her collar. She faltered as she spoke, choosing each word as carefully as a promise before a god.

"Is that...your answer, Yukinon?" Yuigahama asked quietly. Or it seemed like she was asking a question, but her head was hanging, her eyes turned away.

But Yukinoshita turned to look straight at the other girl. "Maybe not..." With a smile that held a hint of pain, she quietly clasped Yuigahama's hand.

Yuigahama raised her head. "So then...," she began, but when her eyes met Yukinoshita's, her words trailed off. The words that would have come next faded out.

I lost my voice, too. I might have even forgotten to breathe.

Yukinoshita's smile was just that beautiful.

Her smoothly combed, long black hair slid away, and when her slender face was revealed, her eyes captured me, clear like crystal.

Her gaze did not waver; she was just taking in the sight of us. The depth of her eyes was like the azure of the sky, so expansive they could suck me in, as if they could not contain a single falsehood. "But I…I want to prove I can do well on my own. I think if I do that, then I can begin properly." I could see no hesitation—not only in her smooth explanation, but in the firm clasp of her hands, her straightforward gaze, and the sharp posture of her spine.

"Begin…properly…," Yuigahama murmured dazedly, almost deliriously.

Yukinoshita nodded. "Yes. I'll go back to my parents' house for a bit and have a real discussion about it, from square one."

"…So we can take that as your answer, huh?" I muttered. It probably wasn't a question—if you can't face the person to say it, you're just talking to yourself.

But Yukinoshita still heard and reacted. She placed her loosely clenched fists on her lap and said quietly, "No matter how much time passed, I've never entirely given up on it…so I think this is probably how I really feel… And I don't think it's wrong, either." She glanced in my direction, examining me.

There was something in her words that made sense—a part I could sympathize with.

If it doesn't change with time, if it doesn't fade despite your attempts to ignore it, then I'd feel ready to call that "something real." On the other hand, if it breaks after time or an attempt to discard it, you know it wasn't real.

If it still won't disappear, even after you turn away, avert your eyes, pretend you don't see, or try to leave it behind, then you should be able to say it's what you really want.

If that was the conclusion she wished for, then there was nothing for me to say.

There was just one thing I'd been fixated on—Yukino Yukinoshita making the decision herself.

This wasn't something to be decided based on someone else's wants or expectations, peer pressure, social vibe, or mood. Even if this would cause something to fall apart, that was still no good reason to rob her of her high-minded nobility.

Wishing not that she would respond to someone's demands, but that she would speak from her heart.

"Why not give it a shot?" I said as she gazed timidly at me, dipping my head slightly. Yukinoshita sighed in relief.

"Yeah, I get it... I think that's an answer, too." Yuigahama, who'd been silently watching Yukinoshita's profile, quietly turned her eyes to the ground. Then she nodded slowly a few times.

"Thank you...," Yukinoshita muttered softly, then lowered her head. I don't know what sort of look she had on her face right then; I'll probably never know. Even if I had seen it for myself, I'm sure I would have forgotten it soon enough.

Because when Yukinoshita lifted her head once more, her expression was so bright and sunny.

Yukinoshita didn't give us the time to say anything else as she hopped to her feet. "How about we get going soon? It really has gotten chilly," she said, taking a step forward—in the direction of the park exit and the apartment where she lived.

As we still hadn't moved yet, Yukinoshita turned back to us.

The swish of her hair, the flutter of her skirt, the sway of her scarf, and her presence as she stood there were all beautiful, and it made me hesitate to draw any closer.

But I'd promised I would be her witness.

So I started walking toward her.

Hoping, without praying to anyone...

...that even if we did regret it, at least there would be words without lies.

## Despite appearances, Haruno Yukinoshita is not drunk.

I'd come here before.

Two tall apartment buildings, similar as twins. In one was the apartment where Yukinoshita lived, on an upper floor.

The last time I'd come over to her place had been during the cultural festival, when she'd worked herself sick and taken time off school. She'd been all alone in that apartment then. And that was when Yuigahama and I had gone over.

I hadn't come since then.

But Yuigahama must have visited her a whole bunch of times before and after that. Maybe she was familiar with the place. She seemed completely at ease, even after she walked inside the automatic doors at the entrance to stand beside Yukinoshita.

I just couldn't settle down, though; I kept fidgeting and trying to find something to look at. *Um, I mean, it's normal to get nervous at a girl's place… And we're still just in the lobby!* With this level of intimidation by proximity, a girl's home is a dangerous place. This was way too "final dungeon" for me, and I think it's wrong to pick up girls in a place like that.

The apartment vestibule was empty and hushed. If I were Basho, I'd even be seeping into stone. What's with this guy Basho—is he Angelo or what?

All I heard was breathing and a hesitant sigh. The automatic doors to the apartment lobby were also closed. The frosted glass of the doors was fairly opaque, decorated with orange plywood that matched the exterior of the building.

When I glanced at the doors, Yukinoshita pulled a key from her bag. But she didn't stick it into the door phone. She just clinked her keys a few times. Yukinoshita lived here alone, so there shouldn't have been anything to hesitate over. But there were others in her territory now.

I didn't know what had led to Yukinoshita getting a solo apartment. I'd had opportunities to ask before, but I'd never taken that step and asked. I probably wouldn't force the question in the future, either.

It wasn't that I wasn't interested—I think it was something else I was lacking. To put it plainly, the problem was that I didn't know how or when to ask.

I've always felt something like fear about accidentally stumbling across something private. You never know where a land mine like that might be.

I know from experience that the most innocuous remark could hurt someone deeply. For example, getting asked in a job interview, *Do you have a girlfriend?* Even if there's no malice intended, the phrasing or the timing can hit pretty hard. Ohhh, here I am again, talking about myself... Well, who cares about me? Basically, there's always a risk in touching on information that hasn't been disclosed.

But right now, there was one thing I could ask her. If it was information we shared, then I could use that as the bridge to a conversation.

"...Is she still here?" I asked.

"...Most likely."

She knew what I meant, even if I didn't expressly state her name. Haruno Yukinoshita had definitely said she'd be waiting in this apartment.

Yukinoshita answered with a slightly weak smile, then jingled the keys in her hands. It seemed she'd come to a decision. Finally, she stuck them into the keyhole in the intercom.

But before she could turn the key, the automatic doors slid soundlessly open.

"Ohhh, if it isn't Yukino-chan!" We heard a sudden bouncy call, followed by light footsteps.

Through the open doors was Haruno Yukinoshita. The shine slanting in from the lobby was just like a spotlight on her.

"…Haruno."

One face was blank and startled, while the other expressed open-mouthed surprise.

I was reminded then that they were sisters, and they looked a lot alike. Oh, I'd been fully aware that they shared similar features—even setting aside my own opinions, tastes, and preferences, they were conventionally beautiful sisters with quite a bit in common. It's just that I normally got such a different impression from each of them; I personally found them each beautiful in her own way.

But in that moment, they honestly appeared so alike to me, that usual impression was overwhelmed. Those blinking, startled faces were like opposing mirrors.

But the reflection was quickly shattered.

"Welcome hooome!" Haruno patted Yukinoshita's shoulder with too much cheer, her expression far softer than usual. Maybe that was what did it.

She wasn't dressed as fashionably as usual, but all fluffy, puffy, and soft. This was probably her at-home wear. She wore a light coat slung over her shoulders and sandals on her feet. She looked homey. I could almost hear the *Just popping out for a bit!*

And there was a moist shine to her hair, a flushed redness to her cheeks. Her big eyes normally seemed sharp, but right now, they were kind of drowsy.

Yukinoshita also apparently noticed the differences, as she scowled in suspicion. "…Have you been drinking?"

"Well, yeah. Just a bit." Haruno gestured with a thumb and index finger pinching at the air. The soft smile on her lips belied that gesture.

She must have drunk quite a lot. Yukinoshita, Yuigahama, and I all stared back at her, unimpressed.

Of course, that made Haruno feel awkward, and with a quiet clearing of her throat, she said, "More importantly, if you're back, then..."

"...Yes. I have something to talk to you about," Yukinoshita said, finishing her sentence. There was nothing nervous or stiff about her expression.

Picking up on that, Haruno let out a little huff. "Hmm." After that brief, disinterested reply, she looked at the elevator, which had already risen upward. "...Anyway, are you guys coming up? We're not going to stand around talking out here."

"Oh, uh, we're totally going home. We were just walking her back anyway," I replied, a little confused by her unexpected offer.

It seemed Yuigahama felt the same. "Y-yeah...and weren't you just heading out?" This issue was really personal, and we obviously couldn't just barge in like that.

But Haruno ignored our reactions, nudging Yuigahama in the back. "It's fine, it's fine. I was just thinking I'd pop out to the corner store."

"U-um...," I said uncomfortably, but if she was gonna poke and prod, I'd have no choice but to move my feet along. With a put-upon sigh, Yukinoshita also wound up following Haruno and Yuigahama into the lobby.

Until the elevator came, Haruno hummed and mashed the button. *Uhhh, pressing it again isn't gonna make it come faster...* Actually, it might even cancel some elevators.

The behavior was more childish than the Haruno I knew. I'd always assumed she could take her alcohol, so it was surprising to see her swaying around.

We got on when the elevator finally came back, but the small space was a bit uncomfortable. Haruno seemed to be the only one enjoying herself, while the rest of us kept our eyes on the numbers shifting on the display. Both the silence and gravity were heavily weighing on my shoulders.

The awkwardness must have bothered Yuigahama, as she tried talking to Haruno. "Were you drinking at home?"

"Hmm? No, no. I was out drinking. So I took a shower to clear my head…but then don't you always want something sweet after drinking?" Haruno looked over at me. *Right?*

"Uh, I don't know…," I replied. *Why're you asking me? We're minors, you know…*

Haruno must have realized that as well, tilting her head with a *hmm*. "Ohhh. Well, you guys'll find out once you start drinking."

"Whoa… Why're you talking like an obnoxious college kid?"

"Ohhh, lookit you being cheeky," Haruno said, pinching my ear. It was still recovering from the numbness of the cold, and this wasn't helping.

*N-nuu! My ears are sensitive!*

On top of that, there was the faint trace of alcohol on her breath and the really nice scent of her shampoo. It was real bad. Why do such nice smells linger inside an elevator?

"You'll want to drink, and you'll want to have sweets," she murmured. The sound was so quiet, it was as if she didn't care if anyone heard or not. There was no time to worry about replying, as the elevator arrived at the floor where Yukinoshita's apartment was.

× × ×

Yukinoshita slowly turned the doorknob, and we entered through the doorway of her apartment.

This was probably a three-bedroom unit. When we'd come before, I'd only ever ventured as far as the living room, but it was fairly spacious, and I remembered seeing from the hallway a door that probably went to the master bedroom.

But something felt different compared with the last time we'd been here.

From the doorway to the hall, and all the way to the living room, everything was perfectly clean and organized; the furniture hadn't changed, either.

Only Yukinoshita seemed to notice what lay behind this feeling of something out of place.

She glanced over to the sideboard beside the sofa, and I spotted something like fried pasta there. There had been something similar in Yuigahama's room. I seemed to recall the general term for this was *diffuser*.

Getting another close look at this thing, I realized it was a wooden stick like a Pretz stuck up in a bottle. *Huh*, I thought. Examining it, I saw that some kind of liquid solution filled up the bottom of the bottle. This would be the source of the smell, while the dried pasta sucked it up to disperse it…or something, I guess?

The wafting fragrance had floral notes. It was sweet and perky, but it also gave off a certain sense of elegance.

But this scent should have been calming, and right now, it made me more restless and unsure. The newness of it, the incongruity, bothered me. Its air spoke of the influence of another. Haruno Yukinoshita's presence had left its faint impression.

*Oh, so this is what felt out of place.*

This scent wasn't really Yukinoshita, and that was what got under my skin. Haruno had probably been the one to bring it over. If I were to make my own assumptions about Yukinoshita, I'd say mint or soap, something clean and fresh, would be more like her.

And Yukinoshita herself was frowning, so this floral fragrance probably wasn't to her taste. She glanced at the air freshener like a cat whose territory has been invaded, but instead of saying anything, she circled around to the kitchen and started to boil water. Maybe she was making tea for us guests.

Despite Yukinoshita's apparent displeasure, Haruno was quite chipper. Humming, she opened the fridge to grab a bottle and a champagne glass, then cheerfully skipped over to dive into the sofa and flop down there. She set the bottle and glass on the side table and flung out her long legs in their fluffy shorts, stretching in a relaxed and comfy way.

I felt my eyes being tugged toward her lazy sprawl, but I yanked them away. As my gaze idly wandered around, Haruno waved her hand like she was beckoning to us. "Well, sit wherever."

"Why are you telling them what to do?" With an exasperated sigh, Yukinoshita returned to the living room and set the tea she carried onto the low table.

There were four cups on the tray, and the way they were positioned told us basically where to sit. Haruno reached out to the cup placed in front of her as well, took a big gulp, and let out a satisfied *pwahh*, then poured champagne into her glass.

Yuigahama watched her with deep interest. "Is that…wine? Do you drink it a lot?"

"I drink anything. Beer, wine, sake, Shaoxing wine, and whiskey."

"Ohhh! Neat. It's kinda cool to know a lot about alcohol!" Yuigahama said.

Haruno giggled. "I don't know anything about alcohol. Go to a decent enough bar, and basically everything there will be good. I just tell them what I like and what I'm in the mood for and leave it to them."

*What the heck? That actually makes her seem like a connoisseur…*

It's like, you know, it's so pretentious when people break into a long-winded explanation. It's ridiculously obnoxious when college kids who've only just learned about alcohol will bring up names like Mori Izou or Maou or Dassai or whatever to show off. So compared with that, you could say Haruno's method of choosing alcohol was clever.

People who effusively bestow their knowledge in an endless lecture while they drink sure are annoying, huh? Like those types who will gush about Belgian beer and trash Japanese dry beer. Symptoms such as these, common in people in their second year of adulthood, are known as A-2 syndrome! Why is it that we boys get this urge to share knowledge nobody's asked for...? What can you do? That's just how we show dominance.

But it's a little sad to be lacking in any knowledge at all. For example...

"Oh! You're a sommelier!"

"Don't blurt out words when you don't really know what they mean..."

I'm also kinda iffy about girls like Gahama-chan, with her wide eyes sparkling with enthusiasm and her nonexistent vocabulary skills. The vocabulary of young people these days is at whoa levels of whoa, I mean, like, dude, it's seriously whoa. Just unbelievably whoa.

But you can't underestimate the effects of alcohol, either. I mean, some people will go on about how sharing drinks brings you together, so I can acknowledge a certain utility there. For example, even if you really run your mouth and say something stupid, you'll often be safe as long as you blame the alcohol. But not always. Since the one who heard it is never going to forget it.

All that aside—right here and now, it was clear that Haruno being drunk had lowered the barriers to contact. Yuigahama felt more at ease about approaching her, too, judging by the way she was acting friendlier with Haruno.

With a swirl of her champagne glass, Haruno inhaled the aroma, then tossed it back. The gesture suited her.

Yuigahama sighed. "Wow, that's kinda cool..."

"...Is it?"

*Well, Haruno is a cool person, but I dunno if it's a good idea to praise this without reservation... If drinking alcohol is cool, then that means the old guys who gather around the Nakayama racetrack who have no front teeth are also cool, right? And the uncles day drinking in Koiwa and Kasai are hotties as well, right?*

But I doubt Yuigahama was imagining such deplorable adults with bad drinking habits; she was looking at Haruno with respect. "Like, women who drink are so cool!"

"You drop that idea right now...," I grumbled. *Geez! It makes me real worried when you talk like that! You'd better pick a decent club when you're in university! Promise Big Bro!*

But I kind of understand what Yuigahama meant by it. All of us probably do appreciate grown-up things in some way or another.

Maybe we just admire things like alcohol and cigarettes because society says that they're only for adults to enjoy. By acquiring such items, you can feel that sense of maturity. The image provides instant validation.

But if you have someone in your life with bad drinking habits, you won't really feel that way... Like at my house, when my dad will come back dead drunk, or when I'm told that he tends to strip when he's out drinking with clients, it feels like...you know.

As I was thinking, a dry sigh slipped out of me.

And I wasn't the only one. When I looked over, I saw Yukinoshita must have visited the kitchen a second time, as she was back with a plastic bottle of mineral water. She handed it to Haruno, holding out her other hand to trade it for the champagne bottle. "Drinking isn't cool in and of itself—the dignified way to enjoy it is with moderation and good sense."

"Yeah, yeah, like me." Haruno chuckled smugly, hugging the bottle tight and refusing to hand it over.

Yukinoshita put her hand on her hip with exasperation. "You're still going to drink?"

"Some days, you want to drink. Besides, alcohol is the lubricant of life."

"...I believe it's more often a source of trouble."

Yeah, yeah, nothing good will be called a lubricant. Like with interviews or job hunts, if you're comparing yourself to something and bring up lubricant, you'll never get hired. Society wants the cogs!

But sometimes there are certain people—those who are as slippery as lubricant or who will smoothly deflect whatever they want.

And Haruno was fluently evading Yukinoshita's nagging with her devil-may-care attitude and another mouthful of champagne. "I'm fine—I'll still be listening to you," she said with a clear, calm tone. She didn't sound drunk at all.

Yukinoshita seemed to recognize that, too. She withdrew the plastic bottle Haruno had rejected and offered a thin smile instead. "...You wouldn't have seriously listened while sober anyway."

"You got it!" Haruno spun her glass around jokingly, then looked at Yukinoshita through its thin lens. Even the filter of its pale golden color did not soften the sharpness of her eyes.

"So? What did you want to talk about?" Haruno asked casually. Her slim finger flicked the edge of the glass. The ring was quiet and beautiful, but with a chill that reminded me of treading on thin ice. All that followed was the sound of the bubbles slowly fizzing, like whispers.

It was only the slightest moment before all the sounds faded out. No new ones could intervene. All Yuigahama and I could get out were choked sighs.

I remembered what Yukinoshita had said—that she wanted us to watch. So I didn't say anything, not even a single word. I was just waiting for her to speak as my eyes wandered around. Even when our gazes unexpectedly met, I tore mine away, until it eventually landed on Yukinoshita's lips.

All the while, Yukinoshita was silent under Haruno's gaze. She cautiously, thoughtfully opened her mouth, then closed it. It was such a small movement, I couldn't tell if she'd inhaled or exhaled.

But that was the only time she showed anything like hesitation.

A faint smile came to her lips as they pressed tight for just a moment, then slowly opened. "About us... About where we're going." Her voice was dignified and crisp—not at all loud, and yet it seemed to echo through the whole room. Or was it the look in her eyes making me think that? She was gazing straight ahead, never looking away. Maybe that was why it left such an impression.

Even Haruno was no exception. "You'll tell me about that, too?"

"I will… Because this is about you and me, and Mother."

Haruno didn't seem to like that, narrowing her eyes and cocking her head an inch. She paused for a few seconds to contemplate this, but eventually she seemed to understand. She shrugged in disappointment. "…Oh. Doesn't sound like what I wanted to hear." Then she sighed and slid her gaze over. "Right?" The one she was asking for agreement was Yuigahama, who froze.

But Yukinoshita leaned forward, blocking Haruno off. "I want you to listen anyway." There was a strong will in her voice. Her tone was no different from normal, and neither was her volume or tempo.

That was how you could hear her determination.

There was no uncertainty or hesitation in Yukino Yukinoshita's words, and certainly nothing wrong, either. Haruno was clearly shaken.

She'd been leaning on her elbow on the sofa the whole time, but now she slowly raised herself up from her reclined position and set the champagne glass in her hand on the side table. With that gesture, she prompted Yukinoshita to continue.

"So I'm going back home. I want to have a proper discussion with Mother about my hopes for the future. Even if she says no, I don't want to regret anything." Yukinoshita broke off.

Her long eyelashes quietly lowered, and she let out a shaky breath. Her narrow shoulders trembled, letting her long, glossy black hair fall to hide her face.

Her expression now unknowable, Yukinoshita continued. "I want to…put at least one thing into words. I need that closure," she said, then combed back her hair. A small, peaceful smile rose on her fair, delicate face.

I swallowed, seeing that expression. I think Yuigahama did, too.

Yukinoshita's bearing was just that beautiful. Her clear, pale eyes showed vivid determination, her smile shy, her cheeks dusted pink.

Maybe that was why none of us could formulate a response.

Just one of us—Haruno—let out a tiny breath like a sigh.

I looked over at the source of the sound, and my breath caught again. There, I saw an expression much resembling Yukinoshita's. That smile was beguiling, kind, and soft—but somehow cold.

"I see. So that's your answer, Yukino-chan," Haruno said gently, a kind of tenderness crossing her face, and Yukinoshita nodded back at her without a word.

But Haruno's gaze remained cold as she silently evaluated her for a while. But when she saw that Yukinoshita's stance wouldn't budge an inch, she let out a short sigh. "Oh well. I guess you've improved somewhat," she said, more to herself than anyone, returning to her aloof manner once more as she reached out for her glass. She tossed back her remaining champagne in one go and lowered her gaze to the empty glass in her hand.

I couldn't know what she saw reflected in that warped glass. A single droplet trailed down from the rim. She watched it with satisfaction, then gave a little nod. "I get what you want to say. If you're serious, then I'll help you out."

"...You'll help?" That word seemed to bother Yukinoshita, and she gave her sister a dubious look.

Haruno grinned back at her. "Yep." Her affirmative reply was straightforward and brief, but Yukinoshita did not appear relieved.

I wasn't, either. I knew a thing or two about Haruno Yukinoshita, including that I couldn't take her words at face value. So even knowing my intervention was uncalled-for, I jumped in anyway. "...Um, how, specifically?" I asked.

"I'm sure our mother won't change her plans so easily, either, which means we have to take the time to talk to her, right? I'll choose the right time to put in a good word with her," Haruno answered with a lighthearted wink.

As Haruno said, their mother's opinion would be difficult to change. I hadn't exactly had a deep conversation with her—I hadn't even known her for very long at all—but I'd heard enough from that exchange between her and Yukinoshita to know this. My incredibly personal impression of her was that she seemed like the type who had no use for other people's opinions.

Her words had been superficially meant for her daughter, but I'd gotten the feeling they had actually been for me. If the two of them always interacted this way, I doubted Yukinoshita speaking with her alone would result in a real dialogue.

She was as stubborn as I'd assumed Yukinoshita was when we'd first met, and the way she could pretend to listen as she ignored you also reminded me of Haruno. Guess I should say they're chips off the old block?

That being the case, Haruno's age would give her the slight advantage of longer association with their mother. Maybe there would be some purpose to having her as backup.

Or so I thought, but Haruno suddenly burst into giggles. "But I don't know if that would work or not." Laughing off her own words, she upturned her champagne bottle to pour the rest into her glass.

*I have no idea if she's trustworthy…*

Haruno's laughter settled down, and then once the contents of her glass were in her stomach, her manner did a one-eighty, and she shot Yukinoshita a serious look. "But you should be ready to not come back here for a while."

"…I'm sure," Yukinoshita replied.

"Huh?" Yuigahama made a startled sound, and Haruno smiled wryly.

"She made me come here because she's worried about Yukino-chan. So if Yukino-chan comes back, Mom won't let her go that easily."

Ah. Surveillance.

Or maybe I should call it management. Well, she is a minor, so some level of that is expected. They're called "guardians" because they guard you.

"Pack your bags ahead of time," Haruno continued. "And make

sure to call Mom, too. If she tells you to come back suddenly, you'll need to be pretty prepared."

*Ahhh, it's like that thing my grandma tells me when my dad gets the idea to go to his parents' house. The thing where she makes me eat enough food to kill me afterward. Grandma, I may be young, but there's a limit to the size of my stomach...*

But this wasn't the time to be pondering the Hikigaya family drama. This was about the Yukinoshita family drama.

Yukinoshita briefly considered this, then nodded obediently. "Yes, I'll do that."

"Then assuming you'll be going back home...I guess I'll be using this place for a while. You're okay with that, right?" Haruno asked.

"It's not as if it ever belonged to me in the first place, so you can do with it what you please," Yukinoshita answered without hesitation.

Giving an overserious *mm-hmm*, Haruno showed her appreciation. "Thanks. It would've been a hassle to pack up my things again. Once you're all ready, then come over."

From what I could tell, Yukinoshita's return home would be a fairly long sojourn. She would be commuting from her parents' house to school as well, and her whole lifestyle base would shift over. I kinda thought, like, *You can't have that much to pack, do you?* But I'm also a guy; I don't think that's how it works for girls. Girls need all sorts of stuff, like clothes and hair dryers and skincare and stuff. When Komachi travels, she carries a lot of bags, too.

I don't understand those struggles, but Yuigahama, being a fellow girl, understood quite well. She raised her hand like she was volunteering in class. "Ohhh! I'll help, too!"

"Oh, I couldn't make you do that...," said Yukinoshita.

"It's totally okay! Actually, I want you to let me help! I like tidying and stuff!"

"But..."

With Yuigahama pushing ("C'mon, c'mon!"), Yukinoshita got more timid ("No, no..."), and they wound up arguing back and forth.

Just as I started to worry it would never end, Yuigahama lowered her head. "I mean, it seems like that's all I can help you with…" Her muttering sounded despondent, and Yuigahama must have noticed that herself. She quickly lifted her head with a weak laugh. Yukinoshita was left in apologetic silence.

Watching was kind of painful for me, too. It would be counter to Yukinoshita's wishes to butt in with my opinions about her own decision. But Yuigahama's noble desire to do something was a valuable gift. So then what should I do?

I didn't have to rack my brain over this. The words came out smoothly.

"Why not? Unpaid labor is hard to come by these days. Even the most sweatshoppy offices these days will have Labor Standards rushing in on them right away," I said the moment the thought hit me—a very Hachiman kind of remark, blurting out nonsense like always. I thought it came out pretty well for an idea that had jumped straight to the conclusion with nothing resembling a process. Exploitation of passion for the job, unpaid overtime, two-day weekends (we didn't say you could take those days off)… Ahhh, what a lovely ring it had.

But I was the only one basking in such self-satisfaction. Of course, Yukinoshita and Yuigahama were both giving me harsh looks.

The one person cracking a smile here was Haruno. "Well, maybe that's a good idea. Why don't you stay the night while you're at it? Once Yukino-chan goes back home, you won't be able to come over so casually anymore."

It was a very big-sister-like statement, far gentler than her usual. Beneath it was something almost mournful. It was true; if Yukinoshita was returning to her parents' house, then Yuigahama would be staying over less frequently.

Even this one fact was a sign of something slowly changing, and it seemed that was enough to soften Yukinoshita out of her stubborn refusal. She'd been drawing back slightly, but now her back rounded just a little as her glance flicked up to Yuigahama. "…Would you…mind?" she asked, soft and reticent with a little blush. She must have felt shy about expressly asking.

With a broad grin, Yuigahama gave her a light smack on the thigh. "Yeah! Of course!"

"Thank you..." Maybe Yukinoshita didn't like having her thigh smacked, or maybe such a direct smile was too much for her to look at, as she quickly said her thanks and sneaked her gaze away. The one that gaze fell on was Haruno. "...But if Yuigahama is to stay over, then we won't have enough guest beds," she said, examining her sister.

Haruno bopped the sofa under her. "I can handle this for one night. Besides, I'll probably be drinking alone the whole time," she replied as she shook her now-empty champagne bottle.

Yukinoshita sighed at her. "...I see. Well then, I'll do that."

"Yeah." As if to indicate the conversation was over, Haruno hopped to her feet. "I'm off to the corner store. You need anything?" she asked.

The other girls shook their heads. Answering with a nod, Haruno snatched up her coat from where it hung over a chair and headed for the door.

As I watched her go, the clock caught my eye. It was getting pretty late, so this was the perfect moment for me to take my leave. "Then I'm going home, too."

If I stayed and took my time hanging around, I'd get stuck helping Yukinoshita pack her bags, too. And if that happened, I'd be touching all sorts of girl things and wind up going *Muh-heh!* like the protagonist from a Mitsuru Adachi manga, and then through gradual erosion, I might find myself staying the night.

*And that can't happen! If I don't escape now, then I'll wind up with the same face as Tatsuya and Hiro! And, like, I just don't belong in a girl's room. It's not very comfortable...*

I quickly rose to my feet to follow after Haruno. As if in response, Yukinoshita and Yuigahama also stood and came after me. It seemed they were coming to see me off.

While I was crouched down to put on my shoes at the step by the door, Haruno shoved her feet into her sandals and went out the door ahead of me. *Lovely. She won't accommodate others even at times like these...*

Not that I wanted to go out with her and have an awkward time in the elevator, either. So I put on my shoes slowly to deliberately create as much distance between us as possible.

Then from behind, a shoehorn was quietly held out to me.

"Oh, thanks." I took it with gratitude and turned around to see a meek-looking Yukinoshita.

After releasing the shoehorn, her hand swayed idly, then went to hug her other arm. "I'm sorry. I didn't mean to make you listen to me rambling...," she muttered, head hanging, and I responded with a shallow nod.

It had been rambling, and it probably wasn't going to change much. It was just that Yukinoshita was going to do what she had decided herself—a confirmation of the obvious.

"Oh, it's fine," I said. "It needed to happen."

For her, and for me, too.

Standing up, I tapped my toes to make sure my shoes were on properly, then returned the shoehorn to Yukinoshita.

"...Thank you," she said with a little smile as she accepted it.

It made me feel antsy, and I let myself look away. "I didn't do anything, though. If you're gonna thank anyone, thank Yuigahama," I said, turning the subject to the other girl behind her. "Good luck with packing."

Yuigahama clasped a fist tight in front of her chest. "Leave it to me! I'm okay with organization!"

*That implies she's bad at other domestic tasks.* ...Well, I'd never had the impression she was great at cleaning and organizing, either. But now that her cooking had improved, she would probably learn to do other things, too.

It was slow enough that you wouldn't notice it, the shift so trivial that you might miss it, but we were changing, bit by bit.

"See you, then." I put my hand on the doorknob, turning back my head.

Yuigahama waved both her hands in front of her chest, while Yukinoshita gave the tiniest wave, half-raised, just over her waist.

"Yeah. See you, Hikki."

"Take care."

Having them say good-bye to me like that was kind of awkward. With a wordless nod in response, I hurried out.

× × ×

I was alone in the elevator, and when I got off again, the lobby was as silent as I'd expected. The time being what it was, there wouldn't be that many people coming and going.

This was a quiet residential area, and since it was a high-society apartment district, well, it was no wonder there were fewer passersby as the night drew darker. I felt that personally as I took a step out into the lobby.

There, I found a woman in attire not very becoming of a high-class residential district.

It was Haruno Yukinoshita, who I'd thought had left ahead of me.

Her pile-fabric hooded parka was striped in pale pastels, fluffy and soft-looking. It had a zipper all the way up the front, but she had it loosely opened at the chest, and her graceful, shapely legs were bared beneath her fluffy shorts. With a coat casually slung over her shoulders, she clashed a little with the stylish interior decoration of the lobby, and there was a precarious beauty to that contrast.

*Her looks already get her attention, so it's kind of unfair for her to be so totally unguarded...*

I wouldn't normally want to start up a conversation with her, but it would be weird to ignore her when she was standing around the entrance. With her grinning at me and beckoning, I had no choice but to approach.

"…I thought you left ahead of me," I said.

Haruno giggled, then whispered like she was sharing a secret, "This makes it like a private rendezvous. It's nice, right?"

"I think that's called an ambush."

Even if both count as "waiting," they're as different as Aming and Yuming. Oh, but when you think about it, those songs "I'll Wait" and "Ambush" are just different routes to the same end, huh? They're both scary, ultimately…

But the scariest of all had to be Haruno Yukinoshita. She started walking like she had no doubt I would follow. The closest convenience store was probably the one by the station, and I was heading in that direction to go home anyway, so it was fine…

Following after Haruno as she walked a step ahead, I went along the street of apartment buildings. When we came out to the wide main road, the nighttime winter breeze blew on through. The coldness stroking her cheeks made Haruno hunch into her coat, burying her face.

Then she seemed to notice something, sniffing. She looked at the shoulders of her coat and immediately scowled. *What is it…?* I wondered, staring at her, and Haruno thrust an arm out at me.

"Mm," she said grumpily as she came up to my side. The hand she'd reached out remained dangling there as if it meant something.

*Uhhh… What the hell…?*

*Wait, calm down… She wants me to hold her hand? Huh, why? To get my fingerprints? That's it. Amazing deduction. Oh nooo, she's gonna break into my iPhone and make unauthorized charges! Stop it! Stop rolling for gacha until you get a five-star!*

Flustered and increasingly uncomfortable, I turned away, and suddenly, I caught the odor of cigarettes. "…Ahhh, is that the smell?"

"Uh-huh," Haruno replied, but her attention was not on me, and she withdrew her hand and sniff-sniffed again.

It had probably gotten into her coat while she was drinking at a bar. I'm familiar with that myself, from the time I had a part-time gig at an *izakaya*. Maybe that shower had been to get the smell out of her hair.

Perhaps smokers aren't really bothered by it after all that time around it, but the smell is gross to a nonsmoker. The kind that was bothering Haruno had a particularly strong tarry odor, very much the old-fashioned pungent tobacco scent.

The menthol type would be bearable, as would the ones with an added sweet flavor like vanilla or something fruity, the slim kind that women seemed to like.

*…So she was drinking with a man?*

*A man? Yep, a man. Her boyfriend, huh? Wait. For real? She has a boyfriend?*

Well, she was an adult; it wasn't strange for her to have a boyfriend, you know? But actually coming into contact with this sort of information felt really harsh for some reason. Like a voice actress announcing her marriage. Just stop titling your blog posts "An Announcement." It gets my heart racing. I have to go lie down. And then I'll even lie about. And then I'll even lie down on the job.

But this was no time to be going through indescribable shock— *actually, I'm not really shocked at all! Listen! It's just that I got a little startled by the news! I-it's not like I have a crush on her, okay?!*

*Phew… If she were someone closer to me, that would've been a solid hit. Specifically, if it were Komachi, or Komachi, or Komachi. Also, maybe Komachi!*

After letting my mind wander for a bit, I reached a momentary calm. Komachi really is great; she works on sudden fevers, heart palpitations, and shortness of breath— Wait, is she some kind of heart remedy?

Anyway, if Haruno's coat smelled this strongly of cigarettes, then she must have been at that bar for a pretty long time. I assumed she'd used some deodorizing spray or something, but the smell was too deep even for that.

"…You were drinking for quite a while, huh?" I asked.

"Yeah. They wouldn't quite let me go. I just about wound up going till morning." Haruno sighed with some annoyance.

"Uh…uh-huh."

Going till morning? Isn't that kinda, y'know, indecent? I mean, like, I totally thought *Live TV Till Morning!* was a sexy show. And then because of that, *It's Morning! It's Live Travel Salad* has a fairly sexy vibe, too.

Anyway, I had acquired information on Haruno I never wanted to know… Has the *Weekly Hachiman* dropped another explosive bombshell?! No, I meant that to be more like celebratory fireworks. Sometimes our scoops are positive, you know? But this was not the time for such lame-ass excuses. In fact, if you considered that it was her drinking that had made her act like this now, then I'd be thankful for it. There was no reason for me to be shocked.

The fact was that normally, I think Haruno would have interrogated Yukinoshita more. But she seemed almost cheerful now.

Because I kept looking over at her face, I wound up a step behind her, while Haruno stretched with a *hnn*. "Good thing I could get back early! Thanks to that, I got to hear what Yukino-chan wanted to say," she said, before letting out a sigh that almost sounded relieved, and I fell silent.

"…"

My lack of engagement must have bothered Haruno; she turned back to me with a "Hmm?" She seemed to be pondering the meaning of my silence.

I gave a small shake of my head to say it was nothing. "…Oh, just thinking it was a little surprising," I said.

Haruno spun on her heel and said in a silly tone, "What is?"

"What's so surprising? I mean…that you'd just listen to her talk."

"Come on. Of course I would. I *am* her big sister." Haruno let out an exasperated chuckle, and I thought she was going to keep walking backward, but then she turned forward again. "You'll hear out Komachi-chan when she has a request, too, won't you?"

"…Well, when you put it like that, I do get what you mean."

If it were about Komachi and me, her point would make sense.

If Komachi asked me for something, something she wanted from the heart, I'm sure I'd try to get it for her without a moment's hesitation. The only answer I had for a Komachi comparison was a groan.

That made Haruno smile. "Right? If that's what Yukino-chan's chosen, then I'll support her in that. Whether it's right or wrong."

"If it's wrong, then wouldn't it be logical to stop her?"

"She wouldn't listen to me. And I don't care either way. It's all the same whether it goes well or whether she gives up on it...," she muttered. I couldn't see her face, but I wanted to know what it looked like right then. I picked up the pace to catch up.

But I didn't get much closer, only enough to get a peek at her profile. Eventually, we crossed the overpass that spanned a major road and came to the side path that went through the park.

Pale-orange streetlamps stood in rows on a field of browning grass. With each step forward, the light swept over her, casting its warm glow and cold shadow on her white cheeks. It was difficult to catch her expression—just like her vague, seemingly contradictory words.

After passing through the trees covering the field, the view opened up again as we came to a promenade that ran through the central area of the park.

When we reached a tree-lined path that ran alongside a long, continuous fountain, Haruno let her pace relax a bit and looked up at the sky. I did the same and saw the crescent moon floating there and, underneath it, the dual high-rise apartment towers wreathed in a hazy, pallid light.

Hopping along the stairs, Haruno turned back to me. "Giving up and letting go is how you become an adult."

"Huh. Is that right...?" Narrowing your world probably is the approach to adulthood. Shaving your options down, eliminating possibilities, carving out a more certain image of the future. This was something I could understand, and maybe Yukinoshita's decision was also of that type.

But as Haruno spoke, there was a hint of something almost plaintive in her sorrowful eyes that bothered me. Maybe it was the distance in the way she was talking, as if this wasn't actually personal to her.

"...Um, so you've experienced something similar?" I asked.

"Oh, I dunno." She chuckled at me. "This isn't about me, is it? Right now, we're talking about Yukino-chan... This has probably been the first time she's actually been open about that. You watch over her, too, Hikigaya." I sensed she was implicitly telling me not to interfere; the nuance here was similar to that other time, when she'd told me over the phone that I'm "nice."

I had no objection to the idea of "respecting Yukinoshita's will" in and of itself. I had no right to interject my opinion here anyway. I could agree with what Haruno was saying. This was probably how I'd wanted it to go. And I wasn't the only one who felt that way. If Haruno Yukinoshita would approve of it, then there was no need to find problems in it.

"...Yeah."

Haruno must have been satisfied with my reply, as she folded her hands casually behind her, arching her back as she laughed happily. "Heh-heh, here I am, being the big sister again..."

"How about you always be her big sister?" I said jokingly.

But Haruno had an instant reply. "Don't wanna." She turned her head in my direction, letting her smile slide over to me. "I'm not like you. You're always doing the big brother thing, though."

"...I mean...I am a big brother." *Why's she saying something so obvious?*

I'm a veteran, having been one ever since Komachi was born. I didn't even have to be conscious of it—I was made to live as a perpetual big brother. I could say that with pride.

Haruno gave me a long look, then suddenly burst into laughter. "I see. What a nice big brother. Wish I could've had a big brother like you." She cackled, although I'm not completely sure it was a joke, then slung an arm around my shoulders as if giving in to the alcohol. She put her weight on me as she leaned in coquettishly.

Her softness and nice smile really made me anxious. "Hey...you're annoying when you're drunk..."

"I'm not drunk! I'm not."

I tried to gently peel her off, but she swayed on her unsteady legs, stepping along beside me, and wouldn't quite back off.

As we continued on, the tree-lined path ended, and we approached the way to the station.

Go over two crosswalks, and that would lead you right to the outlet mall. Though operating hours were over, the avenue that led to the square in front of the station was lit by warm lights. Haruno still had her arm around my shoulders, and I was getting anxious about someone seeing us.

We reached the point where the station was to the right and the convenience store was to the left, and I carefully shrugged her off and scooted a step away. "Um...can you manage to get home?"

"Oh, you're sooo niiice. Wooow. What a gentleman!" She smacked my shoulder like she was saying, *So you're the Gentleman Friend who's good at being nice to women, huh?!*

...*God, she's annoying.* My face stiffened, but I got it moving again to give her a particularly nasty look. "I'm not a gentleman. I do intend to go straight home."

Haruno smiled pleasantly again. "I'm all right." But then she tucked away that smile, and the tone of her response was very cool. I could have sworn her eyes were tipsy before, but now they shone with a bone-chillingly cold light. "That's not enough to get me drunk," she said, but I didn't know how much she'd had.

From her tone, she was already different from before. I could tell this was the usual Haruno Yukinoshita, no twists or trembles or shrillness. She sounded just like always—beautiful, enchanting, with an intoxicating ring to her voice, like it would haunt you till death.

And so, to keep myself from being sucked in, I took my usual stance. I looked away with a sigh, keeping my voice quiet enough that maybe she'd hear, maybe she wouldn't. "...I hear that all drunks say that," I said sarcastically.

"I really don't get drunk... Maybe I can't," she murmured. She'd hooked me in, and I found myself glancing at Haruno again. When I did, she was looking into the distance.

Though her cheeks were still pink, her gaze was utterly cool, and though her lips were drawn, the expression was not a smile. "No matter how much I drink, there's a part of myself behind it that's calm. I can even tell what expression I'm making. I can laugh and enjoy myself, but it feels like it's happening to someone else."

Even now, her words were still distant, as if she were describing someone else. The way she spoke about herself was distinctly objective, and it was vague where the subject of the sentence would be. Her idle, unprompted remark seemed like a mix of truth and lies.

When she noticed I'd fallen silent and was just staring at her, she stuck out her tongue to play it off as a joke. "...So you toss it all back and get sick and puke, then after that, you just fall asleep."

"That's the worst way to get drunk...," I replied lightly, going along with her "joke."

She put a hand on her mouth and giggled. "It really is." Then she started walking again, taking one step away from me, then another. As I watched her go, assuming she would continue on her way to the convenience store, she turned back to me.

That smile seemed to have a touch of affection and sympathy. It was the kindest smile I'd ever seen from her. "But you'll probably be the same... Let me make a prophecy for you. You won't be able to get drunk," she said. The remark was far too unsettling for a farewell.

"Don't, please—in the future, I plan to be either an über-corporate slave forced into drinking with my coworkers, or an ultra-househusband who'll have a beer at lunch in the middle of the day on my wife's dime." I responded with a bold and unpleasant smile, then took just one step forward as well.

When I turned back after that, she was still there, watching me go with an expression that was more innocent than usual. There was a comfortable distance between us, about three steps in total. It made me say too much.

"...And, like, I think you really are drunk," I said.

The words she'd said, that genuinely happy smile. It was as if she was exposing the real Haruno Yukinoshita, and I could only think she was actually drunk.

She gave me a blank look. "Am I...? I suppose I am. Let's call it that, yeah." She brought a hand to her mouth, hiding the quirk of a smile there, and nodded innocently.

As Haruno waved her hand with a "See you," I bowed to her and turned away.

She blamed the alcohol and put on another mask—while telling the great lie that alcohol is a lubricant to open up the heart. She never does show her true face, but she'll deliberately show you the cracks in the mask. I still don't know what her truth is.

If you judged that contradictory nature of hers—perhaps just the way she got by—to be shrewd wiles born from experience, then that would indeed make her an adult. More of one than me anyway. When she can't ultimately accept something, she's capable of pretending she's forgotten it entirely.

The night had grown late, and the town slumbered in quiet darkness. The only lights were the hazy ones from buildings and the taillamps of taxis waiting for customers. As I left the station area, the sounds of the hustle and bustle there grew distant.

It was so quiet, just one thing she'd said to me wouldn't leave my ears.

*You won't be able to get drunk.*

I got the feeling that prophecy would come true.

# Interlude...

I really do like cleaning and organizing.
I'm not good at it at all. But I like it.
When things are all scattered everywhere in a mess, neglected and hopeless, I like to tidy them up one by one. 'Cause while I do it, I can feel good about what I'm doing.
The two of us stayed behind in her apartment, and as we were talking about where to start, she said she had to get some empty boxes and garbage bags and stuff. She went out, and I waited a bit.
I looked around her room, but it was all nice and organized. So organized that it didn't look like you'd need to bother cleaning anything. Unlike my room, it felt like there wasn't much extra junk.
There was just one corner of the space, at the head of the bed, that had a lot of exciting stuff. Stuffed animals, cat merch, and other things—probably stuff she liked, that was important to her. It was a modest little collection. The decorating scheme was basically monotone, mostly cool colors like blue, aqua, and silver, but this one corner was girly and soft. It was cute. I petted the little stuffed panda.
That was when I found a plastic bag behind it, apparently hidden there. The black, square, and flat bag was a little out of place in that charming spot.

I got the feeling I'd seen that bag somewhere, so I reached for it without thinking.

Opening the bag a crack, I peeked inside and saw it was a souvenir photo. I'd gotten one of those a long time ago myself—when my family had gone for a day out together, the one they took at the end of a ride.

I knew I shouldn't look, but I opened it anyway.

I knew the two I saw there.

One was a little startled and kinda silly-looking but clearly having fun.

While the other was all curled up and flinching, eyes closed, hiding behind the other's back but holding that hand tight.

—*Ohhh, I knew it.*

That's all I thought. I'd been so worried about whether they'd been able to have a proper talk, so I was honestly relieved. I thought it was cute—the photo, that she'd held on to it and treasured it like this, and that she'd hidden it.

That was why I quietly pushed it back in the corner where I'd found it.

Forget it.

Make it so you never saw it.

That won't erase it from history—but you can forget it.

I'm sure that's what she intended, too. Not setting it out, but instead tucking it away so very carefully behind her treasures. She never thought to say it out loud or do anything about it.

Maybe I should've asked about the picture. Maybe I should've jokingly teased her. Maybe I should've smiled and said something like, *Go for it! I'm rooting for you!*

But if I did that, it'd probably all be over, so…

If I asked, if I pried, she'd say she didn't. She'd go, *No, no way*, and that would be the end of the discussion. Not acknowledging it, letting it slide by, overlooking it, turning a blind eye. Erase it, forget it, make it go away.

So I'd never ask.

It'd be unfair to ask about her feelings. It'd be unfair to say my own.

But I'm scared to know his feelings.

So making it her fault is the most unfair.

The truth is, I realized a long time ago.

There's a place I can't go. I've come to stand in front of that door a bunch of times, but I can tell that going in is impossible for me. I only ever peek in through the cracks and listen.

The truth is, I realized a long time ago.

I want to go there.

And not just that.

The truth is—

*—I never wanted something real.*

## **Komachi Hikigaya** takes him by surprise and gets formal.

The chilly air woke me up.

The faint morning light was streaming through the window, blurry in my sleepy eyes. The edges of the roofs slowly turned white from the soft reflected light.

The sky was a little cloudy that day—fitting weather for my still-hazy thoughts.

I rolled over and looked at the clock. This late, I'd normally be panicking and jumping out of bed, but fortunately, thanks to the high school entrance exams, I didn't have school. I let my drowsy head and gradually sagging eyelids do as they would, ready to once more indulge in sloth.

But a couple of the words that had just popped into my head raced around my mind once more.

*Entrance exams!* Yes, the second day of Komachi's entrance exams! My parents would have already left the house, so I had to see her off!

I bounded up, and with a *moxie energy wakety!* I shot out of my bedroom and thundered down the stairs. I stepped into the living room, smothering a yawn, right when dreamy-cute Komachi was about to leave the house.

Her favorite hairpin was sparkling, her middle school uniform particularly crisp and precisely worn to school regulation. When my dear little sister noticed me, she raised her hand in a little *'Sup* gesture. "Ohhh. Mornin'."

"Hey," I replied. At the table, I found breakfast and coffee covered with plastic wrap that seemed to be my share.

Komachi was barely finished saying good morning to me when her eyes went back into her bag. She had to be doing her final check before departure. But it seemed about all she was taking was her exam ticket and her pencil case. Once she had that tucked away, she patted her bag to make it flat.

There was something lonely about the empty, flat bag over Komachi's shoulder, and I realized her entrance exams were mostly over.

The written exams for all subjects had ended the day before, and all that was left was the interview. She wouldn't have to bring any reference material or vocab books. And the interview was pretty pointless, too. In Chiba public high schools, academic exams tend to carry more weight, so the first day is what sets you on course.

As is the way of entrance examinees, Komachi would have brought home a problem sheet with answers written on it, and she would be self-grading. If she felt she'd done well, then that was good, of course, but if she got worried over some errors and couldn't concentrate in her interviews—well, I could hardly bear to see that.

Concerned, I tried indirectly inquiring how she was feeling. "How was it?" I reached for the coffee left there and took a sip. I was making an effort to ask completely lightly and cheerfully, choosing words that were vague and nonchalant.

Komachi gave me a blank look, stuck her finger out to touch it to her chin, bent her head to the side, and commenced pondering. "Hmm… Well, so-so. No point freaking out about it now anyway." She sounded particularly calm, a smile in her tone.

*That's some impressive resolve. She's as calm as if she's been told the end of the century's coming. She's so calm, you might even think she's been made into a wax doll. Wait, that was Seikima-II, huh?* Either way, it seemed Komachi was coolheaded now, which was a bit of a relief.

But that cool was not necessarily derived from a positive source.

"Besides, the exam yesterday was basically what decides everything," she added with a wry smile, her words revealing mild unease. A certain type of resignation can occasionally bring a quiet enlightenment. Right now, Komachi was superficially as peaceful as the surface of a placid lake, but a single breeze would churn up the waves.

So I'd bring up something completely unrelated—even if that would just be escapism, even if it was just running from what lay before her. I knew shoving reality in someone's face and battering them with logic wasn't always the right thing to do. "...Once it's over, wanna go out to eat together?" Sloshing sugar and milk into my still-lukewarm coffee, I stirred it into a color that was neither black nor white, but my particular sort of brown.

Komachi grinned a little impishly. "Oh? That's a great idea."

"I know, right?"

"Yeah, yeah!"

I grinned back at her, and Komachi clapped her hands, then put her hands on her cheeks. Then she started twisting around in a deliberately cutesy act. "With a treat from you as a reward, Komachi can do her best! *Blush, blush.* That was worth a lot of Komachi points, *blush, blush.*"

"I'm not gonna treat you. And that scores low..." *I mean, I used up most of my money yesterday...*

But if she was saying this would help her do her best—even jokingly—then I could try scraping the bottom of my wallet. "Well, a date with your little sister doesn't happen every day. I can manage the cost of the food somehow." With a smug chuckle, I jokingly played the part of a rich royal showing off his fortunes.

But Komachi's expression turned suddenly icy. "Yeah, uh, when you call it a date, it really makes Komachi not want to go, though. But if it's all expenses paid, then Komachi'll bear with it."

"Stop it, stop it, don't act so serious... What the heck do you mean, bear with it? That hurts. It was an innocent big brother joke... You're the only one I can say stuff like this to, so it's fine, right...?"

And then as I was dissolving into blubbering tears, Komachi kicked me while I was down. "Whoa, and it's creepy when you get like this, too...," she said, sounding highly aggravated.

*So harsh... Hey, wait, when did it stop being just lunch? Now even the train ticket has wound up on my dime, too... Where did she learn that lingo anyway? Has she reached the age where she wants to act like an adult? Oh no, Komachi-chan is slowly growing up...*

Looking over at my sister, I saw she was giggling. She hefted the shoulder of her bag up again with a *hup* and waved her cell phone before heading out of the living room. "Okeydoke, then I'll give you a call once it's over."

"Understood. When you're waiting for your interview, think about what you wanna eat, just to kill time," I said, with the silent implication, *Don't worry too much*, though I didn't mind if that didn't get across. I followed her to the front door.

She shoved her feet into her loafers, hopping on each foot to make sure they were on right, then turned back. "...Yeah, I will." Her smile seemed calm—mature, somehow.

I knew it was for my own sake, but I decided to believe that even if I didn't say something specific or ask, my intentions would reach just one person in the world, just this girl.

Komachi's earlier smile was tucked away as she drew in a deep breath and sharply saluted with extra energy. "Right then, time for departure!"

"Roger, see you later."

Komachi spun on her heel and pattered away as I watched.

*All right, guess I'll look up some restaurants and get ready for that outing, huh?*

× × ×

Once it got close to lunchtime, I went to the station closest to my school and dawdled for a while.

I wasn't quite sure what time Komachi's exam would be over—partly because the only thing they did on the second day was the interview. You were allowed to leave once yours was done, so I didn't know what Komachi's exam number was. I couldn't guess as to when she'd be out. The examinees couldn't, either—their heads would be full of the test, and they wouldn't be thinking about what time it would end.

So then it was clear what I should do: lie in ambush by the school.

*Hachiman will wait so hard, it'll make both Aming and Yuming blanch. I'll pretend to be cute, and I'll do a good job at it.*

But still, lying in wait behind a tree by the school, murmuring her name like Hyuuma Hoshi's older sister, would be a little uncomfortable. Specifically, socially uncomfortable for me. We'd narrowly avoided yet *another* incident where the son of the Hachiman household got written up in the neighborhood bulletin that was passed around the whole block! You can identify him from his black clothes! We like black clothes too much...

Since I didn't want to get immediately reported to the police, I decided to go kill some time close by as I waited for Komachi.

*And so here we are at the Marinpia right by Inagekaigan Station!*

I went into the old Jasco—now called Aeon—and hung around the bookstore. I bought a few random books there, and then for some really good time-killing, I headed for the Saize not too far from the station. Saize or bust! It's A-OK to go there alone!

The Saize at Inagekaigan is on the second floor of the building in front of the station, so you can get a good view of the people going by. My scheme was thus: Once I started seeing a lot of kids in middle school uniforms, I'd know the exam was over!

*If I could kill time in the Chiba station area, I might just be a genius...,* I thought. Trembling in awe at my own talent, I headed outside.

The chill of the wind blowing through the wide main street of the seaside area made me shiver. *It was already cold out here, and with this wind...* I rewrapped my scarf and buried my face in it.

That was when, out of the corner of my eye, I caught a familiar figure.

She was in the St-Marc Café that faced the street, right to the side of the Marinpia exit. At an outward-facing counter seat, a bluish-black ponytail was restlessly swaying on the other side of the glass.

*Hmm?* I thought with a doubtful look.

I found that Miss Ponytail was fussing over a little girl with

similarly colored, bouncing bluish pigtails, wiping the girl's mouth and having her blow her nose and such.

And if we're talking about little girls I know, I could think of only one. It was Keika Kawasaki. And as for who would be fussing over her… yes, that was Kawa-something!

*Those sisters are really close, huh? Totally unlike a certain other pair of sisters*, I thought as I found myself watching the pleasant scene, when through the glass, my eyes locked with another big, blinking pair.

Keika opened her mouth wide and pointed at me, on the other side of the glass. Then her mouth was moving, opening and closing as she said something. *Aw man, this is so cute…*

But this wasn't the time to be having heart-eyes for Keika's cuteness. Kawasaki immediately noticed me as well, and her eyes met mine.

We exchanged little nods.

Then we both froze.

We were both solidly in Jizo statue mode. We were so Jizo, we could even get little hats to go with the offerings. This Jizo time was a time for seeking, and a bit of a time for thinking. And so of course, we had to make use of this time with a pop quiz!

So here's the question: If you run into a classmate in town, what's the right thing to do? It's a push-button quiz, fastest finger first! Get seven answers right, and you win! If you buzz too quickly three times, then you're out!

But there was no need to answer any questions. The answer here was simple.

If it's someone you've never really talked with before, the correct response is to pretend you never saw them. If it's a classmate you're not really friends with, then it's smart to offer just a casual greeting and leave. If it's a close friend, then you can see them any time, so there's no need to bother getting into a conversation. As before, you can just leave. In other words, with anyone you meet in town, the correct response is to leave!

For this reason, I'd have been glad to have smoothly slipped away, but this was Kawasaki. When I started thinking about our relationship, my feet stopped on their own.

Maybe that was why—even with a layer of glass between us—I could see she was bewildered. The encounter felt similar to running into your cat outside. The distance between both parties feels delicate, like if you take one step closer, the cat'll nyoom away.

Something was seesawing between us, completely bringing us to a standstill—it was so bad, I wanted to call for help like the dude from the insurance ads. *Someone help…!*

As I was mentally seeking help from Axa Direct, the one to come to my aid was not Axa but Keika.

Keika was smiling brightly as she kept waving her hands to beckon me over. I will properly refuse regular invitations with an "I'll go if I can," but I'll easily give in to an invitation from a little girl. Hi, that's me.

*But she's a minor! Oh dear! I may be tempted to accept, but I have to get the okay from her guardian. Otherwise, I'll just be arrested!*

As I was glancing over, thinking, *Oh dear, shouldn't I get permission from her guardian?* Kawasaki appeared to scold Keika with some embarrassment, then started to pacify her. But Keika puffed up her cheeks and jerked her face away, and Kawasaki blew a little sigh.

Then Kawasaki moved the bag off the seat beside her and shot me an examining look. For a moment, she seemed to be muttering something under her breath, before opening her mouth a crack to say just a few words. I think she was saying "Wanna come over?" She immediately jerked her head away, so I couldn't see clearly.

Well, if I had permission, then I would be delighted to oblige. I would go talk with them—just offer a greeting, a very casual two or three words. Here a hi, there a hi, everywhere a hi-hi.

× × ×

When I entered the café, a sigh drifted out of me. Mostly from the temperature and humidity, but I'd personally like to cast a vote for the bright smile before me. The sight of Keika Kawasaki was just that heartwarming.

"It's Haa-chan!"

"Ohhh, it's been a long time, huh?" I said. "Well, guess not really—we saw each other just a little while ago. You doing good?" *Feels like it's been two years or more...*

As I rubbed rough circles nostalgically around the top of Keika's head, she giggled and replied, "I'm good!" She patted the chair to the left of her own.

Guess that meant I should sit there.

*What a smart, cool, and dashing way to make an invitation... Aha! Then she's a "hot stud," eh?* Having a reputation for being weak against hot studs, I obediently sat down where Keika indicated.

*I mean, I had no choice but to sit here. It'd actually be kinda scary to sit by Kawasaki! Just our shoulders lightly touching makes my heart get all fluttery! Stop it! Please don't pretend I did something to you and extort money from me under false pretenses!* Well, I know Kawasaki isn't the sort of person to threaten lunch money out of me; unfortunately, she can be actually rather scary sometimes, so what can you do.

So even as I secured a demilitarized neutral zone by putting Keika between us, I also made an attempt at conversation. "So, like, why are you out here...?"

Neither of us had much to talk about, so in a situation like this, theory would dictate that you engage via an inoffensive common subject that was close at hand. Besides, it was frankly odd for her to have come all the way out here to the Aeon by our school on a weekend. During the exam holiday period, it's customary for high school students of Chiba to lie around at home or go to Destiny Land to do something idle and fun. *...Aha! Then she's an eccentric, eh? Hmm, then what about me...?*

Whether she could guess what I was thinking or not, there was a rustling as Kawasaki indicated the shopping bags she'd earlier moved off the chair and put at her feet. "We came to shop...but then took little break…" Green onions and stuff were sticking out from the openings of the bags.

*But why would she come all this way on a weekend? I thought there was some other supermarket in her neighborhood…*

That thought changed form slightly to spill out of my mouth. "Huh. You came all this way?"

"We always shop here," she said, fidgeting and looking away with embarrassment.

Without missing a beat, Keika shot up her hand. "Point card!" she shouted with a triumphant chuckle. In her hand was a card with a dog character printed on it.

*Ahhh, that thing that barks when you scan it at the register,* I thought, succumbing to the little girl's adorableness.

Kawasaki's cheeks turned pink. "Kei-chan…," she chided quietly.

Keika lowered her hand.

Yeah, well, little kids will want to press the stop button on the bus or offer cards and stuff, huh…? It seemed that at the Kawasaki house, offering cards like that was Keika's job. They had to be stopping by regularly to shop, on the way home after picking her up from preschool.

*But there's other Aeons, too, so isn't the effort a bit much for a school break?* I thought with a tilt of my head.

Kawasaki noticed my confusion and added in a soft mutter, "…Taishi, too, while we're here. Since today, um, his exams are over." She avoided looking at me, turning her gaze out the window.

*Ahhh, I see. So that's why, huh?* I'd heard before that Kawasaki's younger brother, Taishi Kawasaki, was also taking the Soubu High School entrance exams. She'd probably gotten worried over him and found herself coming this way. Or something to that effect. *Whoa… What's up with that…?*

"That's a real brother complex you've got there, yikes…"

"Huh? I don't wanna hear that from you." She shot me a glare, and I automatically cringed.

"Hyerk!" Even knowing she's a good person, that sharpness of hers really is scary, okay...?

As I was curled up and trembling, I suddenly noticed the cold.

The heating at the windowside seats wasn't that great, and it felt like the frigid outside air was coming through the glass. That chilled, shiver-inducing air and the awkward pause in the conversation made me antsy. Kawasaki must have felt similarly, as her gaze kept flitting between the window, me, and Keika. My eyes naturally tended to turn toward Keika, too.

Keika was holding her kiddie glass in both hands, slurping at her orange juice through her straw. When she eventually finished it all, she let out a satisfied-sounding *ahhh*.

Looking over, I saw Kawasaki's cup was also empty. She must've been waiting for Keika to finish her drink. *So then, time to go...perhaps?* I was considering this when Kawasaki glanced at me.

"Um...and you?" Her question was curt, but I could sense the implication: *We're thinking about going soon, so...*

I thought I should use this as my opportunity to obliquely let her know I'd be leaving as well. "Yeah, I was just thinking I'd go get something to eat."

"Oh, huh...," Kawasaki replied disinterestedly. Then she lowered her gaze to Keika and patted her back. "Haa-cha..." She hesitated a moment, then rephrased herself. "Um, Big Bro says he's going."

*I mean, Keika calls me Haa-chan, so it's fine, though. In fact,* Big Bro *is even more embarrassing...*

As I was squirming a bit, there was a tug on my sleeve. "Huhhh, you're going already?"

I looked down beside me to see Keika with her eyebrows in an upside-down V, staring up at me with extreme disappointment. I hadn't even noticed her fingers curling into the fabric. *If she's gonna be like that, getting up is gonna be a challenge...* It's like when you get a full-time job and then they say to you, *You're leaving already?*

As I was wondering what to do, Kawasaki scowled at this little exchange. I was getting the sense she was about to give a low, chiding "Kei-chan..." I'd seen it before during that baking event, but it's still scary, you know...

I didn't want the guilt of turning Kawasaki's ire onto Keika, so for now, I decided I might as well intervene with some random babbling. My special skills include impersonating a lightning rod and also l'Cie heroes. Though I'm not that pretty.

"...Wanna go together? I was thinking about going to Saize," I said.

Kawasaki's eyes widened for an instant as she opened and closed her mouth. "Uh... Huh? N-no..."

"Yeah, figures." I knew that. I read online that girls don't like going with guys to Saize after all. The Internet is so huge, you can learn just about anything there.

Keika was still sulking, so I gave her a pat on the head to pacify her and stood from my seat.

Then a weak voice called me to a stop. "...Ah, hey."

When I turned around, Kawasaki's cheeks were slightly pink, her lips in an aloof pout, her eyes lowered. Then she muttered, barely above a whisper, "...W-well, if it's just tea here, then..."

"Huh? Ah, okay. Right, well, thank you. If it's tea..." Her unexpected reply made me over-polite, and I slumped back into the chair. Keika leaned sweetly against me, like *Yaaay*.

*Aw, now I've totally lost my chance to go...* Now I'd really have to order something. "Want a drink?" I asked as I stood up again.

Kawasaki seemed to snap out of her daze, eyes zipping over to Keika's hands. "Ah, uh, th-then a hot chocolate... And an iced coffee while you're at it."

"Roger."

What a big sister move, worrying more about Keika's drink than her own. Hell, I might even start smiling. I hurriedly trotted off to the register to hide it.

I swiftly finished ordering, picked up the items, then whisked the tray over to the plywood counter seats. On the tray were the hot chocolate and iced coffee Kawasaki had just asked for, plus a hot latte. And a fresh-looking chocolate croissant.

Upon my return, Keika gazed at the croissant with sparkling eyes. A sigh of wonder like Sonny Chiba's escaped her mouth. A weakness for sweets is a classic childish trait. Being that I also have experience with kids, I can recognize such feelings quite clearly. I'm the champion of children.

And so I said the words Keika would surely want me to say at that moment. "...Want some?"

Keika locked on to me with her glittering little eyes. *Heh, my strategy has been a success...* Just like a politician suddenly starts preaching about senior care and pension payment issues right before the election, I will also readily make irresponsible grabs for popularity. While I'm at it, I'll also emphasize my interest in politics to go after a collab on the next "vote at eighteen" campaign. Ministry of Internal Affairs and Communications, are you watching?

Completely oblivious to my schemes, Keika was bouncing up and down. "Yeah! This is why I love you, Haa-chan!" she said energetically, batting at my arm.

"Ha-ha-ha, of course, of course you do! But casual touches will really make boys get the wrong idea, so you can't be doing that so carelessly!"

"Okay! I'll just do it with you, Haa-chan!"

*Oh no, she's already learning how to become a heartbreaker; what a fearsome child... On the day they hear this, the boys of the world will be annihilated on the spot, and Keika's name will instantly go down in history as a mass murderer... And the first name on that memorial monument will probably be me. For the sake of world peace, I must do something about this charming terrorist early!*

As I was burning with a sense of mission, another, stealthier charming terrorist sighed. "What are you teaching to a kid...?" Putting a hand to her forehead, Kawasaki looked ready to click her tongue as she reached out from behind Keika to yank at my sleeve. Then she beckoned me with little hand motions, leaning her face in over Keika's head and lowering her voice to a whisper like she was letting me in on a secret. "Like, um…I'd rather you not do stuff like that."

"Huh?" *What doesn't she want me to do?*

*Oh, that. Does she mean like my own personal Hikaru Genji plan of winning over Keika to try to raise her into a wonderful lady? Right now, I'm making progress to rave reviews like a frantic Columbus.* "Welcome here" *or however that song goes…*

As I was thinking this, Kawasaki glanced out the window and at the climbing sun. "It's not even noon yet…"

"Y-yeah…" *Oh, I see. A kid's stomach is small, after all. If she had a snack right then, she wouldn't be able to finish her lunch. I didn't know what they were planning to eat, but if I caused trouble for the neighbors' children, it might be too much to bear. Maybe not for a bear, though.*

*But still… But still! I went to all that trouble buying this chocolate croissant to score points with a little girl… Whatever do I do?* I was thinking, when it suddenly struck me. I sneakily pushed the plate with the croissant over to Keika and whispered in her ear, "…Let's split it. Keep it a secret from your sister." I put my finger to my lips in a *shh* gesture, and Keika copied it.

"Yeah! A secret!" Nothing unifies people like sharing a secret, especially when it's a conspiracy to commit a crime.

"I can see you, okay…?" I heard a disgruntled sigh as I watched Keika nom away at the halved croissant in satisfaction. Kawasaki shot me a glare. "Don't spoil her too much."

"…H-hey, just every once in a while, you know?"

"Every once in a while? You're always like that."

"I don't think it's *always*… Keika's just special, you know. And Komachi."

"…So you're in denial, huh?" Her eyes narrowed, and the icy chill in them kicked up a notch.

*Whoa… Oh no, it's gotten even colder!* Oh, should I have, like, included Kawasaki in that? I don't get girls, seriously. This question is about as difficult as "Do you know why I'm angry?" It's an unblockable move—no matter how you answer, it's always wrong.

Seeing me flinching and getting flustered, and not knowing what to do, *bow wow wow woooow*, Kawasaki turned her attitude around and lowered her eyes apologetically. She seemed to have trouble getting the words out, but she said, "I'm glad you give Keika attention, but she has to learn restraint…"

"Yes, I'm sorry…" I gave her a proper apology. *Hey, I think it's kinda unfair to get mad and then wilt like that… If you're gonna be like that, then I can't say anything…*

Kawasaki didn't press her point any further, and the silence between us resumed.

Keika must have felt weird about the exchange going on over her head suddenly going quiet; she lifted her head, chocolate on her cheek, and looked between us anxiously. "Don't fight?"

"We're not fighting. Come on, this way, Kei-chan." Kawasaki smiled kindly, then pulled a wet tissue out from one of her shopping bags to dab at Keika's cheek. That seemed to put Keika at ease, and her attention returned to the chocolate croissant.

I don't think Kawasaki was seriously angry. If she were, she'd be even scarier… When sparks are flying between her and Yukinoshita or Miura, you'd think she's some kinda delinquent.

But now, my impression of her had softened.

Before, I'd thought that wooden swords, chains, and yo-yos would be more her speed, but lately shopping bags and green onions have been right at home with her. Actually, maybe I'm getting too used to seeing her carrying shopping bags… The way she came down to the St-Marc with a little kid who looked a lot like her really had a "mah-jongg mama" feel to it. The term *yan-mama* is way too dated.

The whole scene here felt really domestic, me included. Now if I were to be driving a minivan, like an Alphard or an Elgrand, we'd be a common sight at a rural Aeon. Like the type who says his favorite manga is *One Piece* or *Naruto*, with a white fluffy mat spread out over the dashboard and an air freshener in the shape of a hemp leaf hanging from the rearview mirror.

Imagining that created an anxious sort of itch under my skin.

Keika was munching along, chocolate stuck on her face, while Kawasaki watched, leaning her cheek on one hand with a wet wipe in the other. Being there myself, with nothing to do but observe the two of them, just made that unease grow.

It was embarrassing to watch them the whole time, so I jerked my gaze out the window.

Then I saw what looked like a middle school uniform cut in front of the café. Meaning it was about time for the examinees who'd finished their interviews to be coming out. It seemed Kawasaki had also caught sight of it out of the corner of her eye. She sighed, releasing the tension in her shoulders.

I could understand that feeling. Actually seeing the other kids who were taking the exam made me worry for Komachi. Right in front of us were Komachi's rivals, those who would be her obstacles, so a thought suddenly billowed up inside me: *Wouldn't it be best to eliminate them now?*

*Good policy would be to take out the nearest opponent at hand: boys who get near Komachi! Yes, that means Taishi Kawasaki!* And so I decided to gather information on the enemy forces.

"How does it look for Taishi?" I tried asking suddenly.

"...I don't know." Kawasaki tilted her head with a *hmm*.

*My, how surprising. I'd thought for sure this girl with a brother complex—er, worried big sister would know how he self-graded, at least...*

Kawasaki sniffed, then grimaced. "He gets grumpy if I ask about that stuff."

"Ahhh. Guess he's at that age."

Not like I couldn't understand Taishi's feelings. It's not just part of the rebellious phase; when your family—especially when it's your family—needles you about very personal and sensitive problems, you start to shut down.

For example, when you're just chatting with friends, you could say how much debt you have, how low your salary is, or other negative events as a masochistic joke to make them laugh. But you can't bring that up so easily with your family. It really sucks when they get all serious and ask, "Are you actually okay?" You don't want to make them worry, but you also suspect they won't believe you, and that all comes together into a big ol' *just don't ask.*

I was making affirmative noises with a motherly look in my eyes, like, *Boys can be like that, hmm?*

Kawasaki was also nodding with a mom-like expression, but what she said next I couldn't ignore. "But he's graded himself at about eighty percent."

"That's a weird thing for you to know…" Oh man, the moms of the world really are too good. Why do they always immediately notice their sons' secret hiding spots for books?

*Wait, I thought he wasn't telling her? How* does *she know?*

When I gave her a doubtful look, Kawasaki slid her gaze away. "Uh, well, um, Kei-chan said…"

"Yeah, he said it was three hundred ninety-six." Listening from the side, Keika seemed to understand what we were talking about, and she puffed out her chest with a smug chuckle.

"Uh-huh… Oh, Kei-chan asked, huh?" *Ah, maybe the things that are hard to say to an older sister come much easier around his tiny sister? Anyway, little kids will pick up that stuff so fast, hmm. Amazing, isn't it?* I said with my eyes.

For some reason, she turned her head to hide her face again. "…Besides, o-our house isn't that big. You tend to notice."

"Ah, I see." *So she's definitely seen it herself, too.* I didn't even have to bother asking one last bombshell question to nail the perp like Mr. Ukyou. She just confessed herself…

But now I'd found out Taishi's self-grading score. It's typical to go easy on yourself with self-grading, so if I estimated that his actual score was about ten points lower, that would make just over 70 percent.

Comparing that with my own exam score, my slightly harsh opinion slipped out. "I dunno…" Judging from how Komachi had been acting that morning, her scores were probably similar. I had a sense of the average from past data.

Kawasaki had taken the Soubu High School entrance exams like me, so she had to have the same impression. She nodded gravely. "Yeah. The rest is up to the acceptance ratio and his pre-exam academic evaluation." She let out a heavy breath.

The acceptance ratio for our high school most years hovered between one half to one out of five. The feeling you get is that if you can score 80 percent, you can basically assume you've passed. So in that sense, Taishi was right on the edge.

"We're basically fine with private, but I don't think he feels that way." Perhaps thinking about something at the edge of a forbidden borderline, Kawasaki had a slightly pained expression.

I don't know what everyone's family situation is, but it can definitely be emotionally painful for that individual. And not just in the economic sense. You're rejected and branded, and that fact will haunt you and torture you forever. Once you eventually become an adult, you might be able to snap back and say it was nothing, but to a child of fifteen or so, family and school is just about your whole life. The one-two combo of rejection by the school and pity from your family can be too much.

Especially in the case of Taishi Kawasaki, there was pressure of a different type. It wasn't my place to say, but I did it anyway. "Well, you know. Thinking about next year, he'd want to get into public."

"What? Next year?" Kawasaki gave me a dubious look like, *Were you just listening to me?*

*I was listening, how rude...* I responded with a chin-only nod. "Yeah. You want to go for national public, right? That's a lot of pressure, isn't it? Not like I know."

"You're talking about me?" Kawasaki tilted her head, and Keika copied her, cocking her head with a *hmm*. The two of them were such a perfect pair, I couldn't help but let a smile into my voice.

"No, no. Well, yes—but actually no."

"...What're you talking about?" Kawasaki glared at me, looking fairly irritated.

*Whoa, she's super-scary.* "Well, look. The way your brother sees it, if he can go to a public school now, then your options will broaden a little.

I think. Not like I know. But, like, he wants to get in no matter what—not like I know." I rushed to make my point, with a few nice hedges to protect me from responsibility.

Kawasaki blinked in surprise. After a few more blinks, a smile slipped onto her face, but she immediately jerked away. "…Tuition for university is nothing like high school."

*Huh, really? She knows a lot about it.* I have absolutely no intention of paying tuition myself, so I've never looked it up… If I were to casually look into it and calculate how many thousand yen one class cost, I'd be so scared of wasting money that I'd never cut class again.

"…But yeah, maybe he'd say that," Kawasaki muttered softly, twirling the straw for her iced coffee in her fingers. As the harshness faded out of her, my lips were a little looser, too.

"Right? I understand a guy with a sister complex better than anyone."

"What the hell, creep?" Her tone was very light for how blunt the words were.

Keika joined in, innocently chanting, "Creep, creep, creep!"

*Oh, you're quite right. I really am quite creepy.* Observing the face I saw there in the window glass, his cheeks slightly relaxed in a smile, I wholeheartedly agreed.

× × ×

Outside the window, middle schoolers in uniform were starting to catch my eye more and more.

Some time had passed as I was giving Keika attention and occasionally having the odd dribbles of conversation with Kawasaki when the thought struck.

Suddenly, my cell phone vibrated, and I saw a message from Komachi. I replied briefly that I was in the St-Marc by the station. Her response came immediately—not via vibration, but a hard *knock, knock* sound. The source was the window in front of me—where Komachi was. She waved at me.

I beckoned her over, and she trotted into the café.

As soon as she was inside, she spread her arms wide. "It's over! Yaaaaay!"

"Yaaaay!" My voice and hands followed hers as I raised my arms to welcome her. Our palms slapped together.

Before the sound had even faded, Komachi took another step forward, bounding out in front of Kawasaki and Keika. "And Saki and Keika-chan, too! Hello, yaaaay!"

"Yaaaay!" Komachi and Keika transitioned seamlessly into a high five, and that pulled Kawasaki into the mix, too.

*Miss Kawasaki is very confused, isn't she...?*

She seemed to pick up on the vibe, though, and raised her hands just slightly to accommodate Komachi. "Y-yaaaay..." But she was blushing up to her ears in embarrassment, and her voice sounded weak, too.

Komachi leaned back dramatically and took about three steps for emphasis. "Whoa, Saki, your voice is quiet! Okay, one more time: yaaaay!"

"Y-yaaaay!" Kawasaki cried with near desperation while Komachi seamlessly pressed her for a redo. "...What's with your sister?" She was glaring knives at me.

*Hey, I can't fix this...*, I thought, but I'm a big brother, so I've got to deal with my sister's misconduct. "Um, sorry, okay? She's kinda worked up. Komachi, here. Have some water and calm down."

While preparing to hear *Is the water good?!* I held out the glass, and Komachi smiled brightly. "Thanks. But it's kinda gross if you've already drank from it, so I'm gonna go get my own." Komachi smoothly ignored me with perfect finesse, spinning around to trot straight off to the register. Kawasaki giggled.

"K-Komachiii...," I groaned, but Komachi was already too far away to hear as her steps turned to a skip of *run-tatta!*

*Big Bro took quite a lot of damage just now... The* kinda *added a particularly painful realism... That hint of consideration might make me rethink my whole way of life...*

As I was moaning with my face down on the counter, Komachi quickly finished her order and came to sit beside me with an iced latte.

"...Congrats," I offered, and she gave a little nod.

"Yeah. Whew!" She moistened her throat with a *sluuurp* and let out a big *hahhh*.

During the interview—the whole time until the exam ended—she must have felt like something was stuck in her throat. She let her whole body slump onto the counter with exhaustion and the joy of hard-won freedom.

With both brother and sister in the same position, Keika peeked at us curiously. "Ooooh." Then she whispered, "You look alike."

"...Huh?" Komachi wrinkled her face in disgust for just an instant.

Keika let out an admiring sigh. "Haa-chan and Komachi are so alike! Which of you is the copyright fringent?" She tilted her head curiously.

"Where does she learn these words...?" Kawasaki put a hand to her forehead and sighed.

*Yeah, well, little kids pick up new words fast, you know... Anyway, why did Komachi get that nasty look just now? Well, I know the reason, so I won't ask...*

I think it's good that Komachi doesn't resemble me, too... If anything, I take after my father, and Komachi takes after our mother. About the only thing both of us got was the similar hair, I guess. But when she's letting her mind wander or gets a nasty look on her face, she takes after me, huh...?

I was also examining Komachi's face, while she was clearing her throat with a *gfem, gfem*. She straightened in her seat to give Keika a slightly strained smile. "Hmm. Well, since we are brother and sister...," she muttered quietly, the emotion in her voice somewhere between resignation and shyness. But then she breathed it all out in a sigh and dragged the tall chair over right up next to Keika. "You and Saki have a lot in common, too, Keika-chan! You look just like her! You'll grow up so pretty!"

"Tee-hee, you're cute, too, Komachi," Keika mumbled bashfully as she returned the compliment. She must have been used to hearing that.

"Ohhh, she said it! Aw, you!" Komachi said, jokingly poking at Keika's cheeks.

*...Hmm, what a girly conversation.*

The give-and-take of compliments is so nice. It's like getting hit on the right cheek and hitting back on the left. Irresistible.

If in the east, one compliments you with *Cute*, then you say *Cute* to her in return; if in the west one tweets, *I'm so ugly!* then you reply, *That's not true at all, I'm so much uglier than you! Look, I'm fat for real (ded)!*; if in the south you find a classmate from middle school, then you must react with great melodrama: *Yeek! Omigooood, it's been forever! Ahhh, let's hang out sometime!* while touching her arm and making empty promises; if in the north you encounter a hint of femininity, immediately you interject with *I knooow, right.* Or so I assume anyway.

Kei-chan was also glancing over at her spitting image like, *Really? Really?* Miss Saki Kawasaki was speechless (and very shy) in the face of such a compliment.

Hmm, no wonder she would be excluded from girl society. I don't think it's good for pretty girls to have such traditionally cute reactions. The *Kawa*saki family is *ka-wite* cute.

As I was thinking this, Kawasaki cleared her throat with a quiet *hnn* lest we say anything. Then she eyed me and Komachi to strike back. "You guys are close, huh?" she said, attempting to hide her shyness.

Komachi replied instantly—like basically zero frames. "Oh, we're kinda really super not," she denied with utter seriousness, waving her hands with aggressive speed.

"Komachi? Could you pretend to make it a joke?"

And then suddenly, those waving hands cutely went to her cheeks and she smiled brightly. "Frankly, you're sometimes super-annoying. ♡ "

"Yikes..." *I'm speechless! I feel like this is a jab in jest—but could it be for real?!* No words would come out of me anymore; all I could manage was a hoarse and broken *hyrrrgh*.

Kawasaki cracked a smile at our exchange. "We need to get going. I have to get home and make lunch," she said and looked out the window. The sun had risen high in the sky, and lunchtime was approaching. Taishi's exam would be about over, so he'd be going home, too.

Keika's eyebrows turned down again, and she whined grumpily. "Huhhh?"

But Kawasaki patted her back and just whispered, "Taa-kun's waiting."

Keika groaned sullenly, but she folded her arms and nodded. "'Kay. Guess we gotta."

As I was smiling wryly at that gesture, Kawasaki quickly got them ready to go, putting Keika's coat on her, wrapping her scarf, and pulling her gloves on snugly. Once she was done, she gave Komachi and me a casual bow. "Then see you…"

I nodded in return to her very quiet farewell. "Yeah, see you."

"See you again! And bye-bye to you, too, Kei-chan!"

"Bye-bye!" Keika waved energetically at us, and Kawasaki strolled off toward the station with her sister in tow.

After watching her go, I turned back to Komachi. "How about we get some food, too? You know what you wanna eat?" I asked.

Komachi nodded. "Yeah, I was thinking about it to kill time…" She paused a moment. Then with a smug chuckle, she said, "And I came up with eel on the grill, with thyme."

*Hmm, a pun… Normally, I would send this matter to the committee, but she's cute, so I'll let it go!*

"Eel, huh, I'd like eel… They might go extinct soon, and then we won't be able to eat them anymore. It's got that amazing premium, *limited time only* feeling, and it's kinda cool to be the one destroying them…"

"Geez, you're awful… What an awful reason to eat them; the eels will be turning in their graves… Oh, but I hear in Japan they all come from fish farms? Apparently, you can do that these days. I saw it on the news."

*Ahhh, now that she mentions it, she has done a lot of interesting research for the interview part of her entrance exam. But, Komachi—you're too naive!*

"Nah, there's no way," I said.

"Why not?"

"Japan's population is aging because the people can't even manage to breed. We don't have the time to be raising eels," I said with a self-satisfied look.

"Ohhh, you're so socially aware!" With a whistle of *twoo~* ♪ like Cobra, Komachi jabbed a finger at me like, *You nailed it!* Thanks to that, I was feeling very good.

"Think about it that way, and maybe eels won't go extinct that easily. Even made-in-Japan, all-natural corporate livestock are surviving their harsh work environment, after all. You could even say Japan takes better care of eels than workers."

"Maybe both will go extinct…"

Indeed. Both eels and workers are living things, you know? …See how I'm referencing Japan's labor environment every chance I get? I'm demonstrating a deep interest in politics, and in the future a "vote at eighteen" campaign collab (abridged).

Despite the ambition swelling in my heart, Komachi tilted her head with a *hmm*. "But, like, it doesn't have to be eel. I mean, I went out for eel with Mom and Dad the other day."

"You did…?" *Why do they do that stuff without me? I wanted to contribute to the extinction of eels, too, you know? Well, I've been coming home late recently, so I guess I see why. And the three of them went together, huh…?*

Well, I can't hope to match my parents in the area of economic prowess. So maybe it was best to drop the classy, delicious meal options for now.

For this occasion, I should actually be rewarding Komachi in a way unique to me.

A surprise that only I can offer! Not that I really have anything. All I can brag about to anyone is having the cutest little sister in the world. *But I'm rewarding said little sister… What do I do? I'm stuck…*

"Mmgh," I whined, just as the divine revelation came down on me. *Mikooon!* "Oh, I know. How about we go have fun somewhere? Preferably something active. Specifically, maybe tennis with Totsuka. Or, like, just hanging out with Totsuka." *Aw man, am I a genius or what? Hanging out with the cutest friend in the world as a reward for the cutest little sister in the world, I've already got this! It's in the bag, ga-ha-ha!*

But Komachi looked slightly skeptical. "Hmm, I dunno about that…," she said hesitantly, then made a little X with her fingers.

"R-really? Big Bro was really planning to spoil you with this, though…" I dug in a bit. I couldn't just abandon my dream of hanging out with Totsuka, but I didn't have the courage to suddenly invite him out one-on-one.

But Komachi shook her head. "I haven't got my results yet, so I'd rather not do something like that."

"O-oh, I see…" If she didn't want it herself, then it was worthless as a reward. Komachi had the final say on these things. *So now what do I do…?* I was thinking when Komachi tug-tugged on my sleeve.

"Yeah, well, if it's just you and me…that'd be practically perfect. And I think that's worth a lot of Komachi points…," she muttered, sliding her gaze away from me to hide the slight pink of her cheeks. It was so adorable, it made me ask something I shouldn't have.

"Uh, I'm totally fine with that, but…are you?"

Komachi faced me and nodded solemnly. "Mm-hmm. Simple, cheap, and convenient."

"That's not a compliment at all…"

But if that was what Komachi wanted, then my task was clear: present a plan for a brother and sister to have the maximum fun. "Right, where do you wanna go? LaLaport? It's LaLaport, isn't it? Ahhh, LaLaport. LaLaport's our only option. Right now, they have a vending machine with just Max cans. Let's go buy some. I know they'll be great."

"It's not gonna taste any different than it does anywhere else…," Komachi said wearily, her earlier sweetness gone. She wagged her finger at me chidingly. "It doesn't have to be anything fancy, and it doesn't have to be anything special."

"Oh, so then…" I leaned forward eagerly, prompting her to continue.

Komachi sucked a big breath in, then let it out. "I wanna go home and do chores!"

"Huhhh? What…?"

*I've got nothing here. Aghhh, I've got nothing at all…*

As my skin tingled with the presence of a Got Nothing Fairy, Komachi rose to her feet. "So let's go shopping and go home!"

"…Okay."

Well, what makes me happy is letting Komachi do whatever she wants. I stood up along with her and followed her out, heading for the grocery store.

×  ×  ×

We went shopping and came home, and Komachi quickly got started on the chores and cleaning.

Not only did she do the scrubbing and laundry, but she even set to cooking dinner, too. I heard the rhythmic *tap, tap* of her knife, and then immediately the *fshhh* of water flowing from the sink, followed by the clacking of utensils being washed. She was cleaning up everything as she cooked. What an impressive skill.

Meanwhile, I was flopped out in the *kotatsu*, petting the family cat, Kamakura, who'd come to sit on my lap. Anyone who walked in on me would think I was some evil boss.

But as I zoned out watching Komachi rush around, even I started to wonder if I should do something.

"Should I help?" I called out to Komachi in the kitchen.

But what came back was a blunt "No, it's fine. You just stay there. You're in the way."

"Ouch…" I broke down in tears and buried my face in Kamakura's back. The cat turned to me to give me a super-dirty look.

To make matters worse, Komachi sounded so put-upon. "I mean, you always do such a bad job. And when you cook, you never clean up."

"…Yeah, well, that's true. 'Cause it's a hassle… Apologies to my little sister-in-law."

"Who're you calling a sister-in-law? Komachi is your sister." She huffed in displeasure, then turned off the faucet a bit hard. She must have finished most of the cooking, since she wiped her hands on her apron as she circled around to the living room. "And besides, Komachi wants to do it. I couldn't sit down and do it for so long because of exams, and the New Year's cleaning didn't get done right, either," she said as she poured out hot water from the pot to make coffee. The fragrant scent tickled my nostrils, even if it was instant.

As I inhaled, Komachi poured out two cups, ambled over to me, sat at my side, and offered me some. "...Besides, Komachi caused a lot of trouble for Mom, too," she said a bit apologetically.

Accepting the cup, I gave a quiet thanks, then said what I thought out loud. "You don't really have to worry about Mom. You're always doing stuff for her, so it's fine. You worry about it too much."

"Hmm... Well, maybe that's true, but our parents are busy." Komachi didn't seem convinced, a cheerless smile on her face.

Our parents were always occupied, and at some point, it had become typical for Komachi and me to handle the chores that we could.

When Komachi had been small, I'd been the one doing stuff, albeit clumsily. But by the time she'd approached the end of elementary school, her household skills had easily surpassed mine. Ever since, she'd taken over as the main force handling chores. Thanks to her, my chore proficiency was frozen in sixth grade.

Don't get me wrong; I've felt guilty for burdening my sister before. During her exams, our parents had also still been busy—they'd been in a real panic, actually, with the end of the fiscal year approaching—and I had little enough to do that I should've helped out.

"...Sorry. I thought about doing something, too, but, well...you know?" I said, drinking down my bitter coffee. The words came out a bit bitter, too. *I really did, you know? But look, um...when I casually stick my nose in, Mom gets mad at me, okay...?*

Whenever I do chores, she says basically the same thing Komachi did. I can complete them, but not to my mother's standards. I especially can't stand cleaning, and I get, like, one of those early-model Roombas that clean a circle around a square room...

So I'd taken the defiant route. If I was just gonna cause problems, I might as well do nothing—but I really did feel a bit bad for Komachi during her exam period.

But she must not have been that concerned about it, as she laughed pleasantly. "It's fine, it's fine. It's Komachi's hobby."

"Housework?" I asked.

Komachi put a finger to her cheek and cocked her head. "Hmm, well…I guess my hobby is, like, spoiling my big bro?" Then she gave me a cute *tee-hee* sort of smile.

"Aw man, I'm feeling the maternal vibes. The heck. I can experience the ultimate regression. Based… I've achieved ultimate victory. Komachi-mama…" In my heart, I wanted to yell out, *Komachi-mama!* And I didn't yell, but it did escape me.

Komachi's expression twisted in disgust. "God, you're such a creep, Bro! That's sick."

"Shut up, leave me alone. Hey, you're pretty bad, too. What even is that hobby?"

"Right, right? Scores lots of points, huh?" Komachi chuckled smugly, then bumped my upper arm with her shoulder.

*That's not a compliment, ya jerk.*

Though I tried glaring at her out of the corner of my eye, she ignored it and closed her eyes. Then she blissfully put a hand to her chest and let out a long, enraptured sigh. "What an amazing feeling… Ruining someone with my own hands…"

"Hey, that's sick," I said.

Komachi went *tee-hee* ☆ *blep*, sticking out her tongue with a wink as she rapped herself on the head with a fist. A gesture that deliberate was definitely a joke.

We giggled for a while, but then suddenly Komachi's smile faded. Gazing at the ripples on the surface of her coffee, she slowly said, "…But it's true that Komachi likes house chores."

"Hmm?"

"It's kinda, like, different from back when you were taking care of Komachi—now Komachi can do all sorts of things." I gave her a sidelong glance, but her attention was far away, out the window. "When there's something Komachi can do and, like, actually be useful…" I could see none of her usual innocence in her profile. Her clear eyes were so mature. "…It's like…that's not so bad," she added with that mix of jokey and shy blushiness I'd come to expect from Komachi.

I'm sure when she was small, she'd experienced an impatient frustration that I couldn't know. Our parents were often away from the house when she was at the age most kids were getting spoiled rotten. Instead of them, she had me, and I was hardly one to rely on. But though Komachi had grumbled and complained about it, she'd spent that time with me. Before I knew it, she was able to take care of me, too.

"Not bad? Actually, you're too good," I said, thinking from the bottom of my heart, *This little sister of mine really is too good. And this brother is too pathetic.*

Komachi puffed her chest out melodramatically. "Well, Komachi's worked hard. When you have a useless older brother, the crisis helps you grow!"

"Right? I'm the best reverse teacher, aren't I? Look how much I've taught you! You'd better be thankful," I shot back, sweeping up my bangs with one hand as I bent backward to the ceiling in a pose of smug self-importance.

Then Komachi nodded. "Yep, Komachi's thankful."

"Huh?"

*Hey, you can't get so honest when we're messing around… And isn't that the wrong direction to take this joke?* I thought, giving Komachi a look.

Komachi cleared her throat with a *koff*, sneaking her gaze away. "I'm sure it'd be better to do something like this after I actually pass," she mumbled, "but I don't wanna embarrass myself making a big deal out of it, and if I fail, I won't even get the chance, and now is the only time I can say it, so…"

Komachi softly came out of the *kotatsu*, then knelt with proper form on the floor, placing her hands delicately on her knees.

"What? What're you doing?" I asked.

Sitting up straight, Komachi looked me right in the eye. I jerked, startled. Kamakura, who'd been fast asleep on my lap, also woke up confused and padded away from me.

Ignoring both disconcerted human and cat, Komachi grinned a breezy smile. "Thanks, Bro. For taking care of me," she said, then gently placed down three fingers of each hand and slowly bowed.

I stopped breathing—my thoughts had stopped, too. I'd never

expected that from Komachi, but that wasn't all. That bow was so beautiful, I could never imagine it coming from her normally. I think I was entranced.

I realized my mouth was hanging open, and I hurriedly searched for what I should say. "...The heck was that? Cut it out."

"Eh-heh. I kinda wanted to try saying it. Figured it was worth a lot of Komachi points," she teased, rubbing the back of her head, but with those pink cheeks, she wasn't fooling me at all.

*You idiot. Don't say it if it makes you embarrassed; I'm getting your embarrassment secondhand. At least hide it better. You need to say a bunch of stupid stuff as a smoke screen. Your big brother has a lot of experience with that.*

In the interest of leading by example, I said, "It's not worth a lot of points. Besides, it's kinda like you're getting married. Like, really? You're not allowed to go off and get married so suddenly, young lady, so, um, I dunno...... Just don't."

Unable to finish, my voice caught.

There was a prickling in the back of my nose, and my breathing was getting deeper.

I'd just been letting myself babble on and on, but now my voice was going hoarse, and the mindless stream of BS just petered out into a long, smothered exhalation.

Heat was building in the inner corners of my eyes, and I blinked as it became a kind of squeezing pain. A droplet trailed down my cheek.

"O-ohhh...there's, like, water coming out of my eyes... What's this? Why are they doing that; what the heck?" I found myself looking up at the ceiling. I bit the edge of my lip and let out a shaking breath.

Komachi's eyebrows rose in mild surprise, but then she gave a little chuckle. "That's tears, Bro. You're acting like a robot that's learning about feelings for the first time."

"So this...is tears... This is...feelings..."

"Why're you suddenly going monotone...?" Komachi said, sounding exasperated.

What else was I supposed to do? I mean, if I didn't make a joke, I might actually start crying.

It wasn't from sadness or pain, and it definitely wasn't an eye problem. I think I was just happy.

At the same time, there was a trace of loneliness and something like relief.

But that was difficult to put into words. All I could manage was a groan like a really grumpy dog. "Uuurgh."

My voice caught, and I hung my head. Komachi gave me a *What can you do?* smile as she quickly swiped at her eyes. She reached out to my head and gave it a little pat. "Komachi's gonna go get a bath ready. And then go first," she whispered, and I heard a little hoarseness in her voice, too. With a quiet sniff, she rose to her feet and hurried out of the living room without turning back.

When her footsteps grew distant, I finally let out a big breath. No real words or anything else would come out. Just a bunch of sighs.

While I was busy doing that, Kamakura came back from his corner to nuzzle his head against my back.

Whoever this cat was taking after, he was a good cat. He knew exactly what to do.

I took Kamakura into my arms and set him on my lap again. "...Is this that 'weaning off Big Brother' thing she mentioned before? What do you think, Mr. Kamakura? You don't think she's graduating a tad too early?" I asked.

But the cat didn't even meow back. He just let me pet him for a while.

The only other sound was a little sniffle.

**4**

## Until today, he has never once touched that **key**.

It was February, and the grass was still mostly dead. It had been feeling like spring for a while, but the chill often returned, the season passing only on the calendar. It would be a little while longer before the barren, wintry trees would bud. Walking through the park by the river or watching the occasional tree by the roadside, you could just see that it was cold. The path I usually biked to school was extra-wintry thanks to the crisp wind blowing from the sea.

Due to the long weekend, or maybe that thank-you from Komachi, I was kinda distracted until the biting cold air on my cheeks woke me up. The three-day holiday for entrance exams was now over, and the daily grind was back in force.

My body was adapting, too. After nearly two years doing this commute, I turned the corners and stopped at the lights unconsciously. My autopilot was optimized.

And I'd keep doing this for another whole year, so by the end, I'd be able to get to school with my eyes closed. Well, maybe—it'd be more accurate to say I'd have this commute for *only* another year. Sometime in the far future, I might indulge in nostalgia and come down this way on a whim again, but I only had another year to call it my commute.

Nothing ever lasts more than a season, no matter what it is or where you are. Even the cycle of the rising and setting sun becomes temporary once you assign special meaning to it, like the first sunrise of the new year, or the rising sun viewed from the top of a tall mountain or whatever.

And maybe you can say the same thing about relationships. Komachi and I will always be brother and sister, but we both know we're different than we were as little kids. And that means changes in our relationship. I think we'll still be siblings, but just slightly more grown-up. The past fifteen years have taught Komachi and me that time won't cause some massive, critical change for us.

Komachi and I are family, so I don't see a problem with that. I think this is as far as my luck will take me, and I've resigned myself to the inevitability of being attached to her in some way for the rest of my life. All her life, she'll have to accompany Big Bro in hell.

—*But how long could people who aren't her stick with me?*

As I was ruminating, I came up to the back gate of the school.

With a light squeeze on the brakes, I slipped between people and bicycles, turning the handlebars to slide into a free spot.

My bike squeaked as it came to a stop. I locked it up, and when I raised my head again, I found I had way more space here than I'd thought. *Was this bicycle parking area always this big?* I wondered, trudging my way to the school entrance.

Maybe it was because it was after a holiday, but there was a kind of giddiness among the kids in the halls, cheerily chatting as they went. It was like their voices were louder than usual. And I found the answer to my earlier question.

The third-years were right in the middle of their entrance exams, so they didn't have to attend school. Most did not. That's why the bicycle parking lot was empty and the first and second floors of the school building were deserted. All the classrooms I'd passed by on my way from the back door to the stairs were empty, adding to the echoes of the conversations in the hallways. The stillness and the quiet probably encouraged the students to speak louder, too.

It created something vaguely forlorn in this bustle.

But once I came up to the third floor where the second-year classrooms were, I found a warmth in the clamor. Obnoxiously so. *I don't give a rat's ass how you spent the long weekend or whatever, shut up a minute. Come on. You don't have to pull out your phones and show each other photos. And, like, you posted them on your social media anyway, didn't you? That friend of yours probably already saw it, hit Like on instinct, and immediately forgot it. Oh, that's why they go to the trouble of showing each other in person, huh? Wow! So thorough and meticulous! A two-pronged attack that leaves no chance for escape!*

As I was scooting around the sea of Instagrammers in the hallways, light footsteps approached me from behind. When I shifted a half step right to cede the way, I got a smack on my left shoulder.

"Hachiman! Morning!"

When I turned around, I found the loveliest, most Instagrammable subject that could be Instagrammed. It was Saika Totsuka, in his uniform tracksuit with a windbreaker on top.

"H-hey…morning…," I managed to reply.

Totsuka smiled mischievously as if he'd succeeded in a prank. "Did I get you?" he asked in a quiet, teasing voice.

With my breath still caught, I had no choice but to just nod-nod in reply. *Aw, good grief! You teasing master Totsuka!*

*I mean, of course he'd get me—why is he so darn cute? Look at him in his overlong windbreaker sleeves and hiding his smile. He's got way too much girlish charm. C'mon, this isn't the time to be posting food photos of the fancy-schmancy stuff they sell in Daikanyama or Nakameguro. This is what I'm talking about; this is girlish charm. All girls, please take notes. Anyway, I'm slamming the Like button in the Instagram of my heart!*

As I was firing off sixteen shots per second, my thudding heart calmed, my breathing evened out, and I regained enough presence of mind to take in the sight of Totsuka.

His soft, fine hair with its silvery sheen was a little mussed, his movement to adjust the racket case on his shoulder was brisk, the smile on his face was full of life and charm, and the cheeks of his healthy complexion were pink tinged. *Hmm, I'm guessing he rushed over here after morning practice.*

The faintly citrusy scent of his deodorant spray had to be a tasteful post-workout courtesy. And inhaling as much of that scent as possible to get it into my bloodstream meant I was just a man of taste myself. I took a loooong breath in through my nose, then let it out and made an attempt at conversation. "Back from morning practice, huh? It's amazing you can do that in the cold."

"Yeah. But I'm used to it now," Totsuka replied with a cute grin. He didn't miss a beat; instead of deflecting, his delivery told me he was quite confident, actually. "The new students are going to be coming soon, so I have to work hard to show them my best."

He held up two firm fists in front of his chest like he was ready for the fight, and it was so adorable and charming and dependable and cute and basically every positive adjective ever invented. The result was that my full vocabulary capacity died on the spot, and I could do nothing but stare in wibbly-eyed awe. *I don't need words anymore...*

Totsuka seemed confused, as he tilted his head curiously and looked at me through his lashes. "What are you guys going to do about the new students?"

"Huh?" I wasn't expecting that question, even if I hadn't been in a trance.

Totsuka must have thought that meant he hadn't explained enough; he waved his hands and added, "You know, since the Service Club is a real club. Don't you need new students to join?"

Real club *might be a bit of a stretch...*, I thought, but it was a good question. "I dunno... I'm just a lackey, so I don't really know. I don't even really get how the club's supposed to be structured... I was basically abducted into it and threatened into staying imprisoned there."

"Ah-ha-ha, is that right...?" Totsuka said awkwardly.

"So I don't think we need new members," I continued, and he softly lowered his gaze.

"Oh... That's kind of too bad."

If there were no new additions, then the Service Club really would vanish before long. Not exactly a surprise, but something I was being reminded of now. I put one foot forward, walking ahead of Totsuka, where he couldn't see my face, and gave a tired sigh for effect. "It's too bad... Wish I could've been a club elder and talked down to the newbies just once. *You're not the only one struggling; everyone's been through the same. If you quit now, no one else will ever take you in.*"

"W-wow, what a jerky club elder..." I heard a slightly awkward, strained chuckle behind me. "Ah, that's not what I meant to say! The Service Club is a great club, so I'd love if it stuck around..." Hopping a step forward, Totsuka came up by my side again. I saw in his eyes that he was concerned for me.

"...Well, that's up to the club captain and the teacher-advisor. I'm just a minion here. I don't get to stamp approval on anything." Those were the facts, and yet they didn't feel remotely true.

Totsuka giggled. "When you put it like that, it sounds like you're talking about your office job." He seemed close to rolling his eyes, but maybe he was on the mark.

I maintained a very consistent stance on this. Work came about in the form of requests and consults, often accompanying problems, issues, and dilemmas. I would deal with them to the extent I could. My own desires hadn't really had much to do with it. I'd always done it because it was the work expected of me.

So my reply was a slight bit masochistic. "Right? Once you get employed, it's even worse than this. Awful. Really awful. God, I don't wanna get a job."

As we were laughing about it together, we reached our classroom and, with casual waves, headed to our own seats.

The heater in here made the classroom somewhat warmer than the hallway, so the whole place felt a bit lazy. The drafts made the seats by the doors chilly, but as you progressed farther in, the blessings of the heater enabled comfort for many. Saki Kawasaki was at the front right next to the window, leaning her cheek on her hand with her eyes closed, and I wasn't sure if she was dozing off.

On the other hand, when I turned my gaze to the crowd sitting at the back of the class near the window, they were as full of energy as ever. Maybe it was because of how well the baking event went the other day. They were surrounding Tobe, enjoying a lively discussion about whatever the topic of the day was.

Had that event changed their relationships? Yumiko Miura had been unable to figure out the right distance, but she'd closed it just a little; Hina Ebina had placed herself at an appropriate distance, but she'd still made progress forward; meanwhile, Kakeru Tobe...well, who cares? I think he had fun. He's Tobe, so I mean...who cares?

*But what about the one who said it was a "good event"...?* I wondered. Yuigahama was in the crowd, too, and she noticed me studying them. Her mouth opened a bit, and she gave me a little wave. *Please don't; it's kinda embarrassing...* But of course I couldn't ignore her, so I responded with a little nod of my own.

Then, following Yuigahama's gaze, Miura and the others glanced over at me, too. Still sproinging her curls, Miura returned her attention to her phone again, while Ebina acknowledged me with a voiceless *heeey*. Tobe huffed a few *hey*s and *huh*s in lieu of actual greetings.

And then, with just a smile and a glance, Hayato Hayama communicated his good morning. I nodded back, then pulled out my chair.

Leaning my cheek on my hand on the desk, I closed my eyes.

Now that I thought about it, things had changed. We might not both say *Good morning* out loud, but if our eyes met, that was still worth a nod.

When had this started? The answer was actually very simple: since I'd started looking at them.

Hayama's clique had always been present and visible, even when I'd only just joined this class. At the time, they might as well have been classroom decorations. But I'd still remembered their names, and I'd been aware of the peripheral information related to them, like their clubs and stuff. I'd had some awareness of them.

But I hadn't known them.

...Not that I know them well now, either.

I'm not sure if it was this line of thought or the unfamiliarity of exchanging greetings with them, but it got under my skin. The seat of my chair was too uncomfortable to settle into, and I immediately got up again.

Times like these, the best plan is to escape to the washroom. Running is shameful but useful. Like that comedy duo who got into a traffic accident a while back and did a hit-and-run that ended up putting them under house arrest. When they made their comeback, they had a slam-dunk routine!

I scooted out of the classroom and smoothly got my business done. *How about I buy a drink, too...?* I thought, heading for the vending machine at the school store. Late as it was, I caught sight of a sprinkling of kids rushing through the halls to barely make it on time, but it was still very quiet compared with before.

Which was why the footsteps behind me were so obvious. I could feel whoever it was behind me, walking calmly and maintaining a fixed distance.

When I reached the vending machine and stopped, the footsteps behind me stopped after one step, too.

I quickly bought my usual Max can and stepped out of the way, and my stalker leisurely strode forward to press the button for a canned black coffee. "I heard," he said to me as he squatted to take his drink. He didn't turn, as if he was certain I would linger there.

Before, his attitude would have made me sick. I would have snapped at him, probably. But that wasn't the case anymore.

Now, I knew Hayato Hayama was the kind of person who said things that got on my nerves, so I was only a little irked.

I also knew he'd come here to tell me something, so I wouldn't be too mad. *Aw, nooo! Whoops, I think I'm* really *mad, actually!*

*Seriously, where does he get off talking to me that way...? He's just like her, always needling to see how you'll react...* Well, people do tend to pick up verbal habits and speech tics from others. Goes to show how long they've known each other.

In a way, it was completely natural for Hayama to touch on what happened.

"Sounds like you've had a tough time. At least it's a weight off your shoulders, huh?" Hayama continued as he lightly juggled the hot can, until he finally turned back to me with a knowing look.

*Did you know, Raiden...?* I mentally grumbled to myself as I acted confused. "Huh? What is? Oh, my little sister? You're talking about entrance exams?"

"No," Hayama said with a sigh, deflating. "I mean, that too, I guess, but... Oh, tell your sister for me. Congrats on getting through her exams."

"Nope. I don't have to pass on a message from you. But thanks for the sentiment." I met his charming smile with a dull-eyed look.

Hayama blinked, startled. "I never thought I'd get a thanks from you for that." He pulled the tab of his canned coffee with a *pssht* and brought it to his lips with a slightly dark smile.

*Hey, I do thank people, you know? If anything, I'm surprised how conscientious* he's *being, remembering to offer congratulations even now...*

But that conscientious nature was why Hayama also made sure to bring us back to the subject we'd drifted away from. "Your little sister aside...I'm talking about someone else's little sister."

*Someone else's little sister, huh? Who might that be? Keika? Oh, that was a tough time; that little girl has a portentous future...* I should have played dumb, but Hayato Hayama was too serious to allow that.

If I made another joke, I'm sure he would have said something like, *Oh, okay, so that's the kind of person you are* and come to some private conclusion on the matter.

We both mostly knew each other's cards.

The fact was that Hayama and I both assumed we understood each other. We'd been disappointed, then resigned, and eventually accepting—all we'd ever done was make each other deal with our own self-centered sentimentality.

When I vented at him, the words were always directed elsewhere, and they never took the form of questions. I'd never even make sure they reached their target, but I couldn't go without saying them. We knew our stances were incompatible, but ignoring each other would just grate on us, so we just exchanged unsolicited comments and mildly sarcastic insinuations.

"…Well, the tough part is yet to come, right? Not like I know," I said.

"True enough." Hayama broke into a broad, slightly bitter smile as he tossed out the empty can. It flew in an arc to land unerringly in the garbage, the clang echoing through the deserted first floor of the school building. After watching the can land, Hayama let out a faint sigh, as if to get rid of his smile. I couldn't tell if the emotion behind it was satisfaction or desolation.

As I was still puzzling out the answer, he strode off. "…But it's way better than before. I thought things would never change," he muttered over his shoulder without waiting for my response. I don't think he was expecting one.

Yeah, this was how conversations between us always went. Barely even a conversation at all.

We were just wringing out the things we didn't want to say, then taking the other's words and assigning our own meanings to it. It wasn't so much "interpretation" as "decapitation." We cut off the words that could have become conversation and watched their demise.

Hayama was already a few steps ahead. Following him, I thought back on the exchange.

From whom had Hayama heard that Yukinoshita had gone back home? From his parents? Or from Haruno? Or had he heard it from Yukinoshita herself? Or had Yuigahama brought it up? Well, it didn't make much difference, whichever it was. It all meant the same thing.

When you got right down to it, Hayato Hayama had sensed that something was changing due to Yukino Yukinoshita's actions—and it was a change he'd never expected to see.

I was just glad Hayama had taken that as a positive thing. He'd been close with the Yukinoshita family and those sisters for a long time, so his words were worth trusting. My concerns were assuaged a little. I could feel relief that Yukinoshita was doing well, off wherever she was.

When he'd commented on the "weight on my shoulders," I'd deliberately chosen to assume he meant Komachi, but maybe that turn of phrase hadn't been wrong. There was something similar in this sensation, the ache in my chest, to the time Komachi had thanked me.

The ache was the proof that it was right.

On the way back to the classroom, the distance between Hayama and me never shrank.

As the latecomers rushed by in the last seconds before the bell, they all said their good mornings to Hayama. Each time, Hayama raised a casual hand in response.

I didn't even notice when my eyes turned to Hayama's restlessly moving arm.

I suddenly wondered if maybe Hayama's feelings toward her might be similar to mine toward Komachi. They were close in a sense; did he watch her the way I watched Komachi? Did he watch both of them? In the brief time before we reached the classroom, I let myself speculate.

The moment Hayama put his hand on the door, the distance between us closed just a bit.

× × ×

The classroom had seemed quiet that morning, but as the day wore on, the buzz of activity grew, as if a gradual heat was building in the whole school.

During the entrance exam period, none of the clubs had been meeting, so maybe that was why the jocks and their ilk seemed full of energy.

Already, there were calls from the baseball and rugby clubs ringing out from the sports grounds.

Everyone in a sports club was already gone, Hayama's group included, and the other kids were decreasing in number, too.

*Clubs, huh...? We do have club today, right? Or don't we? Might as well just go...* As I wondered, I slowly got ready for the end of the day. Then, right as I was about to rise from my seat, I heard the patter of hurried footsteps toward me. *I know that sound...*

I turned around right as she was tilting her head to peer at me, so our faces wound up startlingly close. "Whoa! Geez..."

"Ah, s-sorry!" Her pinkish-brown bun did a little bob, her big eyes innocently widened, and a gasp left her soft-looking lips. As she jolted back, it was hard not to notice her chest or the citrus smell when she turned her face away to break eye contact.

My heart skipped a beat experiencing all of it so close.

When I breathed a big sigh, Yuigahama flicked a glance at me. "I think you're a little *too* startled." Despite her efforts, a little *snerk* escaped her; then she smacked my shoulder with a giggle.

*Aw geez, this is embarrassing on so many levels. I kinda wanna die a few times... And now people are looking... Anyway, could you stop touching my upper arm? It's super-effective, and it makes me want to store energy to make myself presentable.*

"Going to club?"

"...Y-yeah. More or less," I answered, still a bit stunned as I attempted to calm my racing heart.

Yuigahama seemed to consider for a while. But she quickly nodded. "...Oh. Yeah. Wait there a sec." She rushed back to Miura's group, let them know she was going, and snatched up her stuff—more than usual, like a backpack or something—and then trotted back to me.

"Let's go," she said, then started shoving my back impatiently.

*U-um, I am going, so please don't push...* Remember, kids, in emergencies, it's important not to push, run, or talk. When you get to my level, you have so much fire safety awareness, you'll even avoid talking with people on a regular basis.

And I'm not kidding about this being an emergency. We'd gone together to the clubroom before. But in my recollection, this was the first time we'd ever left the classroom together.

Worried about unwanted attention, I turned back to check. But there weren't many kids still in the classroom, and most of them were focused on those in front of them. They weren't paying much attention to us. I wondered about the pair who'd been talking to Yuigahama just a minute ago and glanced over to check up with them as well—but Ebina just waved *bye-bye*, while Miura sproinged her curls. They didn't seem particularly suspicious of me.

This was a relief.

No matter what I was thinking, anyone else would've said that this was perfectly normal.

Everyone just knew that Yuigahama would go to the Service Club room after school, and the other two girls knew I was a member of the Service Club, too. Of course we'd go to the clubroom together.

I think before, there would have been funny looks—not just at me, but at Yuigahama, too.

Back when they were all just units in a class rank to me, I'd never have considered this possibility. But now that I'd been involved with them as individuals, now that we'd been getting a glimpse into each other's lives, I could make conjectures about all sorts of things. I wouldn't call that understanding, but we'd learned enough that we could make some sense of each other.

Of course, I could say the same about the girl walking beside me.

It was some time after school had ended, so the hallway to the special-use building was emptier than usual. The air was as cold and dry as always.

And yet it didn't feel that wintry and bleak.

The reason for that was Yuigahama beside me…carrying a fluffy blanket in her arms. Glancing at her, I saw Yuigahama burying the end of her chin in it. *Why's she brought a blanket? Linus? Is she Linus? Is this a Peanuts connection? This is Chiba, after all…*

"So, like, what's up with the blanket?" I asked, mainly just to break the silence while we were walking.

Yuigahama tilted her head like, *Huhhh?* "You mean this *buranket?*" She used the English word instead.

"It means the same thing… What, is there some subtle difference? Is it like pasta and spaghetti? Stop using English for everything…"

"Huhhh? But it has *buranket* written on it… And wait, both those words are English…," Yuigahama said grumpily, before she suddenly figured it out and a wrinkle creased her brow.

*So she noticed, huh…?* But I ignored her reaction, staring at the blanket instead. It was folded into a ball, but it wasn't that big. I wasn't sure if it was even enough for a twin bed. I remembered the term that was perfect for that sort of size.

"Oh, it's a lap blanket," I said.

Nuzzling her face deep into the warmth, Yuigahama nodded. "Yeah, yeah. Basically."

"Huhhh…you didn't already have one?"

My mind went back to something that had happened in the clubroom. Yuigahama and Yukinoshita had been sitting side by side, putting a single blanket over their laps to make it like a *kotatsu*. I clearly remembered thinking, *That looks nice and warm. Man, I'm so cold, I wanna go home.*

Feeling slightly envious and extra-conscious of the chill in my usual spot, I eyed the blanket in Yuigahama's arms.

She blinked her wide eyes. "I didn't think you were looking…"

"U-uh, well, more like it's just there in my field of vision…"

"It is, huh…?"

"Uhhh, well, my field of vision covers a lot of things, you know…" I came up with a reply, but I'm not sure if it was actually true or if I had more of a tendency to narrowly focus on things. I mean, even when I self-consciously turned my face away, I could still see Yuigahama burying her reddened cheeks in the blanket.

Our footsteps were loud in the quiet hallway. You could even hear the wind hitting the windows and my own tiny sigh.

*Aw man, this silence is, like, really stressful! I don't even know why, but somehow I've dug my own grave. If I don't say anything and five seconds pass, it'll time out and count as a wrong answer, and I'll get "bad communication"! And that means a reduced reward! Even if I can't get perfect, I'd like to get good—hell, even normal communication, at least. Not that a perfect will help your affection score.*

And so I just said the first thing that came to mind. "Wait, you already have a lap blanket. Why did you get another one? How many laps do you have? Are you a centipede?"

"No! It just came as an extra when I bought a magazine!" Yuigahama shot back, her chin jerking up. But her spirit quickly wilted, her eyebrows sinking into an upside-down V as she despondently muttered, "…So I wound up with a whole bunch, and honestly I can't get rid of them."

"O-oh… Okay…" *So she doesn't actually want it…*

Well, you do get a lot of blankets and blanket-type things in the winter, whether as extras, bonuses, or presents. In fact, I feel like we have a few at our house, too. I see them about as frequently as the plates you get from the spring bread festival. Those plates never break, so you just keep accumulating more…

That made sense to me, so I indicated my understanding, and Yuigahama nodded in return with a smile. "So I brought it from home. It's still cold, and besides…" She suddenly stopped. Her gaze slid up ahead to the Service Club room, and I did the same.

Pausing to choose her words, Yuigahama took a little breath. "…If the club is gonna go on a bit longer, I thought maybe I'd leave it here," she added in a quiet mutter before immediately pursing her lips and staring awkwardly at the ground. All I could do was offer a meaningless *ahhh.*

Maybe I could've come up with something random to say, as I often did. But I couldn't cover at all this time.

*—If it's gonna go on.*

I could hear how certain she was that this was going to end.

By the time we reached the clubroom, I still hadn't come up with the right answer. So instead of giving one, I put my hand on the door handle.

But the door just rattled loudly and didn't budge.

"…It's locked," I said.

Yuigahama peered over my shoulder at the door. "So Yukinon hasn't come yet…," she said. Shifting her things under her arm, she began rummaging around in her coat pocket.

I began ambling off. "I'm gonna go get the key."

"Huh? Ah—" Yuigahama started saying something to me, but I replied with just a hand wave. *It's fine, it's fine.* I was somewhat rushing on my way to the teachers' room. Only Yukinoshita had ever opened the door to the Service Club room.

I'd never noticed until now.

She'd always been the only one to carry the key, and I'd never even touched it.

× × ×

When I cracked open the door to the teachers' room, there was a whole flurry of activity inside.

Mountains of documents covered every desk in sight, and conversations, meetings, and calls were happening all over the office.

*Yikes. Kinda hard to break in and be like,* Hey, where's the keyyy…?

Times like these, the best plan is to talk to Miss Hiratsuka, since she's basically always here watching anime or eating. This was as exciting as startling someone to wake them up. With glee, I said "Pardon me" quietly and stepped toward her workspace.

I'd been dragged out to this desk—er, visited it—plenty of times before. But this time was different.

Miss Hiratsuka's desk was normally a total chaos of documents, envelopes, canned coffees, and figurines having a wild party, but that day, it was neat and tidy. In fact, the only thing on it was a notepad with a black cover, tied with string, and a ballpoint pen.

For an instant, I thought I had the wrong desk. The only sign of Miss Hiratsuka was the rolling desk chair, specifically its backrest tilting way back. But the woman herself was nowhere to be seen.

"Oh, Hikigaya. What is it?"

I glanced around and found the source of the voice a little ways away, poking her head out from behind the partition to the reception space. A cigarette in her lips.

*Oh yeah, she was using that section as a smoking area, huh…?*

Her waving turned into a beckoning gesture, so I headed over. It seemed she'd been doing some kind of writing, but now she was in the middle of a break or something. She held an unopened can of coffee, perhaps to go with the cigarette. What she'd chosen was, of course, MAX Coffee. As for why, because I was someone very special.

Coming in as prompted, I sat down on the sofa in the reception area and told her my business. "Um, I came to get the key."

Miss Hiratsuka gave me a curious look. "Oh? But Yukinoshita just picked it up." Blowing out a cloud of smoke, she tapped the ash off her cigarette. I scowled at the distinctive tarry smell and the suspicion that I'd wasted my effort, and the teacher gave me an exasperated smile. "Why don't you keep in contact to check these things? Reports, communication, and discussion are important."

"Uh, I don't know her number."

"…And Yuigahama?" She gave me a doubtful look.

"Uh, well…" I laughed with a *na-ha-ha* to avoid that question. No way could I tell her I'd just wanted to come get the key.

But even if I didn't say it, Miss Hiratsuka seemed to sense it anyway; she gave me a quiet shrug and a lukewarm smile. I squirmed with discomfort.

Then, in my periphery, I noticed the other teachers and office staff running around, and I took advantage of that to change the subject. "Looks kinda busy here, huh?"

Miss Hiratsuka narrowed her eyes and followed my gaze. "Hmm? ...Ahhh. Well, the school year is just about over. It's par for the course, this time of year."

Huh. I'd assumed they were busy with entrance exams, but it wasn't just that, was it? They had to take care of graduation and students advancing to the next year as well, after all. And since Miss Hiratsuka was in charge of us second-year students, maybe she wouldn't have much involvement with the new first-years.

"I guess everyone's busy at the end of the fiscal year and the school year. My parents had a lot on their plate, too."

"Well, it depends on what time of year a company closes their books, but a lot of places set the cutoff at the end of March, after all. You wind up having to meet their deadlines, so it gets so busy… I want to go home… Closing accounts, end of term, deadlines…all of it can go die…" She hung her head, cursing and complaining.

*And yet you seem to have plenty of time at the moment…*, I thought, giving her a silent judgmental stare, and Miss Hiratsuka noticed my wordless question.

"Mgh, I'm busy, too, you know? I really am!" She suddenly straightened in her seat, dramatically puffing up her cheeks in a pout.

*Hmm, very close. If you were a little younger, I could have honestly found that cute… But when you've gotten to Miss Hiratsuka's age, it comes around full circle to be actually cute again! Aw geez, she actually* is *cute!*

"And now…I'm taking a break. Just a little one? Y'know?" she said emphatically, then pressed her cigarette into the ashtray, crushing it along with my doubts.

But you know what they say: Where there's smoke, there's fire…

"You've made your desk pretty tidy there."

"W-well, when you're busy, you end up trying to escape reality." She scratched her head with an *ah-ha-ha* to cover herself.

*Well, I know the feeling... When you have too much to do, you kinda black out and then suddenly you're gaming! Hmm, can't blame her for that. Not guilty.* Faulting her would be going in the entirely wrong direction. Work is to blame for everything. Work is what's bad. It's important to hate the work, not the person.

As I was folding my arms and nodding, Miss Hiratsuka let out a little sigh. "But I have to get my work sorted out soon, too...," she muttered, and I don't think she meant to say it to me. Or possibly at all. Her gaze was down on the ashtray by her hand. There was no longer any fire or smoke—just the lingering smell.

I'd thought I was used to that stench by now, but I couldn't help but scowl. Maybe it was from remembering my conversation with Haruno. The smell that night had been suffocating and a bit anxiety inducing, just like this one.

In an attempt to forget it, I rose to my feet. "...I'm going to get back."

"Mm-hmm, you should go." Miss Hiratsuka followed me.

Right as I was about to leave the reception area, she called after me. "Hikigaya."

I stopped and turned around. "Yeah?"

Her lips opened slightly, but she just stared at me without saying anything.

Her gaze wasn't sharp like usual, but I didn't see that gentleness she occasionally showed me, either.

I'd never seen this expression on her, actually. I really wanted to hear what came next, and I tilted my head to prompt her.

But she closed her eyes and gave a little shake of her head, then grinned boyishly. "...Nothing. Just make sure to get it! Catch!" And with that, she threw the can in her hands at me in an underhand toss. I managed to catch it, then gave her a silent *What the heck?*

Miss Hiratsuka put a hand to her cheek in a cutesy-wootsy ♪ sort of gesture, tossed me a big ☆ wink, and stuck out her tongue. "No telling anyone I was slacking off here! ☆"

*Whoa, she's obnoxious... What's with that "dreamy-cute!" vibe? Wait.*

*So is this canned coffee supposed to be a bribe to keep my mouth shut? She didn't have to bother, though, since there isn't exactly anyone for me to tell…*

Anyway, I returned fire with a sideways *Peace ☆ capisce!* and left the teacher's room.

If the clubroom door was already unlocked, then there was no rush. Yukinoshita would already have reached it by now, and she'd have let Yuigahama in, too. While juggling the Max can I'd just received in one hand, I strolled casually down to the clubroom.

Unsurprisingly, Yuigahama wasn't to be seen in front of the door, and I could hear two voices from inside. Maybe it was those voices that added the warmth to the bleak sights here.

The door that had only rattled without opening now moved smoothly to the side. The scent of black tea wafted out along with the warm air from the heater. The two girls were sitting in their usual spot by the window.

With a call to them, I pulled out my usual chair on the hallway side. "'Sup."

"Hello." Yukinoshita was just pouring the tea into cups, and she looked up from the desk with a smile. But her eyebrows quickly lowered apologetically. "I'm sorry. It seems we just missed each other… I should have contacted you."

"Ahhh, yeah. It's okay." I waved the canned coffee in the air as if getting it had been my intention all along, and Yukinoshita let out a relieved sigh.

But Yuigahama held her breath instead, puffing up her cheeks. "I told you I'd call her…"

A wry smile slipped out of me at her pouty complaint. "Nah, I don't think you said that…"

"You left before I could."

"Um, but I was getting the Max can? Ah, never mind. Sorry…" With her giving me the stink eye, I tried to make something of an excuse for myself with the coffee in hand, but under the force of Yuigahama's rapidly chilling stare, I wound up apologizing for real.

"…It's fine." She let the air out of her cheeks and brought the mug in her hands to her lips.

Yukinoshita giggled at our exchange and then, teapot in her hands, shifted her attention to me. "Anyway, I did make some tea… Would you like some?"

"Yeah, sure. They say sweets go in your second stomach, after all."

"You say that about coffee?! It really is supersweet!" Yuigahama seemed almost frightened of my Max can.

*Uh, I sure do. I'd even say it's far sweeter than the low-carb, low-fat sweets out there these days…*

Well, I'd save the coffee for when I was more in the mood; for now, I'd have the freshly steeped tea for the after-school teatime.

"Here you go."

"Mm, thanks."

I took a little sip from the Japanese-style cup Yukinoshita poured for me and let out a sigh, feeling the tension of my body unwind.

I didn't even realize how much tension there'd been and what it had taken to relax me.

The random flood of words from my mouth wasn't coming anymore, and all I could manage was a humid breath.

I could have sworn I'd never been bothered by the silence before, but now, this awkward gap was almost terrifying. I cast a sideways glance to check on Yuigahama and found she was looking down at the ripples in her mug. Her mind was in a similar place, I think.

But not Yukinoshita's.

As Yuigahama and I failed to find anything to say, she smiled calmly and broached the subject. "Um, thank you…for the other day." Laying her hands on her lap, she quietly lowered her head in a beautiful, flowing gesture.

I was a little relieved to see it. I couldn't tell you where, but I had the sense I'd seen this before: that beautiful straight-backed posture, the lovely way her hair parted at the top of her head, and her faint smile in front of me. That sense of déjà vu enabled me to speak more gently than I'd expected from myself.

"...Did you finish moving? How'd it go?" I asked. I'd heard about it from Hayama that morning, so I already knew, but I said it anyway. You should hear this sort of thing from the person in question, after all.

Yukinoshita nodded and continued. "Yes. It wasn't enough to call a move, anyhow... And besides, Yuigahama helped." Yukinoshita gave her a warm look, and Yuigahama waved her hands in front of her chest.

"Ah, no, no, no way! I didn't do much at all..." Yuigahama gave a modest, awkward laugh, combing through her bun to occupy her fingers as she turned away.

But Yukinoshita was undeterred. "You really were a help. Thank you..." Her smile was peaceful and dreamlike, making me think of warm sunlight.

As the primary focus of that attention, Yuigahama glanced back at Yukinoshita as well. And when their eyes met, the expression brought to mind a smile through tears. She let out a deep, shaking sigh.

Yukinoshita seemed embarrassed by that reaction. "Should I put out some snacks to go with the tea?"

The room warmed slightly, the smell of tea with a hint of sweetness spreading through it. The rays of the sun were just beginning to slant in and color the air, too.

Suddenly, the air vibrated with a *knock, knock* at the door.

"Come in," Yukinoshita responded calmly, and the door slowly opened.

× × ×

A ray of light from the window shone through the crack in the door, and the cold air coming in from the outside churned up the heat in the room like a burst of wind. One of the windows in the hallway must have been opened for circulation. The clubroom was now filled with fresh air.

"Pardon meeee!" said Iroha Isshiki, the summoner of the recent gust, grinning by the open door. And making no move to come in.

*Huh? Why's she just standing there? And, like, leaving the door wide-open makes it cold...*

As I was shooting her an accusatory look, Isshiki poked herself in the cheek with her index finger and tilted her head. "Ummm, there was a computer here, riiight...?"

"There is...," Yukinoshita replied with slight confusion.

Then Isshiki asked with even further nonchalance, "Can you watch DVDs with it?"

Yukinoshita cocked her head pensively, and she moved to pull the laptop computer out of the desk drawer to check.

But she didn't have to bother—I knew the answer. "It's an old one, so you actually can use it for DVDs."

"Huhhh."

*Why is she impressed by that...?*

"What about it?" I asked.

"Oh, no, just checking."

"Huh... Uh, checking what...?"

With a little wave, she gave us a look that said, *Nothing major.* But it seemed Isshiki finally decided she wanted to come in, as she closed the door behind her, grumbling as she approached. "I'm fine watching it online or whatever, too, but I can't get a receipt for it. You need a credit card for stuff like that, right?"

"I'm not sure why you're asking me..." Yukinoshita was the one to respond. She sounded just as confused as Yuigahama and I felt. *What is she talking about...?*

As we were giving her questioning looks, Isshiki briskly booted up the laptop. "So I rented the DVD, but the student council laptop is too new to play it."

*Huh...theirs is new... Oh, really...? Sure is nice to have money... Well, laptops these days more often don't have disk drives, huh...?*

As I was thinking, Isshiki's bag rustled as she pulled out something. It was a white, square box of about palm size.

"…What's this?" Yuigahama gave it a timid poke with her finger.

*Indeed. What's this, tofu?* Then I noticed the lens and buttons on it. *Okay, so probably not tofu…*

Grabbing that box, Isshiki stuck a cable into it and began connecting it to the laptop.

Yukinoshita made an appreciative *ohhh*. "It's quite small, but it's a projector…"

"Yep, yep. Oh, just gonna pull down the screen, 'kay?" Isshiki nodded back at her, then stood up and went to pull down the projector screen in the corner of the clubroom with a little *fshhh*.

*What's she starting up here?* I wondered, and Isshiki clicked a button on the box. A low, whirring sound started up, and after a few moments, the computer display was projected onto the big screen.

"Oh, wow." Yuigahama's mouth hung open, while Yukinoshita had her arms folded, hand on her chin.

"The image is very clean."

Isshiki waggled a finger at the two of them with a smug chuckle. "Apparently, it can project from phones and stuff, too."

"Ohhh," Yuigahama said. But then a thought seemed to hit her. "Ah." With a little *meh-heh*, she asked jokingly, "But…isn't it expensive?"

Flinging her arms out wide, Isshiki answered, "Act fast, and it's a student council expense, so it's functionally free for me! You won't believe it!"

"That's the worst kind of product demo…," I groaned.

No tagline is shadier than "functionally free." Never naively trust video games that are "functionally free-to-play," or multilevel marketing schemes that claim a guaranteed profit in the long term. I would not be deceived, I would pay no microtransactions, and I would only use the free magic stones to roll for gacha. With that solemn oath in my heart, I patiently observed.

"And, like, what is this projector?" I asked. It appeared to be brand-new; it even had the clear protection seals on it.

Isshiki gave the projector a long look, then tilted her head. "Newly bought equipment...I guess."

*Uh, don't say it like* Jumping abilityyy*...I guess... Big brother Irohasu, I want you to have more confidence when you explain the appeal of the student council's new Friend, Projector-chan.*

"Not that—we're asking what you brought it here for..." Yukinoshita put her hand to her temple like she had a headache.

*Yeah, I wanted to ask the same thing.*

"Well, about that...," Isshiki said as she twirled a DVD around on her finger and set it in the disk drive.

Yuigahama seemed to put two and two together, and she hopped to her feet. "A movie? A movie? We're gonna watch a movie?" She seemed excited, bouncing over to close the curtains and flicking off the lights.

*Uh, we're obviously not going to watch a movie here...*

Then, a distinctly familiar-looking image popped up on the screen. You know the type—a certain freedom-centric statue, or a lion going *grr*, or letters over spotlights, or waves going *za-sploosh*.

*...Huh? We're actually gonna watch a movie?*

Ignoring my confusion, Isshiki slid her chair to a position where she could see the screen better. And then Yuigahama set the desk with snacks on it in front of us, and we were all ready.

*...Huh? We're actually gonna watch a movie?*

After we'd reached this point, Yukinoshita started making more tea. Playing along was her only option now.

*...Guess it's movie time.*

× × ×

In the dark room, with the curtains closed all the way, the only source of illumination was the dim light from the projector. If this had been a

real viewing environment, like a movie theater or a home theater, maybe I would've been able to focus on the movie and get into the story.

But we were currently in the Service Club room. It was an ordinary place where we spent time basically every day, and this unusual version of it really made me feel anxious more than anything else.

Even worse, the only audio output was the internal laptop speakers, so we all had to scooch in to hear it. The population density was really high.

So I wound up fidgeting and squirming, and with each movement, I'd make contact with someone next to me. There were so many little sounds—fabric against fabric, or the surprised gasp of an unexpected touch, or the ticklish whispers of a private conversation.

That was all that my brain was processing, in the end, and I hardly remembered any of the plot.

I did catch the basic story and the fact that it was actually a foreign TV show. It was kind of like a coming-of-age story at an American high school. All I got was that the athletic types were kinda whoa and that the school hierarchy is brutal over there, too. Frankly, my spirit broke halfway into it, and I stopped paying attention. For the rest of it, I became like an ascetic monk desperately fighting worldly desires.

Just as I was starting to achieve enlightenment, the show finally ended. It played all the way through the surprisingly short credits, and with a click, Isshiki turned off the power on the projector.

"Oooh, that was good!" Yuigahama said as she stood up and opened the curtains to reveal it had become dark outside. When she flicked on the lights, I could see Yukinoshita closing her eyes and nodding in satisfaction.

*Seems everyone has quite enjoyed it… My attention was elsewhere, so I only have a vague idea what it was about…*

Isshiki, who seemed to be having a real blast with this, started quietly singing as she started to put things away.

"Dancing queen, hm-hm hm-hm-hmmm."

She was singing the song that had played during a scene I

remembered at the end, but she was just humming the last part instead of the lyrics.

But despite my deepest apologies for interrupting her fine mood, there was something I had to ask. When Isshiki's hands paused in her task, I quickly called out to her, "…Hey, why'd you come to watch a movie here?"

"It wasn't a movie. It was a TV show."

"Same thing…" If it's got Americans being loud in it, then it's Hollywood. Come on, don't make me do more work than that. And if they suddenly start dancing, you can call it Bollywood. That's movies, you know? Although this was a Western drama. When I let out a deep sigh, Isshiki gave me a look of surprise.

"You didn't like it?"

"Oh, I'm sure I would've enjoyed it if I actually watched it, but when you're just zoning out, the brutally painful scenes leave a stronger impression…" And that goes for not just the scenes I'd gotten a glimpse of. The most brutal thing of all had been being so closely surrounded by girls in a private room…

"So, like, you all are fans of these shows, huh…?" I said.

"Well, of course. It's genuinely interesting," Isshiki said as if it was completely obvious.

"Yeah, it was," Yuigahama followed up. Yukinoshita didn't say anything, but she was nodding, too.

"Huhhh, I see…" I've also seen a little of stuff like *24*, *Prison Break*, and shows like that, and I enjoyed them well enough, but the drama they'd just shown me had occasionally gone full soap opera. Wasn't that exhausting? "…I dunno. Maybe it's a girl thing," I muttered.

The girls got huffy at that. "Not just girls. I think it's normal for boys to watch this, too…," said Yuigahama.

"Yeah," Isshiki agreed. "Actually, it's better peace of mind for you if she likes shows that most girls do, you know. If it's the other way, and she says she likes *Mad Max* or *Avengers*, it's absolutely the influence of her boyfriend."

Now that was something I couldn't let pass unremarked upon, and I replied, "Huh? Really?"

Then Isshiki gave me a *nasty* smile. "Well, yeah. Nine times out of ten."

"Hey, you cut that out. Let a guy be happy to find a girl who likes the same movies as him—don't ruin it... Some girls like that stuff..."

Source: Miss Hiratsuka. By the way, Miss Hiratsuka's favorite movies are *Tremors*, *Battleship*, and *Pacific Rim*! When I heard that, I just about fell in love with her.

But you know, the source here is super-untrustworthy. I gave her a questioning glance, like, *So what sort of movies does a "normal" girl watch?*

She chuckled smugly. "You want to find a girl who says she likes *Amélie* or that sort of hipster art-film aesthetic!"

*And now she's launched into a lecture... Also, that's a pretty old choice... Although it is a famous movie and not too hard to find. I guess I get it...?*

"Huhhh... By the way, what's your favorite movie?" I asked.

Ever the sly one, Isshiki put her hands to her cheeks in a coquettishly cutesy-wootsy kind of way. "*Amélie.* ♡"

"Hipster..."

"And I'm not sure that's even true...," Yuigahama commented.

Also, an unbelievably basic pick.

Right as I was about to cut in and say just that, Yukinoshita closed her eyes and muttered around her teacup, "...It's a good movie, though."

*Whoops! Good thing I didn't say it! Everyone has their own tastes and interests when it comes to movies, so I want to respect that stuff, you know! You never know where you might find a land mine!*

But there are people out there who will respectfully walk right over those land mines.

"Ahhh, you *would* like that, wouldn't you, Yukinoshita?" said Isshiki.

"...And what exactly do you mean by that?" Yukinoshita's eyebrows twitched together as she gave Isshiki a cold look. Isshiki shrunk away with a *hyerk*, hiding behind me like a little squirrel.

Yukinoshita rubbed her temple and sighed in exasperation. "More importantly, why did we suddenly have a screening here?"

"Ah, yeah, yeah. Oh yeah." I remembered what I'd been about to ask a moment ago, and I turned my upper body toward her.

Then Isshiki clapped her hands as if she'd just remembered, too. "For reference. If I watched it in the student council room, people would think I'm slacking off, right?"

"I'm not sure that's a good reason to choose to see it here…," Yukinoshita said.

"Watch it at home. Come on," I added.

But despite our candid advice, Isshiki just beamed back at us. "But we went to the trouble of buying that projector, so we'd want to try it out, right? And there's no projector screen in the student council room or at my house. And I have a rule about never working in my off-hours." Not a shred of guilt. At this rate, she might even buy some chic speakers with the student council funds so she could have herself the whole fancy chic-y set. 'Cause, y'know. She's Isshiki…

As I was making horrible puns to myself, Yuigahama raised her hand with an *ohhh*. "Wait, reference material? We were just watching the show like normal, though…"

"The graduation ceremony is coming up, right? And that appreciation-party thing afterward? The student council is in charge of that, so that's why."

"Ohhh…" I knew where this conversation was going now. I inched my chair back and braced myself. *I am absolutely not going to help with this.*

But apparently Isshiki wasn't even going to ask. She folded her arms with a *hmm*, deep in thought. "…Well, honestly, we could just have a normal appreciation party—y'know, just set out some tables so it looks legit and chat about whatever—but when I was thinking about when

I'm going to graduate, I started thinking maaaaybe we should make this one fancy... Oh, and it would make the graduates happy, too."

*Wow! She remembered the graduates at the end! Irohasu sure has grown, huh?!* ...was of course not what I was thinking. In fact, it was refreshing how self-centered she was. If anything, I was impressed.

Then from nearby, I heard a similar sound from someone else. Looking over, I saw Yukinoshita nodding and *hmm*ing with a know-it-all expression. "I see. The prom."

"Ohhh, you got it! I knew you'd figure it out, Yukinoshita!" Isshiki praised her and clapped.

"It's nothing, really. The conversation was obviously headed in that direction." As calm as she was, I could still detect a hint of pride. And a tiny blush. No resistance...

But anyway, thanks to Yukinoshita's correct answer, I'd figured out what this was about, too. This was about the prom. ...*What the heck is a prom?*

"*Puro*? What? Proactiv?" That stuff that works on pimples? I was unfamiliar with the word, but I was asking the wrong person.

Yuigahama turned the question back on me in the same way. "*Puromu*...like a peach? *Momo*?"

"Uh, that's *puramu*," I corrected her English. "You like peaches, huh...?"

"Huh? Yeah. They're great." Yuigahama gave me a big smile and chuckled.

*What the heck? That was so cute. Wait, no. I wanted to know about "proms."* So I looked over at Yukinoshita. *Teach me, Miss Yukipedia!*

She swished the long hair off her shoulders pridefully and smiled an indomitable smile. "A *plum* is the same as the Japanese *sumomo*. They're both Rosaceae Rosales, but strictly speaking, it's another species. In fact, you could say that *sakuranbo* cherries are closer."

"That's not what I wanted to know..."

"Huh? Huh? Some *momo* are *sumomo*...so some *momo* and some *sumomo* are *sakuranbo*?"

*Miss Yuigahama has lost it, huh...? She's gone bananas...or should I say gone peaches and plums?* That was the sort of tongue twister that made me want to say "do it again!" But let's leave that for another occasion.

"So...what's a prom?" I asked.

Yukinoshita nodded. "Yes...," she said, considering her words before she began. "*Prom* is short for *promenade*—it's another word for a ball. I suppose you'd call it...the dance party they have at foreign high schools at the end of the year. You could technically think of it as a fancy graduation party. There was a scene like that in the TV show we just saw, wasn't there?"

*Huhhh...so that really American "Dancing Queen" party scene was that prom thing, huh? I see*, I thought, and then I suddenly realized. "Wait. Wasn't that fiction? Regular people actually do stuff like that?"

"Looks that way. Apparently, it's pretty normal over there. Ummm..." Isshiki pulled out her phone, tapping and sliding her way through an Internet search. Once she found what she wanted, she shoved her phone at me. "Ta-daa!"

"Ohhh..."

On her screen were scenes of fancy parties, with boys and girls dressed up in lavish dresses and tuxedos. The venues for the event were various—a school gym, a club with a DJ booth, a dance hall, outside, but all of them were similarly elaborate-looking. *But none of them even look like high schoolers...*

"See? Think of all the engagement this would get on Instagram! I really wanna do it!" Isshiki gushed.

"What a sucky standard to go off of...," I groaned.

Isshiki was pointing to a photo of women in dresses arriving at a venue in a fancy limousine. As a guy, I get more excited about Gwazines than limousines, you know...

But now was not the time to be thinking about Zeon battleships.

I had an image in my mind of graduation parties, but this prom thing she'd just looked up on her phone was on a whole 'nother scale.

And it had a different vibe from the "nighttime pool party" stuff that attracts the loud types. And it didn't feel very jooshy polly yey, either...

Maybe it was the foreign culture, or maybe it was my own personal tastes and preferences, but this wasn't quite clicking with me. I couldn't imagine our school having a prom. "Uhhh, can't we just have a normal party…? Why a prom…?" I asked.

Sliding her hand across the chest of her pink vest, Isshiki announced with great pleasure, "Eh-heh. Why, you ask? Because I will be the prom queen!"

"Oh…" *What the hell is she talking about…?* I wondered as I tried asking Professor Google what a "prom queen" was.

Apparently, it was basically like, *Let's all choose the coolest girl in our school or grade!* And they also choose one of the boys to be her counterpart, the prom king… "I get it… In our cohort, the prom king would definitely be Hayama…"

"Yeah, I'm sure it would. Hayama is the king, and I am the quee… Ah." Just as Isshiki was saying that, she noticed the time paradox. She then cleared her throat with an *ahem* and smiled brightly at me. "By the way, this has nothing to do with that, but you're not repeating a year or anything, are you?"

"No…"

"Aw, you! You're going to fail your college entrance exams and have nothing to do for a year anyway, so it's all the same. In fact, it's a great deal, since you can still use your student discount."

"Can you not make assumptions? And that doesn't make up for it. I'm gonna have a backup school, too, okay? I'll get in somewhere," I said flatly.

Isshiki pouted. "Oh, really…" Then her expression did a one-eighty, and with a glint in her eye that said, *Well then, I've come up with a compromise just for you!* she nonchalantly added, "Oh, then how about you help me out with the prom instead?"

And to make it worse, that statement was unfortunately not something I could let slide. "Instead? Instead of what? …And hold on a second. Are you seriously planning to have this prom?"

I was glaring at her to make sure she knew these implications were negative, but Isshiki just replied "Yep" like it was nothing.

You can't blame me for sighing over this. "We can't start that now. And I'm not into that stuff. I just don't want to do it."

"H-hmm…" Yuigahama smiled awkwardly. "I think it might be fun, though…but maybe we couldn't manage it."

"Yes, indeed…" Yukinoshita put a hand to her temple and closed her eyes. All three of us were basically in agreement.

Unsurprisingly, with the other two indicating their disapproval, Isshiki seemed increasingly uncertain. "Ohhh, well, I do get that. But I was thinking it'd be nice… You sure we can't?" The spirit from before was gone as she squeezed the hem of her blazer, giving me an imploring look up through her lashes. It was manipulative but so powerful. I almost wanted to hear out her request.

But if I failed to say no to her prom ambitions now, I knew I would pay for it later. The guilt was making my throat tight, but I managed to get out a refusal. "It's more like…honestly, it just feels impossible…for a number of reasons, but… I mean, you get it, right?"

I didn't think there was a need to bother explaining. Time, funds, personnel, experience, information, and everything else—we were lacking too many things. I shouldn't have to tell Isshiki that.

I was sure she had her reasons for coming to make this unreasonable request… Well, I guess the realistic line would be to hear her reasons and search for a potential compromise.

As I was making my guesses as to where that compromise might lie, Isshiki *hmm*'d thoughtfully. "Is that right…? I understand. Then we'll try doing it just with the student council."

"Ah, yeah… Huh?" I did a double take.

But this was neither a mishearing on my part nor idle words. Isshiki's head jerked up, and she glanced at me sharply. She was determined about this.

"…Were you listening to me?" I asked her.

"Yes. So we'll do it ourselves." She grinned boldly.

Now that she'd flatly declared it a second time, I couldn't say any more than that. The usual remark here would be either "Don't bother" for the negative or "Do your best" for the affirmative, but what came out was mostly air. "O-oh... Uh-huh..."

I wasn't the only one with their mouth hanging open—Yuigahama was the same. We exchanged looks. When I asked her ...*What the heck?* with my eyes, she shook her head just slightly as if to say, *I don't know...* Meanwhile, Yukinoshita's eyes were closed, so she did not participate in our silent messaging.

Which meant Isshiki was the only one who could tell us the correct answer. I stared her way.

"Uh, can you not look so shocked...? I knew it would be hard. I've already braced for you saying no. I'm not that dumb," Isshiki said with a sniff.

Yuigahama and I were convinced.

"Ohhh," said Yuigahama, "so you basically came just to give it a potshot?"

"I get it," I said. "So that's why you came into negotiation with nothing really prepared."

Isshiki screwed up her lips and looked away as if she was struggling to find her next sentence. "I—I was thinking watching that TV show together would get you excited about the prom idea, more or less..."

*That counts as nothing, you know... But at least she's being honest.*

As I was giving her a soft, lukewarm look, Isshiki cleared her throat with a *kephum, kephum*. "Well, if you find that you *are* interested, then please come hang out in the student council room, 'kay? We'll welcome you with open arms! We won't let you go home!"

"You're gonna drain us dry... And, like, you're actually serious about this prom thing, huh...?"

"Yep."

Isshiki's answer remained steadfast—she'd already reached her conclusion. And yet not a single one of the proofs that would be necessary for deriving that conclusion had been validated. *This is gonna be a hassle…*

As I was wondering what to do with this, Yukinoshita broke in. "Could I ask why it is you want to hold a prom so badly?"

Isshiki's shoulders twitched with surprise. And from Yukinoshita's behavior, it looked as if she was both talking to Isshiki and thinking about something else the whole time.

That had to be why Isshiki's reaction came late. "Ah, um, well, uh, to be prom queen…"

"But that would be in two years, right?" Yukinoshita deftly slid into the empty silence when Isshiki's words trailed off.

Scratching at her cheek and fiddling with the hair at the back of her neck, Isshiki replied, "Ahhh, um, like, to start laying the groundwork for that now, you know."

"If you were to hold a prom two years from now, you wouldn't have to lay any groundwork to be chosen as queen."

"Uh-huh… Huh?" Isshiki stared at Yukinoshita like she had no idea what she was talking about. Yuigahama and I also exchanged looks.

Yukinoshita breathed a short sigh. "I'm saying there's no reason you absolutely *must* do it this year."

"I mean, I never said *absolutely*…," Isshiki hedged, but Yukinoshita totally ignored her. She just leveled a sharp and patient gaze on her, waiting only for the answer to her question.

Isshiki recoiled a bit, but then she came up with her response with a clap of her hands. "Ah, okay. There's no guarantee I'll be the student council president again next year, right?! So planning now is my only shot…"

"If you're interested, you'll be elected. Not many people run, and even if it does go to a vote, with your ability and accomplishments, you'll win. I don't believe it would be a problem to do it next year." All the words coming out of Yukinoshita's mouth should have been kind in meaning, but her sharp tone made them sound like an accusation.

Isshiki's words trailed off in the face of this interrogation. "Well… um…yes, maybe that's true, but…"

"So then next year, or—"

"We can't," Isshiki interrupted.

Despite Yukinoshita's overpowering force, that one remark of Isshiki's was unshakable.

Yukinoshita silently asked her intentions.

"…If I say we're doing a prom next year, it'll probably never happen. It's like you guys just said. They'll say no, it can't be done, we don't have enough time, and then it'll just kinda die… I know it's hard, and it might even fail, but I have to lay the groundwork for my next move…" As she put the words together, they came out in disjointed bits, then trailed off at the end into a faint, smothered, trembling sound.

I was about to ask if she was okay when her pale hair swished dramatically.

"We have to do it now. If we start now, we might still have time." Jerking her head up again, she leveled a strong, direct gaze at Yukinoshita.

But Yukinoshita's expression didn't change. "…What for? Or who for?" she asked coolly.

Isshiki blinked as if taken by surprise. She seemed to consider a moment, and her lips were slightly open in an innocent sort of way.

But she quickly broke into a fearless grin.

"For me! Duh!" Iroha Isshiki declared, loud and proud, with a hand to her chest and an arch in her back.

Of course. Whether what she'd just said was true or whether it was all a pack of lies to hide something, I had to commend her for her sense of commitment. Asking for her reasons at this point would just be crass.

Yukinoshita seemed surprised, too, as she blinked her eyes a bunch, but that eventually turned to a smile. "I see. Thank you for answering." The emotion was genuine, as if that was what she'd wanted to hear from the bottom of her heart. Maybe she had asked out of pure interest.

What Yukinoshita said next was so smooth, so perfectly planned, that I guessed that might have been the case.

"Then, let's do it."

"What? Huh? You're actually okay with it? Aw geez! I love you, Yukinoshita! But hey, what was all that about, then? You kinda freaked me out and it'd be great if you could never do that again," Isshiki said as she trotted over to Yukinoshita and glomped her with a little squeal.

Apparently quite grumpy about this, Yukinoshita peeled Isshiki away with a quiet and cold "Hey…"

Watching this heartwarming scene, Yuigahama and I sighed at practically the same time.

"Well, once the higher-ups have come to a decision, then there's nothing I can do. Guess it's work time…," I grumbled to myself.

"…Uh-huh, yeah." Yuigahama nodded back with a slightly crooked smile.

Well, the Service Club's plan had been decided. If a task had been generated, then we had to deal with it.

As I was lightly stretching and rotating my shoulders, Yukinoshita called to us with some reservation. "…Um, do you have a moment?"

"Hmm?"

As Yuigahama and I lent our ears, Yukinoshita straightened in her seat with a bit of nervousness. "What I just said was my own intention as an individual, so I won't force you two."

When I stared into her eyes to ask what the darn heck this was about, Yukinoshita took a breath in and out and straightened her back.

"Essentially, um…that's not a decision as club captain. I don't believe I have authority there. So you need not consider this an official club project. Of course, I would be grateful if you'd offer your help. However, I intend to take responsibility for making this prom happen, even if it's on my own. I mean, um…" As Yukinoshita approached the end of her speech, she got quieter and quieter, and her words gradually became vaguer, too. I think she wasn't sure how to communicate it herself. Her hands squeezed her skirt, her head hanging as she bit her lip; she seemed to be struggling to find the words to say.

Her words were a little unclear, and for a moment, I started to tilt my head. But I could remember another incident involving some strained logic. Iroha Isshiki probably sensed that, too.

However, this was slightly broader than the weak logic from back then.

"Basically, you mean club attendance is voluntary?" I said.

Yukinoshita glanced at me and hesitantly started opening her mouth.

But before she could speak, someone else said kindly, "That's not it, Hikki."

It sounded like Yuigahama was pointing out my mistake, but there was nothing accusatory, cautioning, or chiding about her tone. Her voice was like a feather fluttering down, and I looked at Yuigahama. She gave a little shake of her head. She dropped her gaze to the desk and let out a faint breath.

After the slightest pause, she smiled gently at Yukinoshita. "Yukinon…you want to try doing it on your own, right?" she asked, and Yukinoshita nodded instantly.

*Ohhh, I get it.* That made sense, and it was like something stuck in my chest came undone. That really hadn't been it. I'd been wrong.

I always throw so many words on top of each other, wrapping them up in layers and layers, and the result is that I never say the important things. And with just one gentle remark, she had guessed it right.

Yukinoshita's lips trembled, and she sucked in a delicate breath. "And…Isshiki feels that now is our only chance to do it. That if we start now, maybe we'll have enough time… I think I feel the same."

Isshiki was staring in stunned silence at Yukinoshita's profile. I think Yuigahama was probably the only one who was calm. She was always the only one who was really listening attentively to Yukinoshita.

"So I want to properly begin," Yukinoshita continued. "…And I'd be glad if you could see me do it."

"Okay. Then I won't say anything. But promise me." Yuigahama stuck up her pinkie and held it out. Yukinoshita's hand only came halfway to meet it, hovering in confusion.

But Yuigahama waited patiently for Yukinoshita to finish the timid approach, and the two fingers wrapped together. "Don't push yourself too hard. Seriously, don't. And if you need the help, make sure to call for me. Maybe this one isn't a Service Club project, but we're still friends. Times like these, I want to help for real…"

"Yes, I promise… Thank you."

When they sealed their pinkie oath, Yuigahama suddenly broke into her usual bright smile with its hint of childlike innocence. "Mm, good. Then I'm okay. What about you, Hikki?" she asked me in a clear voice like a tinkling bell.

But I couldn't respond right away.

"Ahhh…" My reply was barely more than an exhalation; it wasn't even clear what I was replying to.

Yukinoshita seemed anxious. "…Am I making a mistake?"

"…No. I think it's fine. Not like I'd know."

"Always with the lazy responses." Yukinoshita smiled.

There was a smile in my voice, too. I'd finally understood what I had seen in that beautiful bow. What those circuitous words had been trying to say. No wonder it had given me a sense of déjà vu. And of course it had made sense to me. I'd already gotten a taste of that loneliness and relief.

"…I see. I think I get it," Isshiki muttered. She seemed slightly tired, and there was a weight to her sigh.

Yukinoshita must have picked up on that, as she said meekly, "Um, I'm sorry… I hope you don't mind. It makes sense to worry if I'm the only one helping…" Yukinoshita bowed her head.

But Isshiki smiled brightly back at her. "Oh, no, I'm not really worried about that, so it's okay." She hopped to her feet, took a step toward Yukinoshita, and bent to the side to make their eyes level. "Could you come to the student council room starting tomorrow?"

"Yes. I'm looking forward to it."

"Right. Me too, Yukino!" Isshiki made a joking salute, then with a *hup* took her things in her arms and spun around.

Yukinoshita was nonplussed by that last part, but Isshiki ignored that and strode off.

Then right before closing the door, she waved back with a "Bye!" and left the clubroom.

After watching her go, only the three of us remained. It was late; normally, we would have gone home by now. We really had to get going.

Yukinoshita must have checked the clock as well, as she muttered, "…We should head out." Yuigahama and I nodded back at her, and we quickly got ready to go. Yuigahama folded up the blanket that had been over their laps and carried it under her arm as she left the clubroom. I went out into the hallway as well, and Yukinoshita followed after.

In the darkness of night filling the school building, the hallway was piercingly cold—that threshold was like a gate to another world. But the cold on my skin told me just how comfortable the clubroom was.

Since we weren't taking this on as a job, I wouldn't be coming there tomorrow or the days after that. The thought made me a little reluctant to part.

But this was just what independence was. Just like Komachi's peaceful weaning off her big brother—it left me both lonely and proud. This was something to be celebrated.

As if tucking away something important, the door locked with a click.

Only she ever carried that key, and I had never once touched it.

# 5 Unsurprisingly, **Iroha Isshiki** is the most powerful of underclassmen.

The day after that exchange in the clubroom was a warm one for once. The wind was blowing strong right from morning, and the windows were rattling even after class was done for the day. The sunlight coming in through the glass was enough to warm up the classroom, so the heater was relieved of duty early.

My classmates were not fond of the winter cold and had been reluctant to part with the heat before, but that day, they couldn't get out fast enough.

Left in the sparsely populated classroom, I picked up my mostly empty bag to join the outgoing flow.

I got a tap-tap on my shoulder. Turning around, I saw it was Yuigahama, already in her coat. I knew what she was here for, and I rose from my chair.

Then she wrapped her scarf around her neck as she tilted her head. "What are you gonna do today, Hikki?" she asked.

"…Ahhh." I didn't quite know what to say. Maybe it was because that wasn't quite the question I'd been expecting.

Yuigahama had said that if Yukinoshita needed anything, she'd help as a friend—but I hadn't really declared my plans. And neither of them had asked me about it. I didn't have a job right now.

All this time, I'd always said I just do this stuff because I have to.

None of that was a lie, and that would probably continue to be my stance from here on out, too. I had not accepted any requests, or consults, or responsibilities to fulfill, or contracts to execute, or wrongs to make up for.

I didn't have to go to the clubroom.

As it took me a weirdly long time to derive that conclusion, my expression had shifted into a strained smile.

"Nah, going home." Even as I said it, I wasn't quite sure what the subject of the sentence was or whether it was true, but I swallowed down the uncertainty and said something else. "What about you?"

Yuigahama also paused for a moment, fiddling around with her scarf near her mouth. "Hmm...I'm going home, too..."

"Oh."

"Uh-huh." She nodded, burying her face in the wool, and the conversation trailed off.

It was just for the briefest moment, but the silence there was palpable. I don't think I was the only one bothered by it. It wasn't much in the way of proof, but Yuigahama and I did exchange a few glances back and forth.

*...What?! What the heck is this silence?!*

I was getting confused, so I wondered if I should say something else. Unfortunately, I couldn't really come up with anything. So to smooth over the pause, I hefted my bag up and adjusted it on my shoulder, even though it wasn't really heavy enough for that. "...See you."

"Ah, okay. See you," Yuigahama said, then waved at me. I nodded in return and started walking, then heard footsteps pattering behind me.

I turned back to catch the moment Yuigahama glomped Miura. "Looks like there's no club for me today, either, so I'll go with you!"

"Mmm." Miura was clicking away on her phone and tugging her curls with her fingers, but then she did a double take as Yuigahama's unusual reply finally hit her. "...Wait? Really?! You can come, Yui? Great! Omigod, I wasn't even thinking of anything. Omigod, where do we go?" she said, immediately looking over at Ebina.

Ebina giggled. "You can pick, Yumiko. It's just Chiba anyway, right? Not like I know."

"Huh? If I decide, then our only option's Kushiya Monogatari." Miura's earlier shock had completely evaporated, and she was acting all haughty now.

"Oooh, hype." Ebina applauded blandly. She did not sound hype.

At least Yuigahama was happy to hear this little exchange. "Sooo skewers?" she asked with excited innocence. "Deep-fried? Really?"

And what the heck is Kushiya Monogatari…everyone telling stories about skewers of fried chicken? Or is it the story of fried chicken skewers? I think people would argue over how to read that…

But anyway, Yuigahama's after-school plans were now settled.

As for me, however, I had absolutely no plans. *Now, whatever shall I do?* I wondered as I left the classroom and walked silently down the hallway.

Since we'd just had a long weekend, I'd gone through my pile of recorded TV shows, and I'd read just about all the books I had in my room. *I just gotta catch up on my game backlog, huh…? I was trying not to play console while Komachi was busy studying…*, I thought as I went down the stairs.

I was pretty excited about the opportunity to be a couch potato and game to my heart's content for the first time in a long while, and I was very excited for the new release of a mainline installment in a major franchise; I could even stay up three nights in a row for it… Will the hero Eightman yet *again* save the world?

The more I thought about it, the more excited I became, and I got a bit of a skip in my step.

It crossed my mind that before I'd joined the Service Club, I'd always spent my time like this. Doing what I wanted.

I headed down the stairs and toward the front entrance.

And there, I caught sight of Yukinoshita with her coat under one arm, presumably on her way to the student council room. She seemed to be walking at a rather brisk pace as well, which made me hesitant to call out to her. In the end, I just watched her go from a distance.

From that day forward, Yukinoshita and Isshiki would be planning the prom.

I didn't know the details there. Yukinoshita and I never interacted outside of the Service Club, so if I wasn't going, there was no way to ask. She was in the international curriculum, and I was just in regular classes, so we didn't even wind up together in gym or nonacademic classes.

So the only opportunity for us to interact would be if we happened to run into each other by chance. I wasn't about to barge in and ask about the prom.

Of course, this was partly because I never got a chance to talk to her, but that was far from the only reason. If I just walked up and said *How are things going?* or *Working hard?* when I wasn't going to help, I could imagine what someone would think: *Who the hell do you think you are?* or like *What right do you think you have to be talking, creep?* So I was hesitant to speak with her. Although just thinking about this stuff already made me pretty creepy. Truly a fearsome self-consciousness indeed…

As I was busy getting myself down like this, Yukinoshita turned a corner.

I couldn't see any hesitation in her footsteps.

Her back was beautifully upright, her dignified gaze pointed straight ahead, her long, glossy black hair swaying with each rhythmical step she took.

After she was completely out of sight, I finally remembered that I'd been on my way home.

× × ×

I hadn't played a console game in forever, so I'd stayed up all night gaming. I rubbed my sleepy eyes as I went to school, then went back to my marathon session the moment I got home.

I was whizzing through the story, enjoying the hell out of it, but RPGs always have those moments when you grind to a halt.

Generally, the reason is either underleveling or completionism. As for leveling—this game wasn't particularly brutal, but the completionist elements were the sticky part. Especially because, as someone who was raised on *Pokémon*, I am driven by the compulsive need to fill up the Pokédex, so I was desperately filling out the bestiary like a guy who was a loser in high school seeing he has no plans for the weekend in university and trying to pack his schedule like the cool kids.

You've got trophies, titles, and the bestiary, and then there's challenge runs on your second and third playthroughs of the game, etc....

And the whole "new school, new me" in university metaphor doesn't stop there. After he tries to really cut loose over the summer break after first semester, which makes people say stuff behind his back like ... *That guy's kind of a try-hard*; *Honestly, he's sometimes cringe*; *Sometimes I feel so bad for him*; *He's really got a fundamentally different vibe to him, you know*, he suddenly up and disappears in the second semester—just like my motivation to finish this game... University kids are terrifying!

When you get right down to it, once hobbies and play become quota and routine, they're not much different from work. It took me three days of all-nighters to realize this, and yet again I was heading to school with massive sleep deprivation.

I devoted pretty much every class to napping, and as a result, by the time school was over, my back really hurt.

Once the end-of-day homeroom was over, I somehow sat up and tried to twist my cracking, creaking, and popping back. My spine had so much to say, you could call it a backache *monogatari*.

Between the pain and the fatigue, I fell into pondering the joys and sorrows of life as I turned and twisted my back, then heaved and hoed myself out of the classroom.

That was when Totsuka, who'd apparently been watching me from a distance, trotted up to me. "You've been sleeping all day today, huh,

Hachiman? You've been like this for a little while now. Are you okay?" As soon as he was next to me, he examined my face with concern. The gesture reminded me of a pet rabbit, and I couldn't help but smile.

But at the same time, I felt bad at putting unnecessary worries on him. "I'm fine, I'm fine. I've just been staying up gaming for the past three nights."

"O-oh, really..."

I thought I'd managed to be pretty cheery, but Totsuka seemed a little put off by my declaration. Wonder why. Well, stop wondering—bragging about how you haven't slept would turn off anyone. I was standing there going like, *I haven't gotten aaany sleep; I've been staying up the past three nights gaming and haven't gotten aaaany sleep! Whoaaa, where'd you hear that I haven't been getting enough sleep lately, huh? Where'd you hear that?* Most people find that behavior pretty obnoxious.

Totsuka put his hands on his waist like he was collecting himself and puffed up his cheeks sulkily. "But you have to take care of your health. You should only be gaming for an hour a day!" He wagged his finger at me and chided me with a *Fair play, fair duel!* sort of vibe. He's such a good guy...

Totsuka glanced back toward the classroom we'd just come out of, then added in a quiet murmur, "Besides, if you keep doing that, Yukinoshita and Yuigahama will get mad at you, right?"

I had to smile at that. He was right. They would scold you over stuff like this. "...Well, I can do it because club's not on right now," I replied.

Totsuka nodded a few times, as if that made sense to him. "Ohhh. A holiday, huh?"

"For a little while. So I've got nothing else to do...," I replied, and a big yawn slipped out of me. *I'm getting really sleepy... I can even see angels in front of me. Wait, no, not good! Totsuka only just gave me a reward... Well, that was technically a tongue kis—wait, no a tongue-lashing from Totsuka.* If I showed him I was sleepy again, then I might get another reward. And if I were to force that from him, even Totsuka would eventually start treating me like garbage. Although that could also be a thing…

After earnestly considering these matters, I felt bad for making Totsuka worry. *And I'm acting like a real creep here! This is why you gotta sleep enough! Anyway, I should spend my time in a healthy way today at least, and not go on a gaming bender.* "Well, you're right. Maybe it's not a great idea to be doing nothing but gaming… Are you free any time soon, Totsuka?"

I believe I can safely say that never in my life have I invited someone out in such a smart and cool way. *I just fell in love with myself. Yeek, Hachiman, hold meee!* I had to encourage myself, or I would've died from embarrassment and shyness… If he were a girl, this would not only become my dark past, but it would carve itself into my memory like a graphic war documentary. It would be archived in the history of Hachiman as my loser legacy!

Totsuka is probably just about the only boy I can have a friendly conversation with. I think the actual question of whether I could call him a friend requires his approval, but I mentally categorize him as someone extremely close.

Still, inviting him out one-on-one was a pretty high hurdle. Probably not just for me, but for him, too.

If you're all in a group, and the conversation leads to a big hangout, that's less to worry about. When it's an individual versus the majority, the responsibility of that individual is always dispersed in multiple directions. But when it's one-on-one, all responsibility falls upon you and the other person. Ultimately, this also makes them feel worse for saying no, too. If you're in a group, "I'll go if I can" is a pretty safe bet. After that, if you can reach the point when they realize you always say that and never come, so they should stop inviting you, then you can part ways in a truly harmonious manner. That's my recommendation.

As I was rapidly making excuses to myself, Totsuka's mouth dropped open, and he blinked his big, wide eyes. *Wait, what? What does this reaction mean?*

While I was closely examining this response, Totsuka's mouth kept opening and closing somewhere in between the "ah" and "oh" positions as he flailed his hands. But then he groaned, smacked his hands together, and bowed his head. "Sorry! On weekdays, I have my club... I really can't skip it... Ah, but in the evening...I have tennis school, and that's a little late to hang out, huh...? Um, and on the weekend, I have a practice game... Urk..." He was really racking his brain for a gap in his upcoming plans. It wounded my heart deeply to see him caught between a rock and a hard place with his responsibilities as club captain, but I was also happy that he'd agonize this much for me... I just about got teary-eyed for two different reasons. It's so weird how easily I've been crying lately. Next thing I know, I'll get weepy just from the new episode of *PreCure* every week...

But I was not the uncomfortable one here—that would actually be Totsuka. I don't normally invite people out to things, so the one on the receiving end must not know how to deal with it, you know! *Let's take care of that in the future. Specifically, I'll pin down his schedule about three months in advance...*

While making this new oath to myself, I started in on the groundwork to that end. "Oh, another time's totally fine." I put a slight bit of emphasis on *another time* in an attempt to connect to those future prospects.

Totsuka jumped on that, leaning forward with enthusiasm. "Really? You'd better! I'll text you about it!" He squeezed a fist and looked at me with sparkling eyes, and I floundered a little.

"O-okay..."

Totsuka huffed. "I mean, you hardly ever invite me out! So it's a promise! Next time! You'd better!" He stuck his finger out at me, and I nodded with a little smile. Then he smiled back and with a *hup* adjusted his tennis bag on his shoulder. "Well, I'm going to my club, then."

"Yeah, see you later. Good luck at practice."

Totsuka ran off, and then when he was a little ways away, he waved with his whole arm, to which I responded with a slightly raised hand. I watched him until he was all the way at the end of the hall, then got moving myself.

I think I'd finally figured out how to do something anyone else took for granted. I was still hyperconscious, overthinking, overstrategizing, over-rationalizing, and overexplaining, though, and I still needed to talk myself into doing it at all.

It's not like I'd ever had the desire to change or consciously planned to change; it was mostly just how things had turned out. Totsuka's kindness had carried it most of the way. Still, I was aware that I was actually moving toward a compromise.

But this really had only materialized because it was Saika Totsuka.

In actuality, I hadn't managed to do anything else right.

I didn't feel like going home to play games, so I'd wound up here after school with no plans. When you don't have work, there really is nothing to do. Sleepy as I was, it almost would've been better to have had work.

*My back hurts, so I guess I'll just go lie down now*, I thought as I turned a corner in the hallway and started down the stairs.

That moment, there came a loud, bellowing laugh that rang out all around me. "Fwa-ha-ha-ha-ha-ha-Hachimaaan! I saw! I heard! I knew you had naught to do anyway!"

I didn't have to turn around to know whose voice that was.

Which was why I didn't, and I decided to continue on down the stairs and just go home!

× × ×

But things don't always go as planned, especially with Yoshiteru Zaimokuza. It's what makes him so formidable. So though I should have just ignored him and headed straight home, I instead found myself the subject of coaxing and occasional provoking and eventually tears as a last resort. When Zaimokuza brought me to the Saize at the station, I was still feeling a bit bamboozled. Before I knew it, I was munching on a Milan-style pilaf and slurping at a drink from the drink bar.

Once my stomach was full and I'd gotten comfortable, I sighed. "…Um, hey, I wanna go home."

"Now, now," Zaimokuza replied, "in due time. First, we discuss."

"Discuss what?"

"A light-novel author must have meetings at Saize, after all…"

"Ohhhh."

*Is that right? I thought you normally have them at the publisher's office or at a café, though… Has he acquired some information from the Internet yet again? Hmm, is that it?* Well, it's not like he was doing nothing; it's just that his passion was spinning its wheels in vain, pointed in all the wrong directions and not engaged in any kind of real activity. Oh no! I can't spin any of it into a compliment!

I gave him a look of half exasperation and half ridicule, totaling 100 percent contempt, but the yawn that hijacked my reply somehow made it sound appreciative.

Zaimokuza chuckled smugly like he was pleased, but even he clued in to how hard I was yawning. He pushed his glasses up with a finger and peered into my watery eyes. "What's this? You seem plagued by the sandman."

"Yeah, I've had a lot of spare time lately, so I've been spending all of it gaming. Then I was staying up all night by accident," I said.

Zaimokuza reacted with a twitch. "Gaming because of spare time, you say? Unacceptable. Absolutely unacceptable!" He raised his hands as he shrugged; the reaction reminded me of something from a Western movie or show.

*Aghhh, I can feel a long speech incoming…* Why is it that when our particular field of specialty comes up, we boys will suddenly get chatty, even if we normally don't talk much…? But you know that afterward, you'll go home and regret it. *Whoa, they definitely thought that was weird, and I was talking superfast, too…*

But when in the company of someone he could be a bit at ease with, Zaimokuza didn't worry about that. He raised his hands high and began to sonorously expatiate. "Games of the video are most pleasurable when one is painfully busy and has absolutely no time at all. *Oh crap, oh crap, oh crap,* you say, *I know this isn't the time for video games… Seriously, I have a shit-ton of stuff to do; I can't be gaming. No really. I'm not lying this time!* Making such excuses to no one at all while playing is transgressive, thus bringing the pleasure to its zenith. Source: me. The high when you pull an all-nighter gaming right before exams and then go to school is magnificent!"

"I can't endorse this, but I can't deny it, either…" That very morning on the way to school, I'd smirked to myself and thought, *Oh dude, I haven't slept. Oh dude.* It's such a high from nothing at all. *Aw dude. I'm such a loser. Dude.*

Zaimokuza must have taken my equivocal reply as an affirmative; a smug smirk spread on his face, too. *Dude.*

"So what game playest thou?" he asked.

"Ah, this one." Tapping on my phone, I showed him the title and official game website, and Zaimokuza pushed up his glasses. The vaguely nostalgic little "Ahhh" he gave actually made him sound like a normal person. "Ohhh, this one. It sucks when the heroine leaves the party halfway through, huh?" he said, breaking character completely.

The moment I heard that, my scowl could've curdled milk. "…What? Hold on, the hell? Are you spoiling me? I wasted so many seeds bumping her stats. Agh, now I don't even want to play anymore… If you're gonna write your manuscript, stop playing video games and write…"

"Huh? You haven't finished it yet? Sorry… Um, er, but…but!! This is the fate of those who fail to play a game upon release! Git gud, scrub!" Zaimokuza belted out a loud and triumphant laugh. Well, at least he apologized at first…

Besides, realistically, you should be prepared for that sort of thing once a game's been out for a while. And not just games; the same goes for movies and TV shows, too. You can't read a Japanese history textbook and wail, *No way, that general dies?! I got spoiled for the taiga drama!* Believe it or not, every Sengoku-era warlord is dead.

But even saying that, every experience is different, depending on the player or viewer, and on the environment the work is being played or viewed in. I would hope people keep these things in mind when enjoying content, being considerate where possible so that everyone can have a good experience!

"I bought it right after release, but it's just been in my backlog… Komachi was studying for exams, so I felt bad about gaming at home," I said.

Zaimokuza nodded, his cheeks full of focaccia. "Oh-ho. I see. Now that you mention it, the young maiden was in her third year. So which exam did she take?"

"What? Our school's. Huh, didn't I tell you?"

"Hmmmmm?! I have heard no such thing! Ke-ke-ke-ke-ke!"

"Oh, really? I guess we don't talk about personal stuff. Like university, the future, or family and things like that."

"I *do*! I tell you about that all the time! I share with you my dreams for the future and my career! That's even why I summoned you here today!" Zaimokuza got quite huffy about this, so I asked with a look, *So what do you want anyway?*

Then with a deliberate-sounding cough (*gepkum, gepkum*), he suddenly covered his face with one hand. Between his fingers, I saw anguish.

Eventually, he pulled a piece of twice-folded paper out from his pocket with his other hand and held it up between his index and middle fingers. Under the glow of the electric lights, I could see through slightly to the characters on it. "Before, I made a plan together with thee in the library, did I not? I finished the outline for it…"

"Uh-huh…" *Oh, that thing we talked about around the beginning of February when he burst into the clubroom and wouldn't shut up about becoming an editor? He's always making outlines, huh…? I've never once read a completed manuscript...*, I thought, but nevertheless, I plucked up the paper he offered and decided to read it right there.

Whereupon, fingerless gloves flashed in front of my eyes and snatched the paper back. "W-wait! 'T-tis embarrassing, so wait until you're home..."

"The hell, is this a love letter or what? Stop blushing. It's so gross," I said, stealing the outline back from him. I had been instructed to wait, so wait I would. I solemnly folded it up and let it gracefully sink to the bottom of my bag. I'd probably forget about it later and never even glance at it. So I had to bury it politely, at least...

Oblivious to my intentions, Zaimokuza seemed satisfied as he watched me carefully putting it away, then gazed off into the distance and sighed. "Thanks to next year's entrance exams...'tis my final attempt."

Don't get me wrong—I definitely thought, *His final attempt? Did he even make a first attempt...?* But when he said it with that exquisitely stern and manly expression, I had to swallow my skepticism.

This had to be Zaimokuza's own way of drawing a line for himself.

There's no better excuse for us to abandon an idea than the term *entrance exams*. The word *employment* would probably come to take on the same meaning, too. Dreams, hobbies, clubs, or any of the possibilities that could have been born there would be cleanly melted down to be re-poured into the mold of the adult that society demanded.

This was why he had to do this now; before the world would sweep him away and level him and deprive him, he would challenge, struggle, resist, and try to get a glimpse of becoming someone... And most likely, she would, too.

Lost in thought, I'd fallen entirely silent.

Whatever he thought of that silence, Zaimokuza clapped a hand on my shoulder and gave me a thumbs-up. "Come now, worry not! This is just the final attempt of high school."

*Whoa, really trying to force the cool factor there...*

"Uh, it's not like I'm worried about you…"

"There it iiiis! You *tsundere* boy!" Snickering as he put a hand to his mouth, dear Zaimokuza was so obnoxious…

But if I tried to argue, he'd respond with something even more incoherent. And so I nodded at him with obvious annoyance like, *Yes, yes, you're completely right* and prompted him to keep talking. That little performance just now made me think there was probably still something he wanted to talk about.

And then with a low chuckle, Zaimokuza started talking with maximum manliness. "Make no mistake; I do not intend to succumb. Some things one can write best as a high schooler, others as a university student. The shortest route isn't always the right one, you know. Even detours are a part of my march to victory!"

*That would've been much cooler if he were actually writing something right now…*, I thought, but, well, I was too nice to say so. He wasn't technically wrong, after all.

Instead, I would say something else. With a big, wide smile. "Yeah, and there might be things you can write in the gap year after you fail your exams, too."

"Ha-ha-ha!" Zaimokuza burst out into loud laughter with his face turned to the ceiling, before his expression suddenly turned serious. "…That hits a little too close to home, so let's not talk about that. There isn't not a nonzero chance I'll end up like that, so I don't want to think about it. Nope, nope, nope."

I couldn't help but give a crooked smile. He's so absolutely useless, it's kinda reassuring…

Thinking about it, I realized Zaimokuza was one of the few people who'd known me before I'd joined the Service Club. We'd just been a couple of leftovers paired up in gym class, but still, we were in the same boat. If I hadn't joined the Service Club, maybe I'd have been spending my time after school like this.

…Maybe that actually wouldn't have been so bad, either.

But every once in a while is enough for me! I don't have it in me to deal with him more than this!

× × ×

The morning news had informed me that the plum blossoms were blooming, even in Kanto. The segment had also told me that the winds the other day had been the strongest of that spring. They'd been on and off over the past few days, too. The wind was often warm, signaling that the long winter was almost over.

The god of entrance exams once wrote: "If the eastern wind blows through / then let your fragrance ride them / O sweet blossoms," and around that time came the day when Komachi's exam results would be posted.

*So the plum trees have blossomed, but no cherry blossoms yet, huh?*

But that morning, I was the only one getting antsy, while Komachi was slurping calmly at her tea.

After worrying about what to say to her, all I could come up with was "Um…I'm gonna head out to school…"

But she just shot a wink at me as if to say, *I'm totally fine, all good here.* "Yeah, Komachi's gonna go, too… And once I see the results, I'll text you. Don't worry." She must have been trying to make me feel better, since I was even more anxious now than when I'd gotten my own results. Fortunately, her utter composure helped me finally calm down, too.

Ever since the other day, Komachi had suddenly seemed more mature to me. She was still a middle schooler in the eyes of the world, and she was definitely a minor, but she and I both knew now that she was no longer a child.

She'd always had a precocious side to her, or maybe more like street smarts—but now she had composure and serenity on top of that. This was her growth, the proof that she was starting to become independent. *…It really is like she's weaning off her big brother.*

I suddenly felt a touch of loneliness, but I shoved it behind a smile and rushed out of the house. When I was just out the front door, I called back to Komachi, "Then see you later."

"Yeaaah, bye-bye!" Though I couldn't see her, her voice calling back from the living room sounded carefree.

And then just like always, I rode the same old familiar commute on my squeaky bicycle… If Komachi passed her exam, then would we be going to school together? No, I had the feeling that wasn't how it would go. Maybe we'd occasionally leave the house at the same time when things happened to line up, but we wouldn't try to make it happen. Komachi and I would once again construct an appropriate and comfortable distance between us.

With Komachi on my mind, I spent the whole way to school and homeroom with my head in the clouds.

Around the time second period was almost over, I took a look at the clock. I'd been doing nothing else all day, but the needle had finally reached the number I'd been staring at all this time.

Very soon, exam results would be posted…

I breathed a surreptitious sigh, and then finally, the bell rang, signaling the end of second period. I watched the teacher stride out of the classroom, and then I was rotating my shoulders to loosen them up when my cell phone vibrated.

I snatched it up and looked at the screen. Among the push notifications was the line *You have a new message*, plus Komachi's name. A flash of fear crossed my heart. This message would tell me if Komachi had passed or not, and I hesitated to open it.

But I steeled myself anyway and, with trembling fingers, moved to tap the screen.

But before I could, a graceful beast dashed before me. Her Thoroughbred tail fluttered behind her, leaving a vivid blue streak as the wind of her passing whooshed by.

With a start, I followed it with my eyes to see Saki Kawasaki had already raced off. She'd probably gotten a message from her little brother

Taishi at just about the same moment. I stood up as well and ran out of the classroom.

The two of us were usually on the edges of the classroom; with both of us suddenly bolting, everyone erupted into noise, asking each other what had just happened.

"What? What, what?! Is something happening?! We gonna go?! We going, too?! We're going!" I could hear Tobe getting all worked up behind me. But now was not the time to be turning back. The break was only ten minutes. Kawasaki, with her elegant strides, was already far ahead of me in the hallway.

She was probably headed up to the front gates, where the exam results had been posted. Of course, that was where I was going, too. It took me less than a minute to reach the growing crowd.

The exam takers had already converged there, but I still managed to find Komachi right away. It seemed she noticed me, too.

Unlike her sweaty, winded brother, Komachi seemed incredibly calm as she raised her hand, strolling up to me.

"Oh, Bro. I passed." She said just that with a nonchalant look.

It was anticlimactic for me, too. I was panting after the run, but I let out a deep sigh that helped me get my breathing back under control. What followed was a relief like exhaustion that gradually spread through me.

"Oh…" That was all that finally came out of my mouth. I was so happy, I wanted to gush at Komachi and start jumping around, but she seemed so unsurprised by the results that I felt like I should be the same.

I actually wanted to rub her on the head, but she was too old for that now. As her big bro—the elder, more mature sibling—I'd pull myself together, as was appropriate for her new growth.

I tried to think of a slightly more dignified way to congratulate her—the sort of thing an adult should say.

"I'm glad… I am. I really am glad." But the only words I could find were incredibly clumsy and awkward. I truly am a hopeless big brother. I'm getting fed up with myself, honestly. *This guy hasn't grown at all, compared with his little sister.* I'm always playing with words, and yet I can't put together the right thing to say when it counts.

Komachi had to be pretty fed up with me; I looked at her.

If I couldn't say it quite right in words, then I'd celebrate her with my best smile, at least. The problem was that my smile isn't a very pretty one, but hopefully, she would ignore that part.

She didn't. She just gazed into my eyes with a hint of warmth.

"Yeah, I'm glad, too. Really…," she agreed, her big eyes twinkling in the light of the sun. She sniffed and trailed off. When she let out a long breath, it was shaking, and she sucked in more air to hold it back. When she exhaled again, I heard the beginning of a sob. "I'm really, really…glad… I'm so glad!"

Komachi sprang forward and slammed into me, roughly burying her head into the lapels of my blazer. The damp breaths on my skin hiccuped irregularly, then turned vocal in a way that felt like a punch to the gut.

How long had it been since I'd last seen Komachi bawling like this? This was nothing like how she cried when she was little. *She was so mature this morning, though,* I thought with a wry smile, then suddenly realized something.

*Ahhh, that's not it.* She hadn't been calm at all; she'd just been making an effort to act that way. She'd been smothering her anxiety and worries to keep me or our parents from worrying, or maybe to avoid the stress of any concerned questions. The answer looming before her had been mercilessly clear, but she'd tried to accept it nevertheless, desperately trying to stand on her trembling legs.

From the bottom of my heart, I was truly glad she was rewarded.

My hand reached out to Komachi on its own. I lightly patted her head and ruffled up her hair, and Komachi dissolved into tears yet again.

"Wahhhhh, Big Broooo, I'b zo glaaaad!" She was weeping like a heartbroken celebrity as I patted her back to soothe her.

It seemed she would need a little more time to wean off me. And for me to wean off her. Sooner or later, whether I liked it or not, Komachi would become a proper adult and a wonderful woman. Probably sooner.

But until that time came, maybe she'd let me be her big brother for a while longer…

As I was comforting Komachi, I heard Saki Kawasaki's sharp voice behind me.

"Taishi!"

"Sis, I did it!"

When I turned my head to glance back, I saw Taishi. As he walked towards us, he was holding up over his head a set of the documents they give to the students who passed.

Taishi's proud (and quite loud) voice reminded me of that old classic *Rocky*. *Adrian!!*

That must have reminded Komachi there were others around, as she suddenly snapped out of it and peeled herself off me. She rubbed at her eyes with the sleeve of her uniform. Well, she wouldn't want people she knew to see her bawling. I gave her a crooked smile and cover behind my back.

That was when Taishi discovered me and came over my way. Kawasaki was all alone in the corner, face up to the sky, occasionally bringing her hands to her eyes. *Mm-hmm, Big Sis is glad…*

As I was appreciating the heart of Kawasaki and feeling all the feels, Taishi came up in front of me to pump a celebratory fist. "I did it, Bro!"

"Don't call me Bro—I'll kill you. Just use my name. You did it, congrats. Also, who are you?"

"Thank you very much! I'm Taishi Kawasaki! Um…Hikigaya!" His broad grin had become somewhat tougher than before, and he had the facial features of a grown man. It made me want to celebrate him in a manly way.

"…That's great. All right, time to throw you into the air. In celebration."

"By yourself, Bro?! I don't think it works that way! That's a German suplex! It's concrete underneath!! I'll die!" Taishi thrust both hands out in front of him and backed away. That was a very hard no. I offered a crooked smile, about to say that it was a joke.

"Ohhh, bumps? Yo, for real? We're doing it, right?!" But before I could, Tobe popped in.

Celebration was a great excuse to mess around, and he wanted to take it. Behind him, I could see Yamato, Ooka, and the guys. There was also a smattering of others from our class, and other classes, too. *Oh, and what about Hayama…?* I scanned the area and found him smiling and chatting with a group of teachers. I could infer that he was mediating for the rest of us—since we'd left the school building, even if it was on a break.

*You're wasting your time showing that kind of consideration to Tobe and the guys…*

Tobe hooted ("Whoooo!") as he led Yamato and Ooka, and they all circled around Taishi and started throwing him up like a festival palanquin.

I took the opportunity to turn back to Komachi, who was still hiding behind my back. "Komachi. Go tell your school. And Mom and Dad."

"Yeah…" She was still red-eyed and sniffling, but she clicked away on her phone and started calling the school first.

While I listened to them, I checked the clock. *I really should get back to the classroom now…*, I was thinking as I looked over to Hayama wheedling the teachers, when I caught sight of Yuigahama sliding by them and trotting up to us.

"Komachi-chan!"

Komachi lifted her head, quickly finished her phone call, and rushed over. "Yuiii!"

I'd thought Komachi had finally calmed down, but the moment she saw Yuigahama, she burst into overflowing tears again. She leaped on the older girl without any hesitation at all, sob-sobbing. I almost expected her to cry, *S-Straw Hats…* at being treated like one of the crew.

*…Wait, is she crying more now than she did with me? Is that just my imagination?*

As Komachi reported her results, bawling all the while, Yuigahama nodded back at every word and hugged her tight, then brought Komachi's face up to press their foreheads together and beam at her. "Congrats… That's great… You really worked hard… I'm so happy for you!" she whispered, then finished with the brightest smile.

Face still wet with tears, Komachi gave her a sunburst of a smile in return.

"We've got to tell Yukinon, too!" Yuigahama said.

"Okay!" Komachi nodded cheerfully, taking out her phone. But then she stopped. "Uuurk, I'm crying too much. I can't see the screen…"

"Ahhh… I'll do it." Smiling, Yuigahama started making the call. She held the phone like she was taking a selfie and framed herself and Komachi in the front camera. I think it was a kind of video chat thing. She probably wanted to show her Komachi's face. *…I wonder if Yukinoshita actually knows how to do that with her phone.*

As I was worrying about this, the trio muddled through and finally started a conversation through the screen. Komachi smooshed her face right up against the phone screen as she burst into tears again. "Yukinoooo!"

*So much for calling our parents…*

Our parents, especially our dad, would certainly be quite worried. I didn't want their imaginations running wild with reasons she might not have called and then getting disappointed… So I'd take it upon myself to make the report. But Dad would be like, *I wanted to hear it straight from Komachi, though…* Agh! Such an old block off my chip!

And so…

```
Dear Mother
Cherry blossoms bloom
Regards
```

× × ×

I stayed with Komachi until she left, but even once I was back in class, I still felt kind of restless. The hours passed in a distant haze. The confirmation of Komachi's passing had so utterly filled my heart with relief, most everything the teacher said in class went in one ear and out the other.

*I'm so glad...*, I thought. One, then two classes went by as I ruminated and reflected on this happiness. I'd been taught since childhood to chew my food thoroughly when eating, so I could savor one piece of happy news two or three times. Like a cow.

Even once the bell called *ding-dong-bing-bong* to tell me lunch was here, I didn't feel hungry. Normally, I'd dash over to the school store whether I wanted to or not in order to secure a decent amount of food, but that day, I felt calm enough to take my time.

Wondering what I should eat, I was standing up to go when there was a knock on the door at the front of the classroom, and then it creaked open.

*Maybe you'd knock for the teachers' room or clubrooms, but who knocks to come into a regular classroom...?* I was thinking suspiciously when Yukino Yukinoshita appeared.

The unusual visitor caused a momentary buzzing in the classroom. But even though Yukinoshita was the center of attention, her expression didn't change at all as she stated her business. "Is Kawasaki here?"

"...Huh? M-me?" Kawasaki said, voice cracking slightly. She pointed to her own face and blinked. Yukinoshita replied with a nod.

They were already both pretty enough to draw eyes, and this increased the attention on them even further. Kawasaki scowled and blushed bright red as she trotted quickly toward Yukinoshita. Everyone's curiosity was unbearable for her.

The pair launched straight into a discussion by the door. *Hmm... Kawasaki, maybe it's because you're embarrassed, but I can't hear your voice at all...* Yukinoshita was matching her volume, and the near whispering made their conversation seem extra-secret. I couldn't tell you what it was about. Others around seemed to be perking up their ears as well, but judging from their reactions, they couldn't hear it, either.

Well, my guess is that it was about the prom. It'd be rude to try to eavesdrop on a discussion when I had no plans to get involved.

Leaving my seat for real this time, I headed for the door at the rear of the classroom. On the way, I noticed the side by the window was quieter than usual, and it drew me to look.

There, I saw Yuigahama watching Yukinoshita and Kawasaki. She'd probably figured out what Yukinoshita was here for, too. That was why she wasn't saying anything.

Miura seemed to find this unusual. "Yuiii. You're not going?" she asked brusquely, although there was no real bite to it. I got the odd sense that she was trying to be considerate. I think it was probably a high-context remark, with a lot of meaning expressed in relatively few words. Yuigahama understood it well enough.

"Hmm, yeah." Yuigahama paused like she was considering a moment, but then she smiled and replied, "I don't have to go talk with them. She'll probably tell me after if she needs something. Besides, I'm going to the clubroom after this, so it's okay."

"Hmm?" Miura's reply was so vague, it was hard to tell if she was convinced as she twirled her curly hair. Then she and Ebina exchanged glances, both looking kind of puzzled.

Well, I could understand their reactions. They were in slightly different positions from before, so there would be some confusion.

But I was sure the reason those positions had changed was because they were making progress, even if just a little.

With a sidelong glance at Yuigahama and her friends, I left the classroom.

× × ×

I picked out some random leftover items from the school store and, armed with a Max can, sat down in my usual spot. With the calls from the tennis club doing their noon practice and the cheeps of warbling white-eyes in my ears, I treated myself to a slightly later lunchtime than usual.

The wind was still chilly to be eating outside, but I didn't really feel it. Maybe I had the afterglow of Komachi's success to thank for that.

We'd probably be having a fancy dinner to celebrate, so I could get away with a light lunch. I scarfed down a couple of buns with toppings and followed that with a nice, waaarm Max can.

As my mind drifted into outer space, I heard light footsteps and humming behind me. *This humming…*, I thought, and I turned around to see it was Isshiki.

When she saw me, her lips parted slightly, and she jerked back a bit in surprise. "Oh, you really were way out here."

I suspected I'd just been insulted, but that was par for the course from Isshiki. Instead, I ignored it and asked her business. "Mm, hey, what's up?"

"Oh, no, I just had something to talk about…," she said, but right as she reached my side to sit down, she paused. "…Wait, why aren't you in your classroom? I went all the way there! It was *sooo* embarrassing to ask if you were there, you know!" The mere mention of it was enough to bring it all flooding back, I guess; she went bright red and yanked at my shoulder.

And the whining didn't stop there. "And that wasn't even the worst of it! *Then* Tobe started loudly asking everyone! He kept saying I was looking for you and asking, like, 'Anyone know where he is? Whoo!' Can you believe it?!"

*Whoa, I totally can…* I don't know if he'd go *whoo* there, but that was a very Tobe thing to do. If he meant well by it, then I couldn't be too mad, but in his case, a certain amount of this would be about showing off to Ebina: *I may not look like it, but I'm actually a good guy, see?* So it did actually piss me off, because I just kinda suck.

"I mean…sorry? That's not my fault; it's Tobe's. So then was it like, Hayama stepped in to help you?" I said, anticipating what would follow.

Isshiki snatched her hand away from my shoulder and waved her hands side to side. "Oh, no, Miura snapped and told him to shut up before he could."

*Oh, that routine, huh? I can imagine that, too…*

As the scene played out in my mind, Isshiki added, "So Hayama said, 'Why don't you ask Yuigahama?' and the result is, here I am."

"Hmm, I see… Anyway, did you need something?"

"Yes, I wanted to ask you a favor," Isshiki repeated, straightening her posture and daintily hugging her knees. She cocked her head, and then she was suddenly looking up at me. Her slim fingers plucked weakly at my sleeve, her pale hair swaying in the drifting breeze, and her brown eyes were dewy. "Um…so will you…help me?"

"Not happening. I just don't want to do this prom."

*Your cunning Irohasu attacks won't work on me anymore…* And yet I still had to turn my face away. If I looked her in the eye, I might agree on impulse, so I really had no choice!

And besides, since I'd already refused involvement once, it didn't feel great to flip-flop so easily. If I gave in now, it'd be like I caved to her cuteness…

That would just be too impure, too faithless to the one who had committed her intention to this. To the one who had hung her identity on this, the one who had made a clean decision of her own accord. It would be too insincere. I should at least have dignity in my response. I'd never agreed to help with the prom in the first place. If it was her personal decision and not one for the club, then my answer really wouldn't change.

But sometimes words will completely change their meaning depending on who hears them. I didn't know why Isshiki was smiling with satisfaction after my negative answer. Lowering her eyelids dreamily, she put a gentle hand to her chest, and when her chin came up again, she murmured like a little bird singing a fairy tale, "Or so he said, but he seemed very glad to have me relying on him."

"…Do I?" I made the most aggravated expression possible. If my intention wouldn't get through in words, then I'd use my eyes. No choice but to speak with the eyes.

But Isshiki's reaction was an eye for an eye (or something), as she suddenly turned serious, too. Those wide, sparkling pools of innocence suddenly narrowed, and the light within them reminded me of a blade. "...Should I answer that honestly?" she said. It freaked me out a little.

"Huh? Whoa, don't scare me like this. C'mon, stop." *Time to change the topic!* "Yukinoshita's handling things fine, right? Is there some kind of problem? Ahhh, if the problem is that actually you don't really like each other, then don't tell me, okay? It hurts to hear that stuff."

"Um, I actually like Yukino quite a bit. Just so you know," Isshiki whined. As she went on, her expression turned a little morose. "...Well, whether she likes me or not is a separate question. If you're asking if we're friends, it's kinda...y'know."

*Oh, I think Yukinon likes you, Irohasu... And quite a bit, too...* But as they say, leaving things unsaid is a grace like a lily—er, wait, like a flower. I was sure she'd come to sense that herself anyway.

As I was earnestly pondering such matters, Isshiki's face jerked up. She wagged a finger at me as she filled me in. "Also, we genuinely are making great progress. I knew she was really good at this, but actually working together, it's like...I don't get why she's not the student council president. I wish I could fire the vice president and have her with us forever."

"So the one getting fired isn't you...? I think the vice president is doing his best, too. Not like I know." If he'd just stop flirting with the clerk, then he'd be one of the most diligent members of the team... Far as I could tell anyway. So stop flirting and do your damn job. C'mon. Stop screwing around and work.

Isshiki's replies were giving me a sense of envy, jealousy, and admiration all at the same time, so that meant Yukinoshita was demonstrating her talents and acumen in full. With her competence and experience level, that was easy enough to imagine. I could also easily envision what could well come after that.

"If you're all getting along and things are going okay, then that's fine... But stuff always happens. Even if it is going well," I muttered.

"Pardon?" Isshiki tilted her head and twisted her lips, like, *What the heck is he talking about?* Her eyes were unimpressed.

*That's an irritating way to ask a question...* But it did make sense. She hadn't been student council president during the whole mess with the cultural festival.

So she didn't know anything about how sometimes that smoothness came at a cost.

Actually, none of the people planning this prom even knew about that—Yuigahama wasn't over there with them this time around. She'd made Yukinoshita promise not to push herself, but if things got down to the wire, Yukinoshita could find ways to push herself anyway. She could lie to herself and say, *I can manage this* or *It's just until I finish that.* Someone had to be there who could pick up on that and stop her. If not, then everything would fall apart.

*I should tell that to Isshiki.*

"I wouldn't call this advice, but try not to rely too much on Yukinoshita. She can do most things, so it's easy to depend on her. But if she works herself sick, everything grinds to a halt. She wears out ridiculously fast, so sometimes she'll push herself too far without a second thought... Anyway. Keep it in mind," I said, trying not to sound too intrusive. I wasn't going to be helping with this project. I shouldn't be butting in too much, but I figured that wasn't crossing a line. Isshiki was sharp; she'd get it.

After a bit of silence, Isshiki *hmm*'d in acknowledgment and said, "...I see." Then she flicked me a questioning glance. "I've thought so for quite a while, but you..."

*Huh? What? What...? I'm getting nervous...* I cringed under Isshiki's skeptical gaze.

But her pouted lips suddenly broke into a smile. "...are overprotective." She had a little smile, though it had a bit of a mocking edge and a detached coldness. Then she blinked two, three times, widening her eyes again to communicate that it was a joke.

I found something next to me to look at, until I was finally able to let out the breath I'd been holding. "Uhhh, I don't think I am...," I squeaked.

Isshiki put her index finger to her jaw and tilted her head. "So then what do you call it? You're a big brother type?"

"Yeah, maybe that."

"So you *are* into younger girls?" Isshiki asked, leaning way forward.

"No...," I replied, pulling away by the same amount.

She mock-recoiled and teased, "I don't know about *that*."

"I dunno what you're thinking here—you just get like that when you've got a little sister. It's a habit. I mean, I just wind up acting how I do with my sister," I explained, sticking my hands in my pockets to look cool. Without pulling away or leaning forward, I stood straight and tall. *Being a big brother is a habit, okay...?*

Isshiki let out an exasperated-sounding *hah-ha*—half a sigh and half laughter. A frighteningly quick change of attitude. Anyone but me would have missed it. "I think you should stop doing that," she said coldly.

"O-okay..."

Only a heartbeat after she neatly cut me down, she was sitting with her knees drawn up and her elbows on her knees, chin in hands. She gazed out into the school courtyard, apparently bored. "No girl will be glad to be treated like your little sister." As her somewhat lonely words joined the cold wind and vanished, they felt real and personal.

Maybe she'd experienced something similar before. There had to be older boys who liked her; it wouldn't be strange for her to get treated that way. Though I couldn't understand how you could place an ultra-cunning devilish imp in the same category as a little sister. My little sister, Komachi Hikigaya, is the little sister of the world. There has been no Komachi before Komachi, and no Komachi after Komachi. I don't know any little sisters who surpass Komachi, and my little sister is only Komachi. I mean I've been preaching that a sister's all you need for my past three lives.

No, wait. If she was the little sister of the world, would Komachi have other boys saying she was like a little sister to them...?

*I dunno about that...* Some murky feelings swirled around inside me at that, so I just went ahead and said it. "Well, yeah. A guy who goes and calls himself your big brother is obviously gonna be creepy. And super-cringey. Criminal, even."

"Huh? ...Okaaay. Well, it *is* creepy, though..." Isshiki's eyes darted toward me. She seemed kinda weirded out: like, *What the heck is this creep talking about?!* But then she cleared her throat and gathered herself. "That's not what I mean. It's like...you're not being treated like a girl, right? Wouldn't it kinda bother you if a girl told you you're like a big brother?"

"Uh, I am actually a big brother, sooo not really..."

"Ahhh, maybe it's different for boys. Oh, then..." Something seemed to strike her, and she gave a little *hem*. Suddenly, she closed her eyes to take a shallow breath. She was just like an actress getting into character before a performance. I waited on standby for Irohasu as she slowly opened her eyes and gave me a blank expression. Ready...lights, camera, action!

Isshiki pasted a polite but forced smile on her face, then immediately slid her gaze slightly away. "Ah, ah-ha-ha... You're kind of like a dad. It's like...um, you know... Like, I'm always grateful to you?"

*This report was a shock to Hachiman.*

Yeah, that, uh, that hit me hard. I had to characterize myself like Kong Ming from Yokoyama's *Three Kingdoms* manga and read it out like a narration in my head or I would break. The saddest part was that every word, every hint of body language, screamed that she was trying to avoid being rude or hurting me. Wait, if you're saying that to a teenager, that's *definitely* an insult, isn't it? Even if I were thirty and someone a few years younger than me said that, it would still hurt!

Her act was flawless. *So?* she asked me silently.

I nodded back stiffly. "...That'd hit real hard. Feels like you're in a completely different category. Makes me wonder if I smell like old people. I'd want to die... Yeah. I'd die."

"I dunno about the smell, but yeah, that's the feeling. The different category thing." Isshiki folded her arms and nodded. And then as if to say, *One more piece of advice,* she stuck up her index finger and continued, "And when a guy says you're 'like a little sister,' he'll come on to you later and say he 'can't think of you like a sister anymore.' All this comes as a set."

"Whoa, yikes... The hell...? What do they think a little sister is...? A little sister is a holy, inviolable sanctuary... They should really reconsider the concept of little sisters and think about what they've done..."

"That's not exactly the reaction I was expecting, but I can't complain...," Isshiki grumbled with a dull look in her eyes. "But anyway!" Putting her hands on her waist and posing like she was ready to begin a lecture, she began earnestly admonishing me. "In the future, remember not to go around telling girls they're like a sister."

But then she froze right there and zipped backward with a hand to her mouth. "Wait! Were you planning to say 'I can't think of you as a little sister anymore' later to try to seduce me? Because if you were it would have no effect on my heart whatsoever so please come back and try again later I'm sorry."

"Yeah, yeah, I get it, I get it! I won't say it, okay?"

After saying all that in one big long go, Isshiki was winded. She took a big breath in and out, and her exhalation and my sigh came at the same time.

"What's with that attitude? Geez you didn't hear a word I said!" Isshiki puffed up her cheeks in a grumpy pout.

*Uhhh, I mean, you were talking really fast, and it's always going to end with* I'm sorry *anyway... Of course I'm not gonna actually listen.*

Isshiki gave an extremely disgruntled sniff at my weariness and turned away. "Well, whatever. Just help out with the event, please," she said. Kinda harsh for someone trying to ask a favor.

"Uh…huh? Wait, like I said…" But after how sulky she sounded, I couldn't find the words to refuse, and I trailed off.

In that brief silence, Iroha Isshiki brought her lips close to my ear to whisper, "Because I'm not your little sister."

That sweetly charming sentence sounded nothing like her earlier manner, but you could feel the strong resolve behind her words.

Then suddenly, quicker than I could react, her hands swept briskly over her skirt, and she stood with a grin. The way her skirt trailed behind her, the graceful movements of her slim fingers, and the sparkles of the sand that spilled off her skirt all moved away from me, and the crisp rhythm of her steps reminded me of a waltz.

"I'll be waiting in the student council room after school, 'kay?!" she said once she was a few steps away, fluttering her hand in a wave before she started off again, humming all the while.

She was too distant now for me to say anything back, too far for me to chase after her. She was a whole level or two beyond me; how could I possibly think of her as a little sister?

A reexamination of our views on this matter is in order. That is the underclassman of the world: Iroha Isshiki…

× × ×

After school, I was hauling my legs along the hallway to the student council room.

Since I'd failed to decline Isshiki's request then, I had no choice but to go now. I really didn't have another option, but my legs got heavier as I wondered how I could possibly face them now. But the student council room wasn't that far, and I quickly arrived.

I knocked, and the door immediately opened with Isshiki's face popping out from behind it. "Oh, it's you. You're laaate!"

"Ah, yeah, sorry." I had been dragging my heels, so I offered an apology.

Once I'd been welcomed into the student council room, I found Yukinoshita and Yuigahama inside. I couldn't see any of the other student council members around, but maybe they were working elsewhere.

Yukinoshita would have asked Yuigahama for help first, so I wasn't really confused by Yuigahama's presence. She must have heard from Isshiki that I would come, though; she gave me a little wave and a "Heeey."

As for Yukinoshita, she was not expecting to see me. I heard doubt and confusion in her voice as she murmured, "Hikigaya…"

"Hey. So, like…Isshiki asked me to come. And here I am. To help." Judging from Yukinoshita's reaction, Isshiki hadn't passed along the word. *Heeeey! Irohasuuu! Reports, communication, and discussion are important! Arriving uninvited is painful for all involved, okay…?*

But despite Yukinoshita's confusion, it seemed my presence was not unwanted. In fact, she smiled awkwardly, almost apologetically. "I see. I'm sorry. We're a little shorthanded today, so this is honestly a help. Thank you."

"Oh, I just have the spare time, so I don't mind."

*Well, I'm sure this rushing and heavy work will eat up that time…*, I thought.

Yukinoshita put her hand to her chin with a *hmm*, opening her mouth in a manner that was neither rushed nor heavy. "I assume you'll be having some kind of celebration with your family for Komachi today? I do plan to help us wrap up as quickly as possible, but if there's anything else I need to know about, then I can make adjustments."

My mouth hung open a little. *She's really being calm about this… I thought this place would be a bit more tense…* Confusion made its way into my voice as I replied, "O-okay… Well, my dad gets home late anyway, so you don't need to worry about it too much… Finishing earlier is always better, though."

"Indeed. Well then, let's get started." With a lighthearted smile, Yukinoshita offered me a chair next to Yuigahama. When I took a seat, she slid a stack of papers over to me. "Before you get started, I'll go over the event outline with you." Then she made a fan of the sheets and began reading aloud the details.

I was also hearing a tune in the background. Glancing over, I saw our dear Isshiki humming along as she poured tea, discovered a package of chocolates, and popped one in her mouth.

*…Well, she knows what's going on already, so there's no need for her to listen. And she does get the job done in the end…*

"There's a checklist along with the proposal documents, so if you could take a look at it," Yukinoshita said.

I skimmed briefly over the documents. From what I could see, they seemed to assume the prom format would be somewhat scaled down compared with what we'd seen on that foreign TV show.

They would decorate with flower arrangements and balloon art and stuff, securing the front half of the gym along with the stage to make a dance floor, while in the back they'd set out some tables and chairs where people could eat and chat.

And as for the itinerary: It would kick off with a fancy toast, followed by remarks from the student council president and the captains of all the clubs. Once they'd got everyone worked up, they'd put on some club music, and dance time would begin. A live rock band would burst in at one point, and we'd have a "public confession" event somewhere in there, and then eventually the prom king and prom queen would be chosen, and then time for slow dancing. At the end, everyone would come together for a wild party! There was no set time for chatting with friends, so everyone had to use the chat space at their own discretion…

*I see, I see—yeah, I don't get it. Partly because I don't really know anything about proms. But I also don't do anything with clubs or dancing or that whole culture. This makes no sense. What the heck is a public confession? A new form of execution?*

I'd ask or investigate the stuff I didn't know later; right now, I'd just sweep over the parts I did understand.

"This is gonna cost a lot of money." That was my first thought.

Yukinoshita slid a piece of paper over to me. "I've made a trial balance sheet. The estimates have already been filed, so go look at those, if you're concerned."

"Oh, no, it's fine. You should be the one checking the numbers. Actually, I'm more curious about where you got the funds. Didn't we use up all the budget with that free bulletin before?"

"The actual event is in March, so we've arranged for charges to be made the following month. That way, we can treat it as part of next year's budget. For items that have to be paid in advance, we'll borrow money elsewhere to handle the bill later," Yukinoshita said with a casual shrug.

Me, I was still a little skeptical. The deadline for the student council to close their books was the end of February, so passing the related costs of a March event onto the next semester was understandable. *But more importantly, haven't they already established the budget for next year…?* I was thinking suspiciously when the good old dancing queen Iroha Isshiki-chan started serving tea for some reason. She was still humming. *I see she doesn't have any other work to do…*

"So maaaybe we'll be cheaping out on some stuff next year, but what can you do?" said Isshiki.

"Is that okay…?" Yuigahama asked with a strained smile as she accepted her paper cup of tea.

Isshiki hugged the serving tray to her chest, tilting her head inquisitively. "Yeah, but I figure nobody'll notice, right? I don't think anyone even knows what the student council does."

"T-true… Ahh, yeah, I'd never notice, either. I don't really know, after all…" Yuigahama really did her best to consider the issue, but eventually she set her paper cup back down on the table with a *tup* and weakly hung her head.

*Ahhh, Isshiki argued her down, huh…?*

Isshiki suddenly stepped on the gas, pumping a fist high into the air. "That's why we gotta do it! We're picking the perfect moment to do something high budget! It'll give the impression we're actually doing stuff—we can get away with anything!"

*Nothing she's saying is wrong, and that's what makes it so terrible... Who could present some harsh but honest advice to her at a time like this?* I wondered, looking over at Yukinoshita.

Unfortunately, she was occupied. She had a thick file folder marked *Accounting Documents* in one arm as she flipped through it with a finger, checking it against her computer screen. "At this stage, I've included the full range of expenses in the calculated total, but many elements will be dropped as we go along, so I doubt it will greatly influence next year's budget. In fact, there's been a surplus every year, so I believe that may be enough to absorb it." She closed the file folder with a *tump* and smiled, a hint of pride on her face.

*This isn't good. I do not like where this is going...* I had the feeling this shrewd scumbag / competent airhead partnership would give rise to an indescribable chemistry. Things were going well, but I wasn't so sure of this...

To reduce the anxiety-inducing parts of this proposal, I decided to do a peer review of the trial balance sheet. As I was checking all the billed items, suddenly a question crossed my mind. "You don't need to include an estimate for the costumes? Everyone's dressing up, right?"

"That's right. Attire will be up to the attendees. On our end, we'll just be mediating with a rental company." With a finger, Yukinoshita indicated a catalog of rental costumes—not to me, of course, but to Yuigahama.

*Indeed, she understands very well. I'm not interested in this stuff...*

Meanwhile, Miss Gahama was flipping through the catalog with stars in her eyes.

Girls usually would have some admiration for dresses like this, and I think they'd want to get fancy for the party given the chance. But what about the boys? According to certain Internet discourse, at publisher parties where you find a lot of manga artists, it's mostly the women who dress up, while the men are often in street clothes. They'll even show up in sweats.

"...Will everyone wear stuff like this?" I asked, with the implication *I'd kinda rather not...*

Isshiki caught my drift. "Well, I'm sure some people won't want to dress up. We'll recommend fancy dress, but we won't enforce it as a dress code."

"But everyone will probably do it, in the end. Either the excitement will get them into the idea, or they'll give in to the pressure to conform... There's no need to expressly put it in writing. That will only invite criticism," Yukinoshita added with a lifeless huff. Isshiki grinned.

*Her smile is pretty, physically, and so is she. Why do I feel terror before anything else...?*

Quietly turning away from both their smiles, I dropped my gaze to the trial balance sheet in my hands. Frankly speaking, I couldn't make any judgments about the validity of the figures and sums without more information about where they came from, but everything arranged so far was basically covered. And any additional expenses discovered during the process of planning the event would be secured just in case under the headings *Reserve Funds* and *Miscellaneous Expenses*.

"...Well, I don't see any problems," I said. "If you exclude the fact that you're missing an allocation for personnel costs."

"Yes, thank you for checking. Well then, instead of signing your approval, could you draw a large circle around that item?"

If Isshiki was going to smile at me so brightly and cheerfully, I had no choice but to smile as well.

Yukinoshita was giggling, too, but eventually she settled down and reached out to the balance sheet in my hands and pointed to some of the figures there. "This isn't set in stone. For the catering and related costs, we're switching from the business used for past appreciation parties to a cheaper place, and we're waiting for estimates from various vendors for that. For the decorative flowers, we'll be combining that cost with the bouquets the clubs will be giving to graduates and placing the order in bulk. We're in the process of negotiating a discount."

"O-okay... I see..." *At this rate, the accountant will be on the chopping block, right after the vice president...* I felt like Yukinoshita's business skills had improved, even compared with before—you could even

call her Yukino Yukinoshita RX now. I was really starting to think, *I guess we can just let her handle everything on her own, huh?* Even Isshiki was nodding like, *…Let's leave this to RX.*

*Hmmmm, I think the student council president's job may be in jeopardy, too…*

Anyway, from what I was seeing of the documents they'd put together, it was clear that actually making the prom happen was a more realistic ambition than I'd initially thought. *Apparently, this is actually possible, according to real logic…* What remained was to deal with things reason wouldn't help with. This would probably be the hardest part.

With deadlines, submission dates, schedules, and their ilk, reason will not work. They possess no human hearts. I can see the scene in my mind's eye: *"Wellll, frankly it'd be pretty difficult," "Let's do our best!" "I'm just gonna say it—there's no time," "Let's do our best!" "I'm sorry, there's no way," "Let's do our best!" "…Okay."* It's rare but often happens, and when you hit that point, the only way to deal is to slow down the flow of time by moving at the speed of light. And this is already in sci-fi territory…

*Right, so as far as the schedule goes, the main thing I'm worried about is…* I picked up the next page, the schedule. Yukinoshita had probably made it herself, since it came with a checklist and filled-in cells for completed items.

It provided a clear visualization of progress so far. Everything around the beginning was filled in, but the further you got, the more white space there was. *Seems like we've still got a long way to go…*

But from another angle, this meant they'd finished the planning and drafting of the trial balance sheet and everything in just these past few days, and that alone would be worthy of commendation. It was kinda freaking me out, honestly…

*I mean, it's crazy how much of this sheet is filled. How hard are you working on this?* The completed sections all seemed like pretty difficult issues, too.

For example, one item in the first section: *Proposal/approval of the prom plan by school admin and parents' association.* With this done, you might as well say most of their problems had been dealt with. There was an asterisk with the note *\*Informal consent only, full approval at a later date via mid-project report,* but if they'd already secured it through informal talks, then they basically had it in the bag… *It's in the bag! Ga-ha-ha!*

After that was budget calculation, production of the event schedule, general announcement, song selection, setting up a website, and a meeting of the club captains and everything else, all of it checked off as complete or completion expected. For being at the planning stage, you could call this the best possible start.

What remained was the practical production tasks like making decorations, plus day-of tasks such as setting up the venue—all things that took time and physical labor, and most of which couldn't be started until we were closer to the event.

*Well, with a lot of this stuff, you won't know until you actually do it. If I'm gonna pick out the shakiest elements, this'll be it, I guess…* This was also probably the stuff I'd be sent off to work on.

As I made some general guesses about my own future tasks, I was reading it over again from the top when my eyes caught on a certain heading. "Hmm, 'General Announcement.' You already announced we're doing a prom? I didn't know." The surprise I felt was a fresh and unfamiliar kind, and the remark came out sounding kind of impressed.

A second later, the air in the student council room suddenly froze. Everyone was looking at me like they were eyeing some strange animal from a distance.

The most blatant one was from Isshiki. She was staring at me like I'd just started speaking another language. "Huh? What're you talking about?"

"Huh? You haven't told anyone, right? …Right?" I turned the question to Yuigahama. She would have roughly the same amount of information about the prom as me.

But she twisted around and got fidgety, her lips barely moving as she muttered, "…I know about it."

"Huh? Why? Am I getting bullied?"

"You're not getting bullied! I'm the one wondering why you don't know... Oh, wait." Something seemed to suddenly strike her, and she rummaged around to pull out her phone.

Isshiki soon followed suit and grabbed her own phone with a cry of understanding. "Ahhh!"

""Look!"" they both said, shoving their phones at me simultaneously to show me the same screen. Along with an unfamiliar noise (*liiine!*), on their screens was the messaging app everyone knows: LINE.

"We made an account for the prom committee, and we've been using it to send out information. It's the medium kids our age use the most, so it's our primary vector," Yukinoshita explained, and it finally made sense to me.

High schoolers these days are all connected on LINE, so that would be the fastest way to notify them... *No wonder I didn't know! I have no friends on LINE!* "Huhhh, I see... Wait. You have LINE, too?"

"I just made an account. It's quite convenient, you know? It's an easy way to acquire information and coupons from the shops you like. If you reply, they'll send you photos and things," Yukinoshita explained, extolling the virtues of a messaging app with a warm and fuzzy smile on her face.

With a noncommittal *huhhh*, I shot Yuigahama a sidelong glance. She caught my implicative look and nodded back at me with a helpless smile. *Aha, so it* is *a cat café account!*

*But I suspect we haven't exhausted this topic...*, I was thinking when someone popped up in front of me to do the honors.

"Wait, why don't you have LINE? You can't figure it out? What, are you a boomer? Were you born in the eighties?" Isshiki said, incredibly rudely.

"I'm one hundred percent Gen Z. And that's really rude to old people. You see some of them using LINE with no problem. I just choose not to use it because I don't need it," I said with a shriek. *Yee!*

Yukinoshita put a hand to her cheek and nodded. "Well, that's true enough. I hear these days, even businesses will make good use of it… I'm sure it's not only a tool for young people."

"Yeah. Depends on the person. Old guys will practice or whatever if they *have* to use it, right?" *I'm sure these days, there are plenty of grandparents who message their grandkids on LINE…*

As I was envisioning a mildly heartwarming scene, Yuigahama suddenly seemed dubious and uncomfortable. "But older men on LINE will try really hard to seem young, so it's like…really cringey. They come at you with emoji and stamps and everything… And the casual way they talk is kinda…old…"

"I *sooo* get that. It's like, wow, I didn't know words could have old people smell," Isshiki agreed with a clap of her hands.

…*Why did that just hurt me so much?* "Wait, how do you guys know so much about the ecology of middle-aged men?"

"My daddy's on LINE," said Yuigahama.

"Mine, too," Isshiki piped up.

*Hmm, and what kind of daddies are these…? That does refer to their fathers, right? I'm too scared to know the answer, so I'll ask something else!*

"Are we okay using LINE only for notification? There are people like me who don't have it, aren't there?"

"We've cross-posted on other social media sites, made the announcement on bulletin boards, and set up a website, so I don't believe there will be a problem," Yukinoshita replied smoothly, but then she stopped and giggled. "Besides, anyone who would avoid all those methods of making contact with other people wouldn't have an interest in going to the prom in the first place. As is, in fact, the case with you."

"…That makes a helluva lot of sense." To think my own behavior would be the answer to my own question. I've won yet another argument! I want to know defeat.

As I acknowledged the soundness of this logic, Yukinoshita put on a big sisterly smile. "If you have any other questions, or things you don't understand, please go ahead," she prompted.

I considered for a bit, but I didn't really have any doubts about the materials she'd shown me. So far. But there was something I was curious about. "...I don't have any questions, but there is something I don't understand. Maybe it's a bit late to be saying this, but I don't really get what a prom's supposed to *be*. It hasn't clicked with me. Like, I just can't imagine it. Honestly, that's what bothers me most." I'd thought the same thing back when Isshiki had first come to us about the prom, and then again after looking at the event overview just now.

Yuigahama blinked. "Huh? Isn't a prom, like, the party we saw in that TV show?"

"Yeah, well, yeah, but... I feel like even if we reproduced the prom from that show, it'd wind up totally different." I couldn't quite find the right words for what I wanted to say. I gave a frustrated *mmgh* in thought, while Yuigahama joined me in racking her brain with a *hmm, hmm*.

That was when Isshiki came in with a smug chuckle and a know-it-all expression. "Ohhh, I get it! You want to make the kind of prom we would make, the sort of prom only we could come up with, all for me, right?"

"That's really not it..." *What the heck do you mean, all for you? What does that have to do with anything I said...?*

"Oh really. Am I wrong then. Please explain..." Isshiki shot me a dirty look.

*If I knew that, I wouldn't have spent all this time groaning, okay?* I jerked my face away to escape Isshiki's glare.

And there, my eyes met with Yukinoshita's.

"...Well then, how about we go make the answer to that?" With a rather mysterious turn of phrase, she gave a peaceful smile as she stood from her chair.

× × ×

Leaving the student council room, we headed to the gym.

The indoor sports clubs would normally be practicing there at this time of day, but that moment, we were greeted by an entirely different sight. The front area, including the stage, was a fully laid-out party scene. The flower arrangements and balloon art had been brought in, and a disco ball hung from the ceiling, scattering light over everything.

"Ohhh… This is kinda amazing…" Yuigahama's honest impression slipped out as she took in the tableau.

Personally, I felt like I'd suddenly been flung out into another dimension, and I couldn't even find a simple response. I was just stunned and staring.

"I'll explain in more detail later, but for now, can I ask for you to get changed to prepare? Kawasaki is in the wings setting up the costumes, so please go help her out, Yuigahama," Yukinoshita said casually.

"Okay!" Yuigahama responded energetically and trotted off to the stage wings.

But that wasn't happening with me. *Did she mean Kawa-something? Is she here, too? What's going on?* I was wondering when Yukinoshita gave me a questioning look.

"Isshiki hasn't told you?"

"No…" *Hellooo? Irohasuuu?*

Behind me, I saw Isshiki had a *Whoops!* look on her face. *Well, I can lecture her for real next time—right now, let's try to understand what the heck is going on.* "So what is this? What're we doing?" I asked Yukinoshita.

"We're making a promotional video. We're also making a page for it on the website, so we'll be taking some photos for that, too. And setting everything up to check operations while we're at it." Yukinoshita indicated a few camera tripods that had been set up by the student council.

She seemed to struggle a bit with the rest of the explanation. "And we need some people to star in the video, so I asked Isshiki to handle personnel selection…"

"…Star in the video?" I repeated.

Yukinoshita's and my eyes slid over to Isshiki. With two people's worth of pressure on her, even Isshiki must have felt uncomfortable. She was looking at the floor and dripping cold sweat.

Yukinoshita let out a tired-sounding sigh. "We'll blur faces in the editing, relax. I intend to have you check the footage when we make a rough cut, too... But I imagine it's uncomfortable to have this requested of you when you haven't been filled in." She smiled awkwardly. She was definitely covering for Isshiki with that stuff about editing and rough cuts.

*It's unusual for her to not get mad over something like this... Before, I think she would've said a stern* Isshiki?

Meanwhile, Isshiki took a break from holding her head and groaning to slide forward and bow at me a couple times. "I'm extremely sorry and I really won't do it again but also it's not like that because I was talking about something else and then I got distracted... Also, I got it confused with the stuff I asked Tobe and the guys to help with..."

"Tobe?" I repeated, hearing an unexpected name in the long apology rant.

Isshiki looked up, tucking her hair back behind her ear as she nodded. "Yep. I called over Tobe and some first-years from the soccer club to make things livelier—like, as extras. NPCs."

"And for the girls, I asked some from my class, as well as Isshiki's friends," Yukinoshita added.

"Hmm." If we were making a promotional video, we would need a decent number of people in it to communicate the vibe. There is that saying "dead trees will enliven a mountain," after all.

"So you did get other people, huh?" I said. "...Well, if there's a certain number of people and I'm not noticeable, then fine. I'll do it."

"...Sorry."

"No, I didn't check what this job was." I cracked a crooked grin. There was something kind of funny about Isshiki apologizing with such a meek smile.

Then Yukinoshita smiled for us, too. "Thank you. This honestly helps me a lot. I felt a bit hesitant about giving detailed criticism for the retakes to people I don't really know..."

"Please don't come in assuming there'll be retakes...," I groaned. "Well, anyway, I'll go get changed."

"Oh, the costumes are over here." Isshiki started walking ahead of me. I gave Yukinoshita a *Later* look, and she nodded back *Thank you*.

With Isshiki leading me onward, we headed to the opposite wing of the stage from where Yuigahama had gone. On the way, Isshiki's posture dissolved into a full-on slump. "So...I'm really getting a sense for what you said before."

"A sense for what?" I caught up and came alongside her.

But Isshiki didn't lift her head. "Stuff has been going so well, it's like, I'm letting her handle so much without even meaning to. And now I'm slipping up. I know this can't be the only thing. At this rate, maybe I will wind up entirely relying on Yukino..." Her tone was gloomy, morose, and full of regret. My advice at lunch had come back to haunt her.

Well, if this one mistake was enough to make her conscious of her other failures, I'd call that pretty outstanding. I still can't even acknowledge my own failures, you know...

I couldn't judge her too harshly. "At least you know now, right? If a minor mistake like this makes you more cautious in the future, then that's a small price to pay." But the lighthearted approach had little effect.

"Yeah...I'll be more careful," she answered, pressing her lips in a tight line.

Well, when you get carried away and screw up, it can really bring you down afterward... Like at a job, you know, around the time you're getting used to it and starting to think, *Whoa, I'm totally great at this*, you make an unexpected mistake and the manager kindly helps you out. Then you feel so pathetic and sorry and embarrassed that you wanna die!

Having experienced this firsthand, I wanted to say something to make her feel better. "If something comes up again, then let me know ahead of time... I mean, if you'd told me beforehand, I think I would've complained, but I'd still be here. So, um, well, you don't have to feel—"

"Yeah, of course!" Before I even finished talking, Isshiki's face jerked up, and she beamed at me. I was struck silent. Then she wilted again, shoulders slumping like before. "I'm joking… I'll pull myself together." I could hear a quiet determination in her tone; the joke must've been to encourage herself.

When we eventually arrived at the stage wings, Isshiki opened a door to a side room. Following her in, I saw a disorganized space with lecterns, mic stands, and stuff scattered everywhere. They'd also made sure to leave chairs and full-length mirrors there so it could be used as a green room for events. Costumes had been put together and laid out over the chairs.

"Your costume's here," Isshiki told me. "If it doesn't fit, then… Kawasaki? Was that her name? She can adjust it a bit for you."

"Roger."

I watched Isshiki as she bobbed a bow at me and left, and I went straight to getting changed.

After I took off my uniform, I picked up my outfit. I guess this was a tuxedo? I don't really get what makes it different from a suit, but it brought a wedding to mind… It had a standing collar, with a crisply ironed shirt and a bow tie. I basically knew how all those things were worn. But there was another accessory with it, a pin or a brooch or something, and I had no idea what that was. I'd ask later.

Once I had finished dressing, I checked myself in the long mirror, and I saw a worn-out, dying pianist. *Hmm…is this how it's supposed to look? I've never worn something like this, so I dunno. If you're wearing a tuxedo, don't you have to put on a silk hat and cape and some kind of white mask…?*

Fortunately, the size didn't feel that far off. To complete the outfit, I picked up the bow tie, and after spending a moment doing a Detective Conan impression, I snapped the clasp shut.

Since I didn't have much experience with formal wear, dressing had taken more time than expected. I left the stage wings in a bit of a rush.

I headed back to Yukinoshita first, and there I found an unfamiliar, smartly dressed, and beautiful boy. The hemline of his jacket was long, with a unique shape, so even I knew what kind of suit this was. It's what they call a tailcoat, or tails.

"Good. It fits pretty well," the person said to me, and I finally recognized the bright smile.

"Ohhh… It's you, Yukinoshita… Hey, why the heck are you wearing that?" I asked.

Yukinoshita stretched out her arms, adjusted the collar of her tailcoat, and lifted up the hem a bit uneasily. "Is it funny?"

"No, not at all…"

In fact, it suited her too well. The monochrome palette brought out the beauty of Yukinoshita's fair skin, while the trailing hemline and slacks emphasized her long and shapely legs. She'd tied her hair into a ponytail, and it swayed with every movement, giving her an even more ethereal impression. Together with her delicate build, the phrase *unfortunate pretty boy* crossed my mind. She had such lovely features, it gave her a deviant kind of beauty, an edge.

"You look really cool. Like something out of a movie…" That surreal factor made her difficult to describe.

"Thank you. That's a tasteful compliment, coming from you." Yukinoshita hid a smile behind a white-gloved hand, which further enhanced the illusion.

"Oh, I'm pretty serious. It's like…if you were in a live-action adaptation of the manga, I could say good things about it."

"Your compliments are getting more and more dubious…" The way she sighed and pressed her hand against her temple looked theatrical, too, but her following remark drew me back to reality. "You look like a character from a movie, too. It quite suits you. You're just like the leading…bully who harasses the protagonist, an aristocratic type…'s henchman."

"That's even worse than calling me a pathetic gangster. Don't hurt yourself finding something nice to say."

"I've done no such thing; you're perfect for that role. And besides, you can improve your appearance with a little effort. Lend me your cuff links and handkerchief." Yukinoshita took off her gloves and held out her hand.

Thinking her bare hands had to be much paler, I handed over the handkerchief. I wondered what "cuff links" were, but then I remembered the unidentified accessories. I fished them out of my pocket and dropped them into Yukinoshita's palm. "You mean these?"

She suddenly grabbed my arm. Startled, I tried to pull back, but before I could, she was already rolling up my jacket sleeve and tugging on my shirt cuff. She clicked the cuff links on. Then she quickly folded up the handkerchief and slid it into my breast pocket. "The standard three-peaks fold… This is about right." To finish it off, she gave my breast pocket a pat and smiled with satisfaction.

"O-ohhh… Wait, I've seen one of these before. One of those things you see at weddings."

"I would assume proms were originally an opportunity to learn more formal manners. Although that doesn't have very much to do with us."

"For us, this stuff is basically cosplay."

"I don't like putting it like that, but, well, I suppose it is…," Yukinoshita said with a twist of her lips, then put her gloves on again.

"So why a tailcoat?"

"I wanted to get some shots of the prom king and the prom queen dancing. I couldn't think of anyone with dancing skills, which left me with no choice but to do it myself."

"Huhhh, so you can even dance, too?"

"Just a few steps. The tuxedo isn't especially impressive on me. But the added show of a tailcoat actually might be workable, don't you think?" Yukinoshita said, spinning around in a beautiful pivot. That single turn was such an awe-inspiring sight, it was almost frightening.

*I get it. So the fluttering tail is the added show this coat can get you.*

But her presence was impressive in and of itself. I was sure when it came to dancing, she knew more than just "a few steps," too... "I feel sorry for whoever's dancing with you..."

"It'll be all right. We tried practicing a bit, and Isshiki seems to have a knack for this," Yukinoshita said nonchalantly.

*That's not what I meant, though... This is bigger than dancing technique...*, I thought, but the more startling piece of information was about her partner. "You're dancing with Isshiki?"

"Yes. She's the future prom queen, after all. Perfect, isn't it?"

*There she goes saying stuff like it's nothing again... Normal people can't dance, okay? Is Irohasu gonna be able to handle this...?* Worried, I cast about looking for Isshiki, and Yukinoshita seemed to notice.

"All right, let's step out to meet our princesses," she said and briskly swept toward the stage wings. From behind, she looked just like a prince.

*...The prince has been surprisingly into this.*

× × ×

When we'd first come to the school gym, it had seemed like another dimension. The only feeling it had given me was dissonance, but now that some time had passed and the actors were all there, it really started to get party-like. The windows were all blacked out and the lights turned off, and when the spotlight was switched on, it started reminding me of what we'd seen on that TV show.

All the extras seemed to feel it, too—or maybe that was thanks to Festival Man Tobe, who'd come late and was doing his best to be loud and wild. But they were all enjoying themselves chatting. The boys were mainly in tuxes, and the girls all wore their own dresses. Maybe these costumes were part of it. A lot of the crowd there had to have never met each other, but there was a lot of lively conversation going on. I was getting more of a marriage-matchmaking-party vibe than a prom, but they were both fancy.

And the corner where I stood then was the fanciest. The main reason for this was Yukino Yukinoshita, the cross-dressing beauty, and the bewitching little devil Iroha Isshiki.

Isshiki's dress was mostly orange, and the vivid, cheery color caught your eye. The short skirt wafted outward in a girlish and spritely way, while the decorative lace in suggestive spots like the neckline would go a bit transparent under the light, emphasizing her glamorous charms.

And the little devil now wore a fiendish smile, quite pleased with herself. "Maybe it's an awful thing to say, but wow, this feels like I'm having a beautiful man wait on me hand and foot... I feel great..." Isshiki was so moved by the experience, she was trembling. This visibly disturbed Yukinoshita.

"That really is an awful thing to say... Could you get away from me a little...?"

"This is the duty of a gentleman! You were properly escorting me just now, weren't you?! Oooh, that got my heart pounding a little..." An unpleasant chuckle slipped out of Isshiki at the memory.

I immediately got what she was talking about. When she'd gone to pick up Isshiki, this prince of enthusiasm had been so into it, she'd given Isshiki her arm without any hesitation and escorted her right over to the dance floor.

As a result, the dance floor was now humming with chatter, stroking Isshiki's ego in the process. And now here we were.

"...I'm reconsidering that choice now." The way Yukinoshita said it, it seemed less like she was reconsidering and more like she just regretted it. Her overenthusiasm had settled down; she even seemed a little worn out. We hadn't even started, and I could tell she was tired.

She was aware of that herself, and she sighed before motivating herself again with an *All right*. "Let's get this filming started. We'll be having an initial meeting first, so, Hikigaya, you go and get Yuigahama. She should be about done getting changed."

"Roger," I replied, heading for the wings. I was told Yuigahama had been with Kawasaki, helping the girls get dressed, and now that she was done, she was finally ready to get started on herself.

I knocked on the door of the front room just offstage a few times. I was immediately met with a slightly irritated-sounding "Come iiiin."

*This fear… It's definitely Kawasaki…*, I thought as I slowly opened the door.

Through the door, I saw Yuigahama, just finishing changing into her dress and doing her final check.

The dress was pale pink, almost white, but the translucent-seeming fabric gave the color a far more mature feel to it. Or maybe it was just her silhouette. Her neckline was wide open, the dress coming together around her waist, emphasizing her curves to draw an arc. Though the skirt went well past her knees, the longish slit kept it light—there was even an airiness in the way it fluttered every time she stirred. Her hair, which was usually tied in a bun, was now braided like a flower crown, and the form of address a certain prince had used popped up in my mind.

But that impression only lasted until I saw her giggling in front of the mirror.

Yuigahama stood before a full-length mirror, worrying over the hemline and chest area, prodding at the dress all over. "Wow…this dress is kinda…amazing… Or like, intense."

"Don't move." Behind her, Kawasaki was rustling around adjusting the dress length or something. The chill in her voice made Yuigahama straighten up again.

But then she put a hand to her waist area. "O-okay… Uh, um…I want to tighten the stomach a bit…," she said timidly.

"Huh? …You're gonna be dancing and stuff later. Won't it be too tight?" Kawasaki replied with some irritation in her voice.

But if you listened closely, you could tell she was trying to show consideration. Maybe that was why Yuigahama didn't really shrink away—in fact, she made a noise kind of like a spoiled child throwing a tantrum. "Ah, w-wahhh… I-I'll suck it up!"

"Agh... I'll adjust it a bit." Sighing all the while, Kawasaki briskly met Yuigahama's demand, then gave her a little shove in the back. "All right, you're good. Do your makeup yourself."

"Ah, okay! Thanks, Saki! And sorry to make you wait, Hikki! I'll be ready in a jiffy!" Yuigahama said, then pattered off to the dresser. She slid a scarf around her neck, maybe to keep from getting makeup on her dress, then quickly began laying out makeup tools.

"You can take your time. They're still having their meeting," I called out to her.

Yuigahama only gave me an "Mm" in reply. Probably she was busy putting something on.

Passing behind her, Kawasaki strode up to the exit, where I stood. I could see the fatigue. "I'm heading home, so you guys manage the rest on your own."

"Hey, thanks," I said. "Sorry, it sounds like you got asked to help kinda out of the blue."

"I did." Kawasaki glared at me.

*Wahhhh, I'm sorryyyy,* I thought, cringing away and looking at the ground, and then I heard a short *feh* that could have been a sigh or a chuckle.

"Her skirt is long, and the heels are high, so be careful until she's used to it," Kawasaki said—very brusquely, but also very kindly, as she slipped languidly past me.

My only response to her was a "Y-yeah." *Very cute, Kawa-something.* With that thought, I watched Kawasaki go.

That left just Yuigahama and me in the room. With nothing better to do, my gaze naturally drifted over there. In front of the dresser, Yuigahama was brushing her cheeks like she knew what she was doing.

But then her hand suddenly stopped flat. And then when our eyes met in the mirror, she said hesitantly, "U-um...it's hard to do this if you're staring at me..." The cheek she'd just been brushing was pink tinged, and that made me suddenly feel awkward, too. I looked away.

"Ahhh, sorry. Don't worry about me. Keep going... Wait, aren't you mostly done? Isn't that enough?"

"Huhhh?! ...Not yet." She hesitated a moment and eyed herself in the mirror, and then her hands started moving again.

"O-oh..." *I really think it's enough, though. Well, um, like, I think you're already pretty the way you are*—but I swallowed those words and said nothing more.

Yuigahama swapped her brush for a pen and set it on the edge of her lips. "I mean, we're making a video, right? I don't want it to look bad."

"She said they'll be editing it so you can't see individual faces."

"That's just for the one they're showing everyone, right? We'll still have the original data. That's not gonna get erased. I wouldn't erase it. So...I want to make sure it looks nice," she finished quietly, then drew a faint line of pink. She lifted her jaw, moving her chin to change the angle of her face, slowly, slowly moving the pen to make the line straight. With her lips pink and glossy, the Yuigahama in the mirror looked like a completely different person. None of her usual innocence could be seen in her expression as she gazed into the mirror. She seemed unbearably far away.

Without even thinking, my mouth popped open to say, "Is that how it is...?"

"That's how it is! Okay, done!" Then she spun away from the mirror, back to me, and smiled brightly. That was enough to draw a breath of near relief from me, which was when I realized I'd been holding my breath at all. I'd been mostly unconsciously scratching my head in an attempt to hide it.

"Aren't you gonna fix your hair, too, Hikki?"

"No..."

"Huhhh? But it's a mess. And this is a promotional video, so you can't be a mess. That's really too..." Yuigahama's eyes were locked on the top of my head. And I was already seeing the pity rising inside her.

*I-is it that bad...? I guess so. It is that bad.*

Besides, she was also right to point out that a promotional video was supposed to give a positive impression, so it'd be bad to have me all scruffy in it. "Well, then I'll fix it a bit... I'll grab some wax while I'm here. Gel works, too."

When I went up to the dresser, Yuigahama stepped aside to let me take the seat. With the benefit of Komachi's instruction, even I could manage my hair, at least. I was in a tuxedo, so even a simple sort of slicked-back look should be good enough, right? The problem is that it would only contribute to the crappy gangster image...

I was reaching for the wax that lay among the array of makeup tools, when instantly, it was snatched away from behind me. When I turned back, Yuigahama said nonchalantly, "I'll do it for you, Hikki. It'll look weird if you do it yourself."

"Whoa... You have no faith in my taste... Not that you should... But hey, I can manage this much—"

"C'mon, just leave it to me! I'm good at this, honest!" Before Yuigahama had even finished saying the words, she'd grabbed my head and yanked it around to face the mirror.

*Ow, ow, ow! That's super-embarrassing, and the sweat glands on my scalp are wide-open and leaking!*

But this damn girl was humming and gleeful. "Are there any itchy spots, sir?"

"Uh, you really don't have to do the stylist thing—just get it done..." I was so mortified and bothered by my scalp sweat, I froze, and then Yuigahama's hands stopped moving. *Huh? Does my hair feel gross? Sorry,* I was thinking, when I looked at her through the mirror to see she wore a deeply serious frown.

"Hikki, your scalp is so tough! ...You'll go bald."

"Hey! That's a really low blow... This means war..."

"Kidding, kidding! It's soft, it's soft! Coochie-coochie coo!"

"Thatticklesthatticklesstopstop...cut it out...stoppleasestop..." My hands jerked up to hide my face with a *wahhh*. I didn't need a mirror to know how pathetic I looked, and I didn't want her to see, either. As I was cringing in on myself, her slim fingers twirled through my hair, slowly making separated tufts. Her humming turned into a melody, a soft song.

Between my hair being combed, my head stroked, and an occasional sensation like play bites with fingertips, the tension in my body was gradually unwinding. I was practically helpless as a fish on a chopping block at this point, eyes closed and still.

"…Okay, done."

When I opened my eyes, Yuigahama tilted her head at me in the mirror, asking with her eyes how she'd done. I answered with a couple bobs of my head to say, *Great job*. Really, her skill was wasted on me.

It seemed my satisfaction came out on my face, as Yuigahama smiled and laid her hands on my shoulders. "You make sure to look cool in this, too, Hikki."

"Leave it to me. Lately, digital editing has really made leaps and bounds. Science can do anything."

"Ah-ha! What's that supposed to mean?" She smacked my shoulder with a laugh, and with that, we were both done getting ready. I got up from my seat and took a step toward the dance floor.

Then I heard footsteps clicking across the floor. It wasn't her usual loud pitter-patter, but a slow and graceful sound. That reminded me. "Kawasaki said to watch out for your skirt and heels."

"Ah, oh yeah. It's true—this is pretty tricky. Might be tough to get used to…"

"Yeah… Also, it's dark here," I said, raising up my left elbow a bit. I straightened my back, pushed out my chest, and drew back my chin. Keep your cool, was it? I got the feeling I'd been taught something about that.

Yuigahama gave me a curious look, but eventually, she gave an *ah* of understanding and cracked a smile. Then without saying a word, she laid her hand on my left elbow. Just like that other time.

After these many excuses, we walked a terribly short distance with matched strides.

× × ×

The actual filming went very smoothly. The biggest factor for that had been the faultless conclusion of the dance scene with the king and queen, which had been the greatest concern. Yukinoshita and Isshiki put on a wonderful show for the crowd.

Despite having modestly said she just knew "a few steps," once Yukinoshita got started, her execution was stunning. With sonorous taps of her leather shoes, her clean turns made her tailcoat flutter while her pure-white gloves gently held her partner's hands. Every move she made got the girls all excited.

As for her partner—perhaps Isshiki's comparative lack of experience hamstrung her after all. The whole time, it looked like Yukinoshita was just swinging her around. Isshiki's dancing was somewhat lacking—sometimes she'd mess up and step on Yukinoshita's feet. But she had a cheeky way of wilting and hanging her head every time she made some kind of mistake, and then when Yukinoshita smiled at her to cover those mistakes, Isshiki would beam back at her with perfect charm. As a boy watching, I found that there was something about the way she embodied cute girlishness that made my heart go pitter-patter.

Everyone watching offered applause and ovations, and we all got quite into it.

But as Isshiki was checking over the video while on break, she tilted her head questioningly. "We look great, and everyone around is cheering, too, but it feels almost…hard-core… It's like a legit competitive dance…"

"Yes, I think it was different from what we envisioned, if I do say so myself…" Peeking out from behind Isshiki to look at the screen, Yukinoshita put a hand to her temple and sighed.

Listening from the side, I reflected on the scene from earlier. *Yeah, maybe she's right… It felt less like a fun party with the gang and more like watching a show…*, I thought.

It seemed Isshiki had reached the same conclusion. She nodded and turned back to Yukinoshita. "Well, this'll be fine for what it is, to show off the slow dance portion. But I also want some footage with a more *Whoo, let's go* vibe."

"Something that feels casual, with lots of energy, hmm…? How about we take a video of everyone dancing? Could we try doing it mostly following you and Tobe as the main focus?"

"I guess that's how it's gonna be, huh…? Agh…"

*Isshiki really seems like she doesn't wanna do it, huh…? Well, Yukinoshita can't really do the party vibe, so we don't have much choice…,* I thought, smiling. Not my problem.

But then for some reason, Yukinoshita's gaze slid over to me. "…And one more scene, just for extra footage. Yuigahama, can I ask you to join in? And Hikigaya as well."

"Huh?" Yuigahama's face went blank.

My jaw dropped. *What is she talking about…?* "Um, I've never danced before…," I said, raising my hand slightly, and Yuigahama agreed with big nods. *Listen, this isn't a ballroom, okay?* I was thinking when Isshiki strolled over.

"Whatever is fine for this video. Just imagine, like, what they do at a club, you know," Isshiki said, putting a hand on her waist and sticking up a finger to wave it around.

*She's acting like she's explaining something, but that's not an explanation at all…*

As the weariness settled in, Yukinoshita came over to cover for Isshiki. "You can just copy what you see everyone else do," she said with a sympathetic smile. "This is ultimately just to have the footage, since it's always best to have excess material for the editing process. If you like, you can focus on making Isshiki and Tobe look good."

"O-okay…that's something I'm supergood at…" I have a lot of experience foiling other people's fun, after all.

Besides, what Yukinoshita was saying made sense. You could never have too much footage, and we probably wouldn't get another opportunity to do a large-scale filming like this. It would cause problems if we realized too late that we didn't have enough of one thing or had to throw out another thing. It wasn't a bad idea to film as much as we could now.

Despite the logic of it, though, something felt wrong, or really out of whack. Like the pieces required to make this logic work were missing.

"Um…and you think we're the ones to do it?" Yuigahama asked tentatively, and that was when I felt like the pieces clicked together.

But that feeling was immediately drowned out when Yukinoshita replied instantly. "I think so. The role will draw more attention to you, so I feel a bit hesitant about asking others to do it. That being the case, it would help a lot if you could. If it's too much, though, I'll look into some other way…" She said it so smoothly, without even a thought.

"Oh, no." Yuigahama gave a troubled smile, giving a little wave in front of her chest to accept the job. "I don't mean that… If you're okay with it, I'm good."

Well, if she was going to ask like that, then we couldn't refuse. The people there had mostly come out of good intentions and kindness, so it was hard to ask too much.

"Then first, let's just try filming a shot!" Isshiki clapped her hands. Yuigahama and I joined all the others shuffling out. When we went to our designated positions, Yuigahama was there at the front.

"…Can you dance?" I asked quietly.

Yuigahama made some mumbling, uncomfortable movements with her mouth. "I dunno… But if it's a, like, *whoo!* kinda feeling, then, like, I can get into the moment!"

"A *whoo* kinda feeling, huh…?"

"Yeah, yeah! Whoooo!" Yuigahama forced some excitement into her voice, adding in some idol-esque moves. I didn't really get it.

As I was sighing, the tuxedoed Tobe next to us was drawn to all the whooing and slung an arm over my shoulder. "C'mon, Hikitani! Dude, ya gotta have fun with it! It's like—whoo, whoo! C'mon, whoooo!"

I had no idea what he meant—however, this was the one time when his vapid energy was a lifeline.

"O-okay… Guess you're used to all this…," I said, half feeling like I was talking to myself.

Tobe gave a toothy and smug grin. "Right? Hey, dude, you don't gotta worry—it's all good. It's like, dude. You gotta groove on the off-beat. It's like…like taking a shower in the sound? Once the music's on, you dance! You with me?"

"Tobe, please be quiet," Isshiki snapped.

"Dude…," said Tobe before dejectedly going into standby.

His advice had not been useful at all, but his stance was what we needed right now. There was nothing to do but vaguely imitate Tobe's vibe. It's like if you go to a concert, even if you've never heard the song before, you can still chant along when they call "One, two!"

Once I was done getting myself mentally prepared, I quietly waited for the music to start. Then the lights went out.

What eventually started playing was a standard number at dance parties. The spotlight swung around, and the disco ball rained down its glow.

At first, everyone was awkward, just swaying shoulders along with the rhythm. But when Tobe and a few others started the fist pumping, some more followed. They clapped loud enough to echo off the gym walls, gradually bringing everyone closer together. Taking a step in to do a twist, another step in and high five, doing a joking robot dance. Some people were even brave enough to entwine their arms.

As the crowd slowly succumbed to the intoxicating music and atmosphere, it led into the next song. Though I wouldn't call it a ballad, it was a mellower song than the last one.

So far, I'd just been, like, glancing around at everyone else as I swayed my shoulders and snapped my fingers, but I just couldn't quite manage to join in any more than that. My feet and the shaking of my head marked the rhythm like a metronome. And then there was a tug on my free hand.

Looking over, I saw Yuigahama smiling shyly. My heart rate was up from the exercise, but that didn't explain the *badum* when it skipped a beat, and I instinctively glanced out of the corner of my eyes at everyone else.

Everyone was either jokingly dancing random waltzes or stubbornly staring at each other and dancing at a metaphorical arm's length apart.

Which meant nobody was paying any attention to us. And all I was looking at was Yuigahama. I gently laid my now-free hands on her shoulders. I didn't know any steps or anything. I just swayed my body with her; if she stepped forward, I went back, and if she moved to the side, I followed. The places where she touched were hot, and I was so worried about my hands being sweaty, and I didn't even want to breathe with her face so close.

*This is more brutal than I imagined, mainly mentally...* Instead of an excuse, my mouth decided to say, "Sorry, I'm sweating a lot."

"Ah, yeah. It's a lot of exercise, huh?"

"No, um, like, I—I mean, it's gross, right? I mean, like, I should die, right?"

"Huh?! Why so dramatic?! And so down on yourself!" Yuigahama laughed, and the song changed again. I'd heard this one before. It was the song that had played at the end of that TV show. Yuigahama's gaze slid to the side.

I followed her and saw Isshiki and Tobe dancing wildly. Their rhythm and moves were all over the place, but they seemed to be having fun anyway. When Tobe tried to put his hands around Isshiki's waist, she smacked them away and then spun as if she were going to give him a roundhouse kick... The dancing queen indeed.

When the song was over, applause and a cheer went up. And then everyone went off to enjoy their own chats or eagerly started taking pictures of themselves, their friends, and their dance partners.

*So now the dance scene we were so worried about has basically been filmed. Okay*, I thought, and the exhaustion hit me all at once. I wobbled away from the circle of people and toward the tables where the catering had been set up.

With a sip of my drink, I surveyed the dance floor and the decorations on the stage.

*I see—so this is a prom... Well, I kinda get the vibe now. Really not my thing.*

# 6  Yui Yuigahama's thoughts happen to turn to the future.

The day after the filming, Yuigahama and I were once again summoned to the student council room.

Isshiki, sitting opposite us, tap-tapped a stack of papers to arrange them and gracefully held them out to Yuigahama. "I've made a list of the photos to be used on the website, so if any are no good, then please cross them off. If you could handle the check for me."

"Roger. Um…wanna look together, Hikki?" Yuigahama asked as she accepted the pages and fanned them out.

I shook my head. "Nah, I'm good. Worst case, I'll want to label them all as rejects… I'll leave it to you."

"I see… Sure thing, I'll take a look." Convinced, Yuigahama gave me a wry smile, then pulled out a pen and started going over each picture. I could hear her squealing and aahing over every single one. Girls really do worry about how they look in photos, huh…?

But this left me a little at loose ends. I was leaning my face on one hand, gazing out of the corner of my eye at the catalog of photos in Yuigahama's hands, when Yukinoshita's voice reached from the other side of the computer.

"So? Has that resolved your concerns?"

"Oh. Well, a little, once we actually tried doing it. We really did just make the answer." Thinking back on the mysterious turn of phrase

Yukinoshita had used then, I went on. "Before, we only had that foreign TV show for comparison, so I couldn't really imagine it. Yesterday helped me build a clearer image. It sounds bad to put it like this, but it's lowered the bar for the prom. I think the people who've seen this video will feel the same way."

"I see. So then making that video has been a meaningful endeavor. If it were purely for promotional purposes, we could have found an existing video online, but I wanted it to feel familiar to the audience. Otherwise, they wouldn't be able to imagine it," she said, preening a little. There was something funny about her pride, and I chuckled.

I had to admit, it was decently effective. And if it worked for a naysayer like me, that would go double for people who actually wanted to go.

Yukinoshita had probably wanted to make this video as a sort of localization. Most of the information, images, and video we had about proms were from a foreign country, and those cultural and racial differences create a wall you have to overcome to picture it. If we just put ourselves in the image, it would only express more vividly the differences in body type, extravagance, and scale. And then when we made our own version, people would think, *This is different from what we imagined* or *This is kinda pitiful*, stuff like that. So you had to give them the image by presenting a Japan-style—or rather, a Soubu High School-type—prom as a model case.

"You're not the only one—everyone who came to the shoot apparently had a pretty good impression of it, too. It was all over my timeline. Look." Isshiki showed me her phone screen, with photos from the filming the day before. The participants had uploaded them to social media, with comments like *It was sooo fun!* added to photos of girls in updos and dresses.

But they're still kinda hiding behind all the cat ears and fake mustache filters… And they've made their eyes really big with ultra-black irises. And their skin is so washed out, you have no idea what they looked like to begin with.

"Ahhh, I saw that, too. Some people were really into it, huh?" Yuigahama said, raising her face from her stack of paper.

Isshiki replied with a "Yep, yep," swiping her phone again to show me more pictures uploaded on various accounts. Most had been edited and tweaked on apps like SNOW or BeautyPlus, so I had absolutely no idea who was who, but they all seemed to be having a glamorously good time.

However, there were also some slightly bolder photos of boys and girls together, leaning on each other's shoulders or with their faces close. Some people might not be happy to see those, especially when some of the girls were wearing more revealing dresses with low necklines. People like me. I wanted to be like, *Huh? Why the hell're you flirting during filming?* but I couldn't even talk! *Gaaah! Just remembering is making me embarrassed! I wanna die!! And so let us leave those matters unquestioned...*

But anyway, the posts had mostly positive remarks, and the responses on the timeline were all along the lines of *I like it!* and *I wanna do it, too!* Of course, there were some negative comments, but they were the vast minority, so few you could just ignore them.

"If it's led to some secondary promotion, then the budget investment was worthwhile." Yukinoshita closed her eyes and nodded, then once again returned to her clicking and clacking on her computer.

Meanwhile, Yuigahama had finished selecting photos; she swiped her pen along the sheet at the end, then held the stack of papers out back to Isshiki. "Hmm, if this is good?"

"Thank you very much. Well then, I'll get straight to making that page on the website." *Hmm*ing to herself, Isshiki checked over the stack of papers and drew the laptop toward her, then started to spin the trackball.

"Thank you. I'm sorry for having you come all the way here. We'll be all right now." Yukinoshita's hands paused for a moment, and she gave a light bow of her head.

I blinked, and it took me a few moments to understand what those words meant. "...Huh? We're done?" I asked.

Her face went blank for an instant, and then she put a hand to her chin thoughtfully. "Yes. That was my intention… The student council is handling production of decorations, so for now, there will be no other work that requires your help. Isn't that right?" Yukinoshita turned to Isshiki.

"Huh? …Uhhh, uh-huh. W-well, if you say so, Yukino. Yeah, of course." Isshiki must have been working on figuring out the process in her head, as she stared off in another direction and gave an inarticulate answer.

Regardless, the calculation of tasks had been worked out in Yukinoshita's mind, and she nodded. "If it turns out we absolutely need more people, we may ask for your help again, but I'll let you know if that happens."

If she was gonna smile that brightly at me, then I had no choice but to agree. You'd think I'd welcome not having work and getting to go home early, but being released so easily kinda didn't sit well with me.

When I was trying to work through whatever that meant, Yuigahama, sitting beside me, rose to her feet. "Yeah, okay. See you! And good luck! If there's anything I can help with, let me know again." She quickly got her things together, then poked my shoulder with an elbow. "Come on, let's go, Hikki," she prompted.

"O-okay." I finally got up, too. "Then see you."

When we called to them, Yukinoshita and Isshiki leaned out from behind their computers.

"Yes. Thank you for today," said Yukinoshita.

"Thank youuuu!" Isshiki echoed, and then they quickly got back to work. We didn't want to get in the way, so Yuigahama and I briskly left the student council room.

We trudged along the hallway, heading for the front entrance. The light pouring in through the windows was brighter than it usually was after school, letting us know the sun was still high in the sky.

"Nothing to do now, huh?" Yuigahama murmured, walking beside me.

"...Well, I always have nothing to do. You're not gonna hang out with Miura or whatever?"

"I told them I was helping today. Besides, they had plans, too," Yuigahama said. She smiled like she didn't know what to do.

"Huhhh...," I replied listlessly.

After that, the conversation petered out, and the only sound was our footsteps ringing through the hall. I remembered experiencing a weird silence like this before. Had that been the day we'd stopped going to the club?

Thinking back, I glanced at Yuigahama beside me, which happened to be right as she was glancing at me. I kinda felt like I couldn't just look away again, so instead, I decided to say something. "...Wanna go stop by someplace?"

"Huh?" She wasn't surprised, exactly—more like utterly baffled. This wasn't so much unexpected as incomprehensible to her.

*Duuude. I've really blown it now, huh?* Feeling my face overheating, I tugged up my scarf to hide it. "Uh, um... I was thinking about getting Komachi something, like to congratulate her or for her birthday...or something," I mumbled through my scarf. I needed to use all my brainpower to find a plausible-sounding reason.

That seemed to be enough for Yuigahama, as she clapped her hands, then went straight to enthusiastically smacking my shoulder. "I like that idea! Let's go, let's go! I'll buy something, too! Hey, where are we going? Where d'you wanna go?"

*I'm thankful you're excited about the idea, but please give me a little time to think...*

"Huh? Uh, I dunno... Oh! I remembered I wanted to go to LaLaport." My hand curled into a fist as I was struck by a divine revelation. *Yeah, yeah, that's actually a place I wanna go.*

As I was mentally celebrating, Yuigahama tilted her head curiously. "LaLaport? Sure, but why?"

"I heard there's a vending machine that only sells Max cans, so I wanted to buy one there." As soon as the words were out of my mouth,

I remembered how Komachi had lambasted me before. *I've done it agaaain...*

Or so I thought, but Yuigahama immediately accepted it. "Sure. So then let's go to LaLaport... Geez, how much do you love Max cans?" she added with a snicker. Probably a little weirded out.

But I was surprised that she'd agreed so readily. "Huh? That's okay?"

"Huh? Is it not?" She gave me a questioning look in return. Her eyes were loudly saying, *What're you even talking about? You suggested it...*

I took a breath to calm myself. "No, it's okay... LaLaport, then. Guess we go to the station first."

"Yeah! Then let's go," she replied with a big grin and a bubbly tone. The trademark patter of her footsteps bounded down the hallway a few steps ahead of me. Following her, I picked up the pace, too.

× × ×

The Tokyo Bay LaLaport is not that far from our school, just four stops from the closest station. It takes just over ten minutes in a car. Even if you include all the waiting time and walking, it's under thirty minutes by train.

That meant that on our way there, there was never a real silence. Occasionally, the conversation would run dry, but the riders getting on and off or changes in scenery immediately gave us fodder for trivial conversation, like "It's pretty empty, huh?" or "They had an event over there a while ago" or whatever. Technically, Yuigahama was the one talking to me about lots of stuff.

And even after arriving at LaLaport, our meandering conversation continued in dribs and drabs.

"Oh, yeah, so what're you planning to get, Hikki?"

"What do you think I should get?"

"You're not even gonna try thinking yourself?!"

"Uh, I mean I don't know the stores around here or anything…"

Yuigahama jerked away in shock and turned back down the street we'd come. This area was lined with clothing stores, but being ignorant in these matters, all I'd managed to do was zone out staring at the window displays.

What's more, the first store you see when you walk into LaLaport is Peach John lingerie, and that really kicked my embarrassment and shyness up a notch. Before long, my spirit was broken. Now I was just following after Yuigahama, kind of in stalker mode.

If I'd been shopping for myself, I'd have briskly made my purchases without really worrying about it, but we were here now to buy a present for Komachi. She may be my sister, but she's still a girl. With my sense of taste, that's enough to make me throw in the towel.

Yuigahama must have understood that. Strolling ahead of me, she tilted her head with a *hmm*. "Ummm…I dunno, this is Komachi-chan, so a hairpin or something?"

"Ahhh, hmm. She has a pretty clear sense of her own taste, so I don't think she'd be glad to get something she doesn't like."

"Oh, huh…" Yuigahama seemed like she wanted to say, *I think she would, though*, so I kept going.

"Yeah, she'd probably be like, *Ohhh, thanks, Big Bro! Komachi's so happy! Blush, blush*, but then she'd never use it."

"What's with the weird impression of her…? Well, maybe you're right. If I got a weird present from my dad, I don't think I'd use it. I'd be happier to get cash."

"Your poor dad…"

As we talked, I tried peeking into a bunch of different storefronts, but nothing screamed *Komachi* at me.

Around the time we'd done a round of the floors close to the station, my legs started getting tired. When I came to a stop, I saw a corner I recognized from a photo online. "Oh, that Max can vending machine is supposed to be around here, so I'm gonna go buy one."

"Oh, is it here?"

"Yeah, this is definitely the place. I made sure to look it up beforehand."

"You researched that part?! What about the present?!"

While her very reasonable suggestion was sliding in one ear and out the other, I slipped through the waves of people to the vending machine. At one of the entrances facing the road, among its more conventional brethren, was that yellow machine.

"O-oh…so this is the Max can vending machine. I heard it was only out for a limited time, so I thought maybe it'd be gone, but…" I was brimming with emotion, but that didn't stop me from snapping photos. *Hmm, I like how yellow it is!*

"Huh, wow. It really is shaped just like a Max can," Yuigahama said with utter disinterest as she came up after me. She didn't take any pics, nor did she upload anything to Instagram for likes, either.

*…I'm left with no choice. Allow me to explain.*

"It's not *just* in the shape of a Max can. You can tell if you circle around, but on the back, it actually has the nutritional information written on it. Isn't it detailed? You can feel the love."

"Huhhh."

*…She doesn't care at all!*

*Well, of course. Most people wouldn't get the point of a vending machine specifically made for Max cans. Makes me happy, though.*

Once I'd taken a bunch of pics, I took a selfie with the vending machine in the background, going *Yaaay* ♪ with a sideways ☆ peace sign.

Yuigahama suddenly giggled. "…Okay, so maybe the design is kinda cute."

"Right?! The design's been changed a bunch of times, but the current one has got way more pop appeal! It's ridiculously cute!" I gushed before I could stop myself.

"Why's this the most excited you've been today?! And, like, I don't know what it used to look like…" Yuigahama sighed in exasperation. "Well, whatever. I'll take one, too," she said, pulling out her phone to hop a step closer and stand at my side. Coming up beside me where I'd just been taking selfies, with no warning at all, she took a photo with a *snap*. She was so smooth about it, I didn't even have the time to protest. I probably had a really dumb look on my face. Although if she'd asked me first, the blushing and refusal to look at the camera wouldn't have made for a good picture, either.

So, well, this photo would be a little better.

"...Send me that one," I said.

"Yeah," Yuigahama replied, as if this was perfectly normal. Her eyes were still on her own phone. Only a moment after some swiping and tapping, my phone vibrated. When I looked, there was a message from her.

In the attached photo, we were totally bleached white with sparkly stars flying around, and also both of us had dog ears, dog noses, and dog whiskers... *Well, with this much editing, I can't complain of illegal use of my image.* Smiling wryly, I put password protection on the file.

"Okay," I said. "I got what I came for, so time to go home."

"We haven't done it, and I'm not going home..." As I was about to cheerily withdraw, Yuigahama grabbed my sleeve with a sigh and stopped me. "Oh, then wanna go try that IKEA? They have lots of random household stuff."

She was pointing ahead to another building. IKEA is a furniture and interior decoration warehouse store from Sweden that has outlets all over the world. The first outlet in Japan is in Funabashi in Chiba. Fantastic as always, Chiba, number one in Japan.

Well, wandering around a big place like LaLaport with nothing in mind wasn't the most efficient use of our time. Maybe it'd be a good idea to change tacks. I agreed with Yuigahama's suggestion, and we immediately set off for the IKEA.

Since this commercial area was near the ocean, the sea breeze was still chilly around this time of year, and you could really feel it coming out of the warm shopping mall. As I was quietly chanting "Cold, cold, cold," Yuigahama and I crossed the pedestrian bridge at a trot.

Before long, we were inside the IKEA, and we both sighed at practically the same time. Of course the warmth was part of it, but also because the sofas and rugs and stuff at the entrance looked so cozy.

"How about we just look around?" Yuigahama suggested.

She took the elevator up with the confidence of a pro. I followed, and we came to the open area of the showroom space. There was furniture, interior decoration, and miscellaneous items arranged so that you could pick them up and check them out. There were also themed booths with selections of furniture, like "A family of three in a Kachidoki apartment" or "An LDK that makes you smarter," so it had a bit of a theme park feeling.

*Huh, this is the first time I've ever come to a furniture store, but it's pretty interesting. You could practically live here if you ever got tired of home. Living space runaway Ikeon…*

I browsed around the store. *Yep, guess this is what an IKEA is like.*

Right as I was passing by a booth labeled LAID-BACK SINGLE LIVING IN URAYASU, Yuigahama popped in to take a peek.

*What is it? Is there some wonderful curio she wants to investigate? Like an armchair that won't break, even if you sit on it six million three hundred thousand times…?* I followed her into the booth.

The interior decoration was white in theme, with a tidy wardrobe and storage shelves, and the space felt big for the square footage. It made good use of the vertical space on the walls and shelves, and the small articles placed about came together neatly, too. In the back of the booth was a kitchen—though a small one—and a spot for a washing machine.

*You really could enjoy some laid-back living in a place like this, even on your own. Hachiman, you should live in an apartment like this!* whispered the mom in my head, but I shooed her away.

Meanwhile, Yuigahama was strolling around the booth, making noises of appreciation. After a little while, she plunked down on the bed by the wall with a tired-sounding *phew*. Then she twisted back to face me and opened her mouth nonchalantly. "Hikki, are you gonna live on your own, once you're in university?"

"Depends on the school and the faculty. If it's in Tama or Tokorozawa, I really wouldn't want to commute from my house. The places I want to get into right now are basically all within commuting distance, though," I said, picking up the fancy-schmancy empty bottle placed on top of the desk and examining it.

Yuigahama seemed both impressed and surprised. "You've already decided you'll pass…"

"With my grades, there aren't many options at just the right level for private humanities. I'll just take a few exams for faculties in fields that seem like they could be interesting. So it's not like I decided it. More like a process of elimination." I put the bottle back where it had come from, and though there was nothing inside, it made a heavy-sounding *clunk*. To cover for it, I added, "It's not like there's anything I really want to do."

I wasn't able to say the last part: *That's why I'm going to university. To find it.*

I'd kind of realized it myself. Even at university, I probably wasn't going to meet destiny or find a dream that would decide the course of my life.

I've never really devoted myself to anything in life before, so I don't think I'm cut out for the pursuit of dreams. Even if I did find something I could have an interest in, I'd screw up somewhere along the line, or give up, or bark about how I didn't like it that much in the first place anyway. I could basically see how it would end.

But I think most people are like that. It's not really something to be pessimistic about.

Haruno Yukinoshita had said that you become an adult through giving up on many things.

But some people don't even reach that stage, since they don't even try in the first place. Like me, for example. So what happens to the people who couldn't even give up?

I realized with a start that all this pointless navel-gazing had made the conversation grind to a halt.

When I looked over at Yuigahama, her gaze was focused on the empty bottle near my hand. "Yukinon's decided on her future, huh? She's fast...," she muttered in way that could be taken as deploring or sorrowful. I didn't know what to say in reply.

But then, as if to reassure me that I didn't have to say anything, Yuigahama let out a little breath and grinned. When our eyes met, she seemed to notice I'd been on my feet this whole time. She shifted over with a *hup* to open up space for me to sit.

The creak of the springs was weirdly vivid, and it startled me. But it'd be awkward to say no when she'd made room for me. *Besides, like, acting hyperaware of it would be creepy! And I am hyperaware of it and creepy!* Wearily, I sat down on the bed.

"What was your dream when you were little, Hikki?" Yuigahama asked like a kid pestering me for a bedtime story. Maybe that was because of where we were sitting.

I didn't have a big repertoire of fanciful ideas to respond with, but I took a moment to consider. "Depends on your definition of *dream*, but... If just something like a whim counts, then, well, there was lots of stuff. I wanted to be a CEO or a millionaire...pro baseball player, superhero, manga artist, idol, police officer... Also a doctor, lawyer, prime minister, president. And an oil baron."

"Those are all money related. They're not dreams at all..."

"Yeah, well, now that I've said it out loud, even I'm wondering what the hell was wrong with me..." It made me kind of depressed. Not a very cute kid. Still not, if I do say so myself...

Yuigahama seemed to pick up on my calm little bout of self-loathing. "Oh, but!" she hurried to say. "When you said *idol*, I thought, *That's a real dreamer!*"

"That doesn't make it better. Just so you know, I was supercute when I was little, okay? If I'd just had a reason to, I'd have become an idol. And, like...what about you?" I asked.

She folded her arms with a *hmm* and tilted her head. "I… Yeah, there was a lot of stuff. I wanted to be a florist, a pastry chef, or an idol!" she said energetically, just like a kid with dreams.

"In a way, those aren't too different from mine," I replied, a crooked smile tugging at my lips.

But her innocent grin only lasted for a moment, and her expression quickly turned more mature. A smile crossed her face, and she stood from the bed. She took one slow step after another, as if leaving her childhood dreams behind there. "…Also, a bride and stuff," she said over her shoulder, then spun around to face me again.

She was standing in front of the kitchen, which was in the back of the booth. The tile on the wall was completely white, and the light coming in through the glass square that was made to look like a skylight rained down on her like a veil.

Her words felt too real to be called a dream, and I couldn't laugh them off or make a face.

Instead, I slowly walked into the kitchen, using that time to think up some joke. "That's not much different from me… A househusband has dreams, you know."

"When you say it like that, you totally don't…" Yuigahama's shoulders slumped, and she let out an exasperated chuckle. I think she laughed for my sake. Even under a source of light so bright it seemed deliberate, I could still feel something gentle in her smile. I was too bashful to raise my eyes.

You couldn't actually use the kitchen in this booth, of course, but they had a full set of everything, from cooking implements to utensils. It felt real, like you could start living here right now. I mean, they were selling these things, so obviously they should feel real—but they didn't quite, not in that way.

The furniture, the utensils, the kitchen, and the bed were all real, but fake at the same time. Wondering what made that distinction, I touched a cupboard.

Then Yuigahama clapped her hands. "Oh, wouldn't something handmade be a good idea?"

"Huh? Furniture?"

"No, the present. Like a cake."

For a moment there, the wheels of my brain were really spinning trying to figure out what the heck she was talking about. But when she said *present*, I suddenly remembered. *Oh, the present for Komachi! I knew that, I knew that. That was not because I forgot, okay, look.* While I was mentally generating a flood of excuses, Yuigahama's revelation showed no signs of stopping.

She started lining up the plates, knives, and forks, and then a mug, too, as she began an impassioned speech. "And then when we serve the cake, we put out a drink with it, in a mug…and that mug is actually the present! Wow! Yeah, that sounds kinda chic!" She put both hands to her cheeks excitedly. "Yes!"

"…You think? Is that chic?" I asked coolly, and her confidence in her design sense wilted a bit.

"I-it's fine! It's a bit like a surprise! It'll work!" Her cheeks flushed a little pink, and she began timidly returning the utensils to their places.

"Well…handmade actually isn't a bad idea." Her sulky reaction was so charming, I had to smile, and then I even said something sweet. In the most literal sense. "How about we go eat some dessert? For research purposes."

"Ohhh, that's a great idea! Let's go, let's go!" Yuigahama got real excited about that, poking and prodding me in the back, and we left the display booth.

Making something myself actually wasn't a bad idea. Some things will really appeal to the heart of the receiver, and the fact that they spent the time on you is touching. And if it's someone you feel affection for, then all the more so.

It really will sway your heart.

…Guess I'll do my best to make a cake for Komachi! And maybe through this process, I might just discover a new dream.

Yes, my dream of becoming the legendary Cure Patissière…

× × ×

Du Fu once said that the nation is crushed, but the rivers and mountains still remain. On the other hand, someone else once said, "My dreams are crushed, and I remain at my parents' house." Of course, that's me.

My dreams have been crushed. Though we went to have some nice desserts, nominally for research, I discovered the obvious fact that I could never make any of this, and my dream of becoming a Pretty Cure came to an end. After returning home, I went to bed in a huff.

But night would still turn to dawn.

The next day after that outing with Yuigahama, another school day passed without incident, and eventually classes were over.

There must really have been no real work to do for prom planning, just as we'd been told the day before in the student council room. There was no summons from either Yukinoshita or Isshiki, and here we were.

*If it's this late and nobody's messaged me, then can I just go home?* I wondered, feeling just a little uneasy. I couldn't help but glance over at Yuigahama. If anyone would be contacted, she'd get a message first.

Yuigahama nodded back at me. Then she waited for a moment when her chat with Miura and Ebina reached a lull before slipping away to come over to me. "What're your plans today, Hikki?" she asked with a cock of her head. If that's how she was asking the question, then she wasn't going to be helping with the prom.

"Going home. There's nothing to do."

"Oh…same here, so I'm going home," Yuigahama said, then immediately pattered back to her seat, waving at Miura and Ebina with a "See you guys!" before she got her stuff, threw on her coat, heaved on her backpack, and wound her scarf around her neck. "Then let's go."

"Okay…" I was completely confused as to how this had led to us walking back together, but I headed to the front of the classroom.

Then the door rattled violently. I'd just barely registered the sound when it was smacked open with a loud rolling of ball bearings that startled me.

Isshiki appeared, panting as if she'd run all the way there. The moment she saw us, she slumped limply, letting out a big sigh. "Phew, you're both still here…"

"What's wrong?" Yuigahama asked.

"…Can you just come with me?" As soon as she said it, she spun around the other way.

Yuigahama and I exchanged confused looks, but Isshiki's grave expression gave us no choice but to follow her in ignorance.

Isshiki rushed down the hallway, and we had to hurry to keep up with her. As we descended the stairs, I came up next to her and observed her profile.

Isshiki noticed my eyes on her, but her sharp gaze remained firmly ahead as if she didn't have the time to explain. Her feet were still picking up speed. "So we're kinda in trouble." With just that remark, she drew her mouth in a tight line. The harshness of her expression told me that this was serious, whatever it was.

Before I could ask for any details, we arrived at the room she wanted.

It was in the hallway that had the teachers' room, the admin office, the principal's office, and other rooms like that. I'd never gone in there before, but the plate read RECEPTION ROOM. Isshiki knocked on the door, then opened it without waiting for an answer and strode in.

I hesitated for a moment, wondering if I should follow her.

The moment the door had opened, I saw them: Miss Hiratsuka and Yukinoshita seated on the sofa nearest the entrance. They were facing away from us.

Opposite them was Haruno Yukinoshita, with her mother.

I didn't just have a bad feeling about their presence here. This wasn't a premonition. This was certainty.

Yukinoshita's back was hunched slightly in the face of her mother's calmness—or maybe I should say her detachment.

Her mother lifted her face to the open door. Her soft gaze, her mild smile, came from eyes so beautiful that you could get trapped in them.

The attention directed at us was the same temperature as it had been when it was directed at her own daughter. It made something cold run up my spine.

Isshiki reacted by bobbing a bow. "I'm very sorry for making you wait. About the prom, all of us discussed it together to make the decision… So I want all of us to be involved in any disputes about whether it will go on as planned," she said with determination, almost yelling it. Her hostility bled through in her voice, her manner of speaking, and her eyes. She didn't try to hide any of it.

Mrs. Yukinoshita smiled as if to say, *Oh dear.* "A dispute? Oh, it's nothing so dramatic. We just came to share our opinion with everyone," she said in a slow, gentle tone as if soothing a small child, then smiled brightly as she prompted us to sit.

Miss Hiratsuka turned her head toward us as well, nodding to indicate we should do so.

There were two black leather sofas with a low table between them. There was a three-person sofa facing the door we'd come in, while opposite that was the L-shaped sofa where Yukinoshita and Miss Hiratsuka were sitting. Of course, that was the side we went to sit on, which put us across from Yukinoshita's mother and Haruno.

Yukinoshita, who hadn't looked toward us even once since our arrival, got things started with a stiff and formal introduction. "…Well then, would you mind reiterating what you have to say once more?"

There was a hint of tension in Mrs. Yukinoshita's smile. Haruno was apathetically swirling her stir stick around in the coffee she'd been served.

The room was dead silent, almost frozen by the chill around the three Yukinoshita women.

Mrs. Yukinoshita seemed to sense that, and she smiled with extra gentleness. "About this prom—it has been expressed to me that the event should be canceled. Some of the parents have seen the photos that were posted online and have come to us. They've said that it doesn't seem very decent…that they're worried that perhaps it may not be appropriate for high school students." She carefully chose her words, then glanced over at Haruno, on standby beside her.

Haruno breathed a beleaguered sigh. "And the reception among the alumni is…mixed." From the way she was supplementing her mother's statement, I figured out the reason Haruno was here. She'd been sent in for supporting fire.

But the hint of a challenging smile showed in the corner of her mouth as she added, "…It's mostly positive, though."

"Even if it is a minority opinion, that doesn't mean it should be cast aside. If some people are saying they don't like the idea, we should be attentive to that," her mother instantly shot back. Her manner wasn't sweet enough to call chiding—*accusatory* would be more accurate. There was something authoritative about it. But Haruno let it slide over her with feigned ignorance, closing her eyes to bring her coffee to her lips again.

Yukinoshita's eyes were cold, and I could hear it in her voice when she replied. "…So then why are you here, Mother?"

"I am a member of the parents' association… And when the request comes from someone with a relationship with your father, we can't reject it out of hand… You understand that, don't you?"

Her face was smiling, her tone warm. Her manner was peaceful. She chided in a kind and understandable way. This was like scolding a child, not the way she'd treated Haruno before.

When Yukinoshita lowered her head, squeezing the hem of her skirt, her mother continued gently, "Of course, as long as things are done in moderation, I don't think they'll mind?" Her seemingly considerate smile, her slow and graceful tone, and her apparent willingness to compromise were all incredibly polite, but she was implying the complete opposite of what she'd said. And the words that followed expressed that directly.

"But we've looked into proms as well, and issues such as drinking and improper sexual conduct do occur. Some believe it's inappropriate to hold one as has been proposed for the appreciation party. Not to mention that when problems do come up, you won't be able to take responsibility for it, will you?"

"I explained this! If we work together with the parents' association and the school administration, we can prevent issues of that nature…" For just a moment, Yukinoshita raised her voice, but she quickly settled down. Her voice turned weak, almost sulking. "And we've received informal permission for it, haven't we…?" she added in a mumble, and then her gaze fell to a corner of the floor as she gritted her teeth.

Yukinoshita's mother listened with narrowed eyes, but once she was done hearing everything, she nodded. "I believe the parents' association was also careless in this matter. But it was ultimately only informal approval after a review of the documents, wasn't it? The ultimate decision was postponed until you actually tried doing it…"

"That doesn't make sense," Isshiki jumped in before she was even done speaking, ready to start a fight. "We talked about it beforehand so that the decision wouldn't be overturned later. And, like, isn't it the parents' job to discipline their kids so that they don't cause problems?"

Yuigahama's eyes widened at her determination.

"Isshiki," Miss Hiratsuka reprimanded her.

"…Sorry." Isshiki seemed to think she'd said too much and grudgingly apologized. But the pout on her lips showed she wasn't satisfied.

Haruno quietly turned away and tried not to smile. Of course, she was the only one.

Miss Hiratsuka bowed her head to apologize for her student's rudeness, and Mrs. Yukinoshita gave the smallest shake of her head to say she wasn't bothered.

"Of course, I believe the parents and guardians will have a variety of opinions. I doubt they want to forbid everything and restrict your freedom. I'm sure they're simply worried. If there's an uproar about it on social media, or individuals are identified and come to harm…such incidents are quite likely, aren't they? That's why parents are even more sensitive to such a big event," Mrs. Yukinoshita said, focusing her gaze on Isshiki. Her eyes flashed. She almost seemed to be enjoying how unusual she was.

"You said your name was Isshiki, is that right? As you've said, I believe parents and the school should make sure to teach their children about how to manage such situations and how to appropriately use the Internet. There are such initiatives happening in school education, and they're often incorporated into business seminars these days as well," she explained passionately, almost gleefully. That excitement when she was explaining something resembled her daughter Yukinoshita a lot. It was almost charming.

However, the moment that smile faded, so did the resemblance. "...But it's still difficult to say it's enough. Even adults who have studied the matter and should have sound judgment in that area will still cause online debacles and issues."

*And that went doubly so for children. So you shouldn't have this prom.* She didn't have to say it; I knew where this was going.

The students who had taken part in the filming had, quite honestly and without any pretensions, posted photos on social media without anticipating that it would become a matter for concern. Some parents were connected with their kids on LINE, and some parents would be snooping on their kids' Instagrams and other social media. And we on the student side hadn't been paying attention to that. Meaning some people *would* see this event as indecent and get aggressive about it.

"...Once you start talking hypotheticals, you can worry about anything," Yukinoshita said bitterly. She must have arrived at the same thought as me.

Indeed. It was ridiculous to worry about every single possibility, then cancel it because there was risk. If you were going to be like that, then you could also say the catering might cause food poisoning, so cancel it. No matter how many precautions you took, nobody could say for sure that it would be absolutely safe.

Yukinoshita's mother should, of course, understand that herself.

"With these negative views, I really do think there's no need to force the event. If the community is talking behind your back, it will hinder your opportunities right when you're entering a new stage in life."

So next she changed her approach, bringing in emotional arguments. With her eyebrows turned down in an expression of concern, she made her appeal. "An appreciation party is for the graduates, but it's also an important event for the parents, teachers, and other members of the community… No one was dissatisfied with the old appreciation parties, were they?" she said, turning to Haruno beside her with a tilt of her head. Haruno gave just one cold nod.

Yukinoshita couldn't say a word. *Critical hit*, I thought, and a bitter taste spread in my mouth.

If we'd come at it with the goal of addressing complaints about the old appreciation parties and then had decided to have a prom instead, that would have made it easier to gain understanding. But we'd come straight from the concept of prom. This would be difficult to push back on.

Isshiki leaned forward. "If you're talking about graduates, then we're future graduates, too. We absolutely have a right to make proposals about the appreciation party."

Her backward argument was actually brilliant. *Nice one, Isshiki.* When I stared at her, impressed, she glanced back at me with a triumphant chuckle. That seemed to get her going, too. "The other students at this school see the prom favorably, in fact. Most of the opinions on social media are positive…"

But she wasn't able to finish. The moment Isshiki took a breath, Mrs. Yukinoshita smiled and cut right in. "Perhaps that is the case with social media. But it's also important to listen to the opinions that aren't made public. Someone with authority, someone with everyone's trust, has that responsibility… You two make sure to remember that, too," she added to her daughters at the end. Same tone, same manner, but that last sentence was a very different temperature. Maybe that was why—Haruno snorted and let out a bored sigh, and Yukinoshita just froze.

At this point, I had a whole new perspective. I was really getting what Haruno Yukinoshita had once said about the one "scarier than herself." This was bad. It wasn't getting anywhere.

You couldn't fight this woman with logic.

At first, you would only see her listening with a meek smile and apparent understanding. She might even convince you she was lending an ear to your opinion and engaging in discussion.

But she wasn't. This was a style of counteroffensive. She'd turn your point aside with a smile, see how you would respond, then cut you with the return strike. If she'd just been using this to out-argue you and make you yield, that wouldn't have been so bad. But she didn't fixate on such matters—she drove you into the trap she'd set at the beginning.

She would not concede any part of her final conclusion, and to that end, she would feign sorrow or introduce emotion into her logic.

Yukinoshita's mother had said that it was nothing so dramatic as a dispute.

She was completely right. All along, she'd never had any intention of disputing anything, and she'd said at the beginning that there was no room for argument.

I was sure there were contradictions somewhere in her objections, some holes, but she covered them up with that mild smile and gentle tone. Even if you did find a hole to pierce, it would change nothing. She would take it with a smile and agree, right until she brought it to the same conclusion from a different angle.

It would be bad strategy to let her talk too much right now. The more she spoke, the more potential openings would vanish.

Isshiki must have sensed this danger as well. She glanced at me. I caught her look out of the corner of my eye, but all I could do was make a face. Sorry if she'd been expecting something from me, but this opponent was really too much. All I could do was direct her attack elsewhere.

"The school administration has given its informal consent, right? What's your view on this?" I asked Miss Hiratsuka, and all eyes gathered on her at once. Yuigahama and Isshiki seemed faintly hopeful. Haruno seemed vaguely amused as she committed to spectating, while Yukinoshita closed her eyes and waited for the words to come.

Yukinoshita's mother, on the other hand, leveled her with eyes as peaceful as calm seas.

Now the center of attention, Miss Hiratsuka smiled with her lips only. "Personally speaking, I would like to avoid instantly deciding to cancel the event. Our school has a tradition of valuing autonomy. My suggestion would be appropriately revising the problematic areas of the event plan while engaging in continued negotiations. That way, we can obtain cooperation and understanding from all parents and guardians."

As expected of a reliable adult. I was grateful she could end this sham dispute here and now.

Mrs. Yukinoshita had no objections to this suggestion to start over. "I believe that's a very reasonable view. Well then, I'll visit again. In the future, would it be possible for me to speak with the school administration?"

"I've informed my superiors. We'll confirm the date as soon as possible and touch base with you."

When that businesslike exchange was done, Mrs. Yukinoshita bowed. "I'm sorry for the trouble. Thank you very much… Haruno, let's pay our respects to everyone and get back."

"Ah, I'll leave once I've finished my coffee." Haruno pointed to her coffee cup, smiled as if she hadn't been paying attention to any of this, and fluttered a hand in a wave.

Her mother sighed with exasperation. "I see. Well then, I'll head back without you," she said, rising to her feet. Even after sitting for a long time, her kimono was not the slightest bit ruffled, and her bearing was just as dignified while standing. And with equal dignity, she called the name of her other daughter. "Yukino."

Yukinoshita's eyes only flicked away. Noticing that little reaction, her mother spoke slowly and gently to her. "I understand that you're doing your best. But come home a little earlier. There's no need for you to push yourself."

"…Yes. I understand." That was all Yukinoshita said before she closed her eyes.

Her mother smiled, seemingly at a loss, but eventually she seemed to come to a decision and began walking off. She bowed good-bye to us, and Miss Hiratsuka stood and followed to see her off. The two of them continued out of the reception room.

Once the door of the reception room was closed, a number of us sighed.

On the other side of the door, I could hear Miss Hiratsuka exchanging a few parting words with Mrs. Yukinoshita.

"Agh, I'm tired," said Haruno quietly. Maybe she didn't want to be heard. "Getting dragged along for this stuff is such a hassle…," she said. She drank down her probably cold coffee and made a face at it. Yukinoshita seemed to be swallowing something, too, although I didn't think she'd had anything to drink. Her lips were pressed in a hard line. The two of them had very similar faces.

Although, if you're talking about resemblance, then I'm sure it was their mother they took after.

The feeling of something foreign, or twisted, that I sometimes sensed in both Yukinoshita and Haruno, I could also see in their mother. That was what made me want to probe it. "Um… She said one of the members of the parents' association, but was it the chair of the association or someone like that?"

"No, no, it's some ridiculous honorary position, like trustee or something. Their job is to write authorization forms, because they have membership. But our father has strong community ties because of his job, and both his daughters are from this school, right? So we were asked to come out here."

*I see. A situation specific to someone in a position of local power, huh? To draw an example from my own life, I guess it's like the company exec at my dad's job or whatever. Apparently, if you go report to him when there's trouble, he says, "I'll go have a talk with them, too." He's eager to barge in on that person, even if you never asked him to. Although with Yukinoshita's mother, it's local people making requests to her, so I guess that's a little different, huh?*

As I was thinking, Haruno's voice suddenly turned glum. "...So what she wants basically doesn't matter. Since she got the request, she had to come here and say her piece, for appearances' sake," Haruno said as if it bored her, then snorted.

But I didn't think I could laugh it off. Something about it—something about that stance—reminded me of what a certain someone had said before, and it made me feel a bit sick.

As I sighed out the feeling, the reception room door opened, and Miss Hiratsuka returned. "Oh, damn" was the first thing that came from her mouth, along with a wry smile. She pulled a crystal glass ashtray from the shelf in the corner of the reception room, went to stand beside the window, and lit her cigarette.

Apparently, this reception room was exempt from the general no-smoking rule in the school building. Well, anyone brought to this kind of room would probably be getting VIP treatment, and some of those types would be heavy smokers. By meeting with them in a special space that lay outside the rules, the school would show their good faith and respect.

In other words, Mrs. Yukinoshita was being treated as none other than a VIP, and that was enough to tell me where the school administration would stand on this.

And perhaps Yukinoshita, who'd been a part of this discussion from the very start, felt that the most. Her straight-backed posture was no different from before, but there was darkness in her voice. "...How do you think the school administration will handle this?"

"I couldn't say. If it's just pictures on social media, then… Well, my bosses don't see it as that much of a problem, either." After a series of quick drags on her cigarette, Miss Hiratsuka smiled to put Yukinoshita at ease. But then she tapped the ash off the end and continued quietly, "…It's just that there are many fine people out there who will oh-so-graciously offer their opinions. We sometimes get e-mails or phone calls. *'Goodness me, those skirts are too short'* or *'They were out on the street being loud'* or *'They looked at me and laughed.'* Usually, we'll just say, *'Thank you very much for your valuable opinion; we will take it into consideration when disciplining students in the future,*' and if necessary, we carry out the discipline, and that's the end of it, but..." Miss Hiratsuka trailed off, blew out a puff of smoke, and sneered. "But when it's coming from this angle, it really will be seen as a bigger problem... We'll be forced to deal with it accordingly."

She was dancing around it, but that only meant one thing: The prom was canceled.

If you were to come up with similar cases for this sort of problem, you'd be counting forever. For example, once, there was a recruiting ad for a certain company posted at a certain train station. The ad had punch, with a slightly novel twist in the copy writing, so it went viral on social media and got a big response with tens of thousands of likes. Most of the responses were positive, seeing it as unique and fun. But within a few days, the company that had produced the ad wound up withdrawing it themselves. They'd gotten negative feedback via phone and e-mail and such, enough that it had become a problem for the company.

This happens a lot these days: Even if the reception is overwhelmingly positive, just a little bit of criticism is enough to warrant consideration and action, and not always by choice.

The ideas of compliance, political correctness, etc. have started to take root, and companies are now more strongly aware of areas where they should show consideration. Though that in itself is something to be glad of, this change in perception is still in a transitional period.

For that reason, terms like *inappropriate, inadvisable,* or *indecent* have sometimes been utilized excessively, and there have been some extreme reactions. You could say the same of the environment surrounding this prom. I think that's enough to understand the concept.

The problem here was what would actually be done.

"Can't you put pressure on the parents from the school side?" I asked. Since we'd received informal permission to hold the prom, sending us back to the drawing board didn't reflect well on the school. Even from this one point, I'd try being like, *Isn't there any way we could win you over?*

Miss Hiratsuka's eyes fell to the cigarette in her hand, and she paused for a moment of consideration. "I wouldn't call it absolutely impossible…but if you kids want to have the prom next year and beyond, then I think I shouldn't intervene." She crushed her cigarette in the ashtray, and when its flame went out, she turned back to us. After the smoke was gone, that distinctive smell with a heavy hit of tar wafted around. It stirred up my anxiety.

I didn't understand what she was saying, and it was showing on my face.

Then Haruno raised her voice in surprise. "…Shizuka-chan, you still haven't said?"

"I couldn't tell them when it hasn't been formally decided," Miss Hiratsuka replied calmly.

"You just couldn't say it," Haruno deadpanned, and the teacher averted her eyes awkwardly.

"…Urk, well."

Moving in for the next blow, Haruno let out a deep sigh and continued. "I mean, it's a public school, and you've worked at this school enough years. Last year was right on the borderline, so this year is definitely the last."

The fragments of their conversation basically told me what the situation was. But I couldn't bring myself to put that into words. All I had was an understanding that still felt unreal. *Oh, is that right?*

But Yuigahama tried to put it into words. "Um, does that mean…?" she began hesitantly.

"Well, that talk comes later." Miss Hiratsuka smiled brightly at her and brought an end to that line of discussion. "Let's leave it for next time." Then she turned her gaze to Yukinoshita and Isshiki. "So…what will you do?" she asked.

Both of them jerked their faces up. I scratched at my head as well, as if I could erase the shock from my face.

"What do we do…? Revise the issues in the plan…," Yukinoshita started to say, but then immediately shook her head. She must have realized herself that was meaningless. Impossible.

If you took out the dresses and dancing and the fancy party, then it wasn't a prom anymore. That would never satisfy the people who wanted it. But we couldn't just make some half-assed revisions to the areas where there had been complaints; it wouldn't get the okay that easily, not after having gotten off to such a rocky start. You couldn't please everyone involved. We were stuck.

"As the parents' association discusses continuing the prom, I'll think of some way we can gain their understanding…," Yukinoshita said, but her face was so pale and her voice sounded so feeble, she had nearly given up hope. But there was nothing else we could do.

I agreed. "Yeah, you're right. For now, we get what we need to convince them, and then…"

I stopped there. Yukinoshita, sitting next to me on the sofa, had grabbed my sleeve to stop me. Though the pull itself was weak, her squeeze wrinkled the cloth. "Wait. Anything beyond that is my job… It's something I should do."

"…This isn't the time to be fixated on that," I said, and Isshiki nodded. Miss Hiratsuka was watching over us, as she always did. Yuigahama didn't say yea or nay, or anything at all. Yukinoshita was choked silent, her lips pulled tight. I waited for her answer.

But someone else was the one to speak. "…You're gonna be the big bro again?" Despite the playful, teasing smile in her words, they left me cold. Haruno Yukinoshita, lounging on the sofa opposite us, almost seemed to pity me.

"Huh? What are you talking about?" It took me a second to register the anger in my reply, but I knew I wasn't being polite.

But Haruno giggled, as if my reaction amused her. "When Yukino-chan says she can do it herself, you can't just barge in and lend her a hand. You're not her big brother or anything."

She was just messing with me, but it bothered me enough to keep me from responding. From behind, I could hear Isshiki faintly sighing, and I found myself looking away. "That's not...what this is." My voice was weak and trembling, but also a clear denial.

I felt something like a gentle rub on my back, and when I lifted my head, Yuigahama was glaring at Haruno. "...She's important to us. Of course we'd help her out."

"If you care for her, then I think you should respect her will." Haruno's sigh revealed her irritation. "If the prom happens, that might change our mother's view of her somewhat. If she accomplishes it herself... Do you understand the implications if you interfere?" Her voice was hostile toward Yuigahama and me. Her sharp gaze seemed to shoot us down; her pointed words dug into our skin.

It was a heavy question. If you got down to it, I think she was asking if we could take responsibility for her future, her life. I couldn't answer that lightly. We weren't little kids who could act without considering the consequences, but we weren't grown enough to shoulder the full burden.

So Yuigahama, Isshiki, and I could say nothing.

If anyone here had the answers, then it would be Miss Hiratsuka. But she kept her silence and let the smoke rise from her cigarette, watching Haruno with an aged, stern smile.

Haruno seemed to notice, and her face softened. She was much gentler when she spoke to us next. "No matter how much you care for someone, it's not necessarily the right thing to always give them help... Do you know what a relationship like yours is?"

"Haruno, stop it... I understand." Yukinoshita didn't cut off the question—she spoke slowly, in a calm tone. When she gave a smile clear as crystal, Haruno didn't press her any further.

Yukinoshita was staring at her hands in her lap. Eventually, she quietly put together the words she wanted to say. "I want to really prove that I can do it myself. So...Hikigaya, I won't ask for your help anymore. I'm sorry it's such a selfish request, but...please. Let me do it," she said, lifting her head. Her expression was pure and calm, just like her voice.

But when our gazes met, her eyes grew dewy. Her faint smile was trembling now, and sorrow was bleeding through. She gulped a little, and her voice shook. "If I don't, I'll get…worse and worse… I know… that I'm being dependent. On you, and on Yuigahama—I say I won't rely on anyone, but then I always end up forcing you to take that role anyway." Yukinoshita's voice faltered under its melancholy weight.

Yuigahama lowered her gaze, quietly listening. Miss Hiratsuka silently closed her eyes, while Isshiki awkwardly looked away. Haruno watched coldly, but then she let out a faint breath, breaking into a smile.

But I couldn't help but say it. Even if the words were empty, if they meant nothing, I couldn't *not* reject what she'd said.

"That's…not true… That's totally wrong," I somehow managed to say.

But Yukinoshita slowly shook her head. "It's not. That's always how it winds up. I thought I could do better, but I haven't managed to change anything… So please."

Her wet eyes, her fragile voice, that ghost of a smile on her lips—all of it left me unable to speak. All that came out was air.

"Hikki…" Yuigahama tugged at my sleeve.

Still trying to respond, I let out a long breath to rein in my shaking and finally managed to nod. I meant to say *okay*, but I don't know how much of my voice even got out. But she had heard me anyway.

Yukinoshita smiled, nodded at me, and rose to her feet. "I'm going back to the student council room to consider how to deal with this moving forward." She bowed to Miss Hiratsuka, then started walking. There was no hesitation or faltering in her stride as she left the reception room without turning back. Isshiki jumped off the sofa as well, bowing and hurrying after Yukinoshita.

Once the two of them were gone, Miss Hiratsuka let out a sigh like air coming out of a tire and lit another cigarette. "Hikigaya. Let's talk again later. Go home for today. Yuigahama and Haruno, too," she said with a puff of smoke and a harsh, tired smile.

"…I'll do that," I replied, with the sense that my face mirrored hers. Extremely tired and extremely bitter.

It was too much trouble to put on my coat, so I held it and my bag under my arm as I gave Haruno a nod and stood from the sofa. I had to get moving, no matter what it took, or the exhaustion and despondency would keep me here forever.

Beside me, Yuigahama was there, getting ready to go. I turned my face toward her, speaking as gently as possible and smiling as best I could. "…See you, then."

"Huh?" Yuigahama's chin rose, and for an instant, she seemed surprised. But she appeared to quickly intuit my intention. She swallowed her bewilderment, grinned, and replied, "…Ah, yeah. See you…"

I took advantage of her kindness, giving a listless nod back at her, and left the reception room.

I wasn't confident I could have a real conversation with Yuigahama at that moment. It would've been better if I just couldn't speak—worst case, I'd run my mouth and say things I shouldn't say or shouldn't ask.

I left the school building, practically dragging my heavy legs as I headed for the parking lot. I unlocked my bike and pushed the old creaking and groaning machine toward the back entrance. It wasn't just my legs that felt leaden—my bicycle, body, and mood were all weighing me down. Hell, even my shoulders.

I felt a tug and turned around to see Haruno Yukinoshita, who'd apparently come running to me, with a hand on my shoulder as she let out a breath. "I caught up with you! Walk me back," she said, pretending to wipe the sweat off her forehead melodramatically. Then she just came right up by my side and started walking with me. Frankly, I was already exhausted, so I couldn't bring myself to fight it.

"Is just to the station okay?" I asked.

"Yeah… Since we were all there, I wanted to go back with Gahama-chan. But when I tried to invite her, she slipped away from me. She's got a good intuition, really."

"So do they usually try to run?" I quipped with a dry *ha-ha*.

But she giggled and shot back, "I don't usually let them get away."

One idiot with bad intuition had been trapped like this, so perhaps you could say Yuigahama, who had eluded the net, had good intuition.

Haruno gave an appreciative *hmmm*. "She really is sharp. She understands everything. Yukino-chan's thoughts, how she really feels, eeeverything."

I couldn't let that slide, and my feet stopped. I found myself turning toward Haruno.

She chuckled. "Oh, I guess it's not just her intuition that's good. She's got a good face, personality, and figure, too… She really is a *good girl*, huh?"

"You say that like it's a bad thing." She'd weirdly emphasized that last part, and I'd sensed she was smirking, too. The comment was malicious.

But even after I pointed that out, Haruno didn't seem in the least ashamed, hopping up onto the curb and facing me. "Oh? Doesn't that depend on who hears it? It's your fault for taking it that way."

"…You have a point."

What Haruno had just said seemed clearly insulting. But it's true I have the bad habit of reading too deeply into what people say. So she wasn't wrong about this.

Haruno stepped carefully along the curb as if walking on a balance beam and stabbed a finger at me. "Yep! So you're a bad boy, Hikigaya! Or maybe a boy who thinks he's a bad one. Who always thinks he's wrong… Just like right now."

She grinned as if to say, *Got you!* then hopped down from the curb. "And Yukino-chan is…," Haruno began, then suddenly raised her face to the red of dusk. Her eyes narrowed, as if the sky had burned her with its brilliance. "…a normal girl, you know. She likes cute things and cats, she's scared of ghosts and heights, she's worries about who she is… You'd find a girl like that anywhere." She cocked her head to the side in a silent question: *Did you know?* But she didn't say that out loud, of course, so I tilted my head back. *No, I don't.*

I didn't know if Yukino Yukinoshita could be called a normal girl. Beautiful, elegant, intelligent, athletic, etc., etc.—if you were to list every way in which she surpassed the rest, you'd go on forever. I think Haruno Yukinoshita, being the Perfect Devil Superhuman she was, was about the only person who could call her normal. Most people would see her as a totally different kind of creature.

At least, I've never thought of Yukino Yukinoshita as a normal girl.

But this sort of voiceless answer to a voiceless question did not meet the approval of the Perfect Devil Superhuman, and she sulked at me. She strode right up to me and glared. "Yukino-chan is a normal girl… Well, Gahama-chan is, too."

Haruno and I were face-to-face, with the bars of my bike between us. You may be forgetting this, but I am a normal boy, so when a pretty older lady gets this close to me, I get nervous. As my cheeks burned, I turned my face away just as she murmured softly, "…But when the three of you get together, you each play your own roles, huh?"

I didn't see her expression, but her sympathy and sadness showed in her voice. That lonely, gentle sound surprised me, and I looked right back at her again—but there was the usual Perfect Devil Superhuman fortified armor shell. Her face was frighteningly beautiful, and her smile was malicious.

"Now then, time for a question. What do you call the relationship between these three people?" She circled back around in front of my bike and leaned her forearms on the bars and front basket. I couldn't go back, and I couldn't go forward. She was staring coyly at me; she wouldn't let me go until I answered.

"…A good kid, a bad kid, and a normal kid? Is this the Imo-Kin Trio?"

"Boo. Wrong. I'm talking about *your* relationship."

The answer may have been wrong, but I had answered the question, more or less. But Haruno wouldn't release me, nor would she tell me the right response. ...So then I can't leave until I answer? Or until I give Haruno what she wants? Or is it the same question she asked in the reception room?

But if you've got a hint as to what sort of thing Haruno would like, then it wasn't anything that difficult.

The problem was that saying it was difficult. That was why it took so much time to brace myself. And all the while, Haruno was staring right into my eyes, making my task even harder. When I finally spit it out, I wound up surreptitiously turning my face away, and my voice squeaked.

"..................Like a...l-love triangle."

Haruno gave me a blank look. Mouth half-open, she tilted her head like, *What?* But suddenly it clicked; she spurted and then burst into loud laughter. "Ah-ha-ha-ha! So that's how you see it! Pff! And you said it yourself! That's hilarious! Ah-ha-ha! Ohhh man, my stomach hurts! I'm gonna pull a muscle, ow, ow, ow, ah-ha!"

"You're laughing too hard..."

Haruno released my bicycle, still holding her side as she kept on laughing. As my self-respect and self-consciousness were ground down to dust, I wanted to go home immediately. But I did have to ask, just in case. "Um, is that...the right answer?"

"Huh? The right answer? Ahhh, the right answer, huh...? The answer is..." Haruno wiped away the beading tears in the corners of her eyes, beckoned me with little motions of her hand, and put the other hand softly to her own lips. *Come listen.* Though I wondered why it was necessary to be so secretive about it, I leaned forward.

Her face drew close. A sweet scent reminiscent of flower nectar drifted past my nose, and the soft breath of her chuckle stroked my cheek.

It was so ticklish, I turned away instinctively. But Haruno took my chin with her other hand and wouldn't let me. Holding me fast, she brought her lips close to my ear to murmur, "It's called codependency."

The chill in her whisper felt more like truth than any "something real."

I had a dim grasp on the meaning of the term itself. I'd read before in some book that it was when you and another person are excessively reliant on your relationship, when you're addicted to being a captive in that relationship.

"I told you before that it's not trust." She giggled gleefully, and then suddenly her smile twisted obscenely. "Feels good to have her need you, doesn't it?"

Her enchanting voice hit my earlobes, and my skull tingled. I remembered now—there'd been more written in that book. What makes it codependency is not just the one depending, but the one being relied on as well. Being needed by someone is where they find their own value in being, gaining a sense of satisfaction and peace of mind.

As the mental images from every word tied themselves to my circumstances, it felt like the ground under my feet was shifting.

I'd been told many times. It had been pointed out to me that I was spoiling people without being aware of it. I'd been told I seemed happy to be relied on. And every time, I'd gone on about how I have a big brother nature or it's my job, so that's the way it was.

I felt nauseated with shame and self-loathing. How ugly and shallow, to play up my status as the aloof loner, while I was actually not so displeased about people making requests of me. I even felt pleasure from it. In so doing, I reinforced my raison d'être—it was beyond disgusting. I enjoyed being relied on without even knowing it. I wanted it, to a slight degree. Then when they didn't want that from me, I would tell myself I was just feeling a little lonely. What a repulsive, despicable character.

And then I was making excuses to myself through self-criticism, which was sincerely gross. I felt as if something under my ears was cramping, and saliva overflowed inside my mouth. I swallowed it down and let out a ragged breath.

If you wanted to call Yukinoshita's and my relationship codependent, then yeah. It was. And even if she wasn't actually relying on me, my old self would've wondered what was wrong with me, the way I'd been acting lately. If I was going to do some kind of codependency check now, a number of items would fit.

A sneer passed across Haruno's face, and then she immediately went off ahead. When I dragged myself after her, we eventually arrived at a small path by the park between the school and the station. Haruno glanced up at the wintry-looking trees on the boulevard, still barren of buds, leaves, or flowers, and murmured, "But that's now over. Yukino-chan will go on to become independent and grow up a little." Her proud words, her happy tone, and her sad profile as she spoke of her little sister gave me a sense of déjà vu. She'd said something similar on a night a little colder than this one.

Just like now, she'd been walking a few steps ahead of me as she had been talking about that.

I clearly remembered what she'd said then. Sometimes I would notice that and jokingly pretend I didn't, act smart, put on a show of throwing it away, and pat myself on the back for doing the right thing, but I'd never forgotten it, in the end.

The sun was descending, and the city was submerged in the twilight. Before I knew it, the path had come to an end, and we were approaching the main street in front of the station. At sundown, it was filled with people hurrying to and fro.

"This is far enough. See you," Haruno said with a casual wave, and she strode off.

"Um..." Staring at her feet, I called out to her hoarsely.

Haruno turned back to me midstep. She tilted her head with a grin and wordlessly asked for me to continue. It was so gentle that for a moment, my breath caught.

"So...what will she give up to become an adult?"

That smile, so much like hers, crinkled in sadness. "...A lot. About as much as me."

She hadn't told me a single thing, and yet her short answer could not possibly be clearer.

Haruno Yukinoshita disappeared into the crowd.

# 7 Even knowing that he will regret the **decision**...

That day was part of a warm spell, with a smattering of rain in the morning. Unlike the other day, it went by peacefully.

School was over, and sleep beckoned. With a big yawn, I was lazily getting ready to go when a loud pitter-patter of footsteps ran up to me.

In keeping with the mood of the past few days, Yuigahama tap-tapped on my shoulder. "Hikki, let's go!"

The moment we'd left the reception room crossed my mind, and all that came out of me was a sigh. When Yuigahama tilted her head owlishly to silently ask, *You're not going?* I quickly understood that was her way of showing concern.

"...Yeah, then let's go." I did a long, wide stretch like a cat and slowly got up.

We left the school and headed down the road to the station. Thanks to the morning rain, the two of us were taking the same way back. Yuigahama was quite chipper today, swinging her umbrella, chattering to me about various things as we walked.

"Oh, we talked about baking a cake, right? When I told my mom, she said we could use our place. She actually got pretty excited about it, um, and it was, like, really embarrassing..."

"I dunno if I could go over there... 'Specially after what you just told me...," I said.

Yuigahama smiled awkwardly, then stuck a hand in her pocket and pulled out her phone. "Hmm, but if it's your house, then Komachi-chan'll find out." Her eyes dropped to her phone. "Huh?" She stopped walking. "...I think the prom is in trouble," she said, showing me her phone. It displayed a screen from LINE—a "group chat," I believe. The header read *Service Club*, with the names "Yukino Yukinoshita" and "Iro-Iro Irohasu." I could make a lot of jokes about this, but when I saw the most recent message, they all evaporated.

"...The school administration has decided to cancel the prom? What the hell? What happened to that meeting about continuing?"

"Wanna try messaging them to ask?"

"...No, it's fine. It's faster to talk to the higher-ups when it comes to this. I'll make a call." And with that remark, I took a few steps back from Yuigahama and turned away from her. While I was waiting for the other end to pick up, I glanced over at her to see she was staring gravely at the LINE screen, occasionally shooting me anxious sidelong looks.

I was listening to the call sound with impatience when Miss Hiratsuka's sigh came from the receiver.

"What's going on with the prom?" I demanded before she could speak.

After another long sigh, she irritably said, "I'll give you the full *rundown* another day. Right now, we're in the middle of handling it. Once everything's blown over..."

"How many days do we lose, then? If you wait that long, we won't be able to recover."

"There's not going to be a recovery. Besides, do you even want to help with the prom?"

"A-ahhh, well... If they say down the line that it's on again, actually, think of all the work we'll have to do."

"...I'm not so sure about that. I don't think that'll happen."

There was certainty in her voice, but I instantly rejected that.

Even if the situation was dire now, would Iroha Isshiki give up that easily after digging in so hard? And Yukino Yukinoshita had finally stated her wishes out loud, so she would never let go of it without a fight. She wouldn't let that happen.

Miss Hiratsuka must have noticed my irritated sigh, as she groaned and gave up. "Guess I can't keep you in the dark, huh…? Yukinoshita was the one to request that I not tell you it's been canceled. You can put two and two together. Now that you know, tell me: Do you still have a reason to help with the prom?"

The moment I heard that, the words I'd been meaning to say all left me. I think I even lost my concept of time.

I didn't come back to earth until Miss Hiratsuka started calling "Heeeey" at me. "We're on the phone. I can't know what's going on if you don't use your words… I'll wait."

When she restated herself in an easy, calm tone, I finally adjusted my hold on the situation. *A reason, a reason, a reason.*

"The reason is…well, partly it's just my club, but also, like, we've gone too far to turn back." I was rambling as I quickly searched for the words, but there was no answer from the other end. Just a sigh and nothing after. It was irritating. *You get me, don't you?*

"You don't put these things into *words*. It's important—that's why I don't say it. I give it adequate consideration, then go through due process so that I don't screw it up… You're like that, too, aren't you?" *You didn't say you were being transferred to another school. Isn't that important?* I almost said. But though I clenched my teeth to keep it back, I could tell it had come out in my voice.

"…Hikigaya, I'm sorry. But I'll keep waiting until I hear it… Put it into words."

This was the first time I'd ever heard her apologize so gently, so sadly.

All my reasons had just vanished. Everything I could think of was tied to work or the club or Komachi. Even if I changed the phrasing or the terminology, I realized that everything came down to those.

So even when I tried to say something into the phone, my mouth just changed shape a bunch of times and wouldn't form words.

All that was left was about us. Saying "because we're codependent" would be amazingly easy to understand. It would be easy to say that I validated my existence by being relied upon. I could even convince myself of that. But it wasn't an answer. Codependency is a structure. It's not feelings. It could be an excuse, yes, but it wouldn't be a reason for me.

I wrung it all out, considering everything up to that point, exhausting every other option, until all that remained in my heart was regret.

But that was the one thing I didn't want to say. Because that was the most pathetic reason. But if I didn't say something, my damn teacher wouldn't let me get anywhere—or that was the excuse I knew she was letting me use.

So I pressed my forehead, letting her know with a dramatic sigh that I really didn't want to do this, and said quietly, "…Because I promised that I'd save her someday."

"Because she asked me" was just too obvious. There was no logic or lyricism in that utterly cliché turn of phrase. I absolutely loathed using it to say I would save her.

"That's fine… I'll make the time. Come right away," Miss Hiratsuka said with satisfaction, then hung up on me.

I put away my phone and returned to Yuigahama, a little ways away. With her eyes, she asked me, *How'd it go?*

"Sorry I made you wait… I'm going to see Miss Hiratsuka for a bit." After excusing myself, I said what had been decided and nothing more.

Yuigahama blinked. "Oh really? What're you going to do?"

"For now, just figure out what's going on. Honestly, there's nothing else I can do until I've got the facts," I replied. A pretty hopeless answer.

But Yuigahama cracked a smile. "…Oh. But if you'll go, I feel like things will work out somehow." Then she offered a few big nods of approval. As her head moved, a shining drop streaked down her face.

My breath caught.

That startled reaction was enough to draw Yuigahama's attention to her own eyes, and she immediately wiped her cheek with her fingers. "Huh? Ah! Like, it's just such a relief. Whew, dunno where that came from..." With a long sigh, she rubbed her fingers together.

She said it like it was obvious, so I tried not to be too shaken. "No, I'm the one who's surprised... Are you okay? Want me to walk you home?"

"Huh? Oh, I'm good, I'm good! It's fine. Happens all the time with girls." Pulling the sleeve of her cardigan over her hand, she dabbed at her eyes, then fiddled with her bun bashfully. "I just had no idea about anything, so...like, just that one tiny thing really is a relief. Actually, like...I feel okay now."

Well, she had seemed really serious when she checked LINE earlier. When you're really tense and then it all comes unwound, maybe you do get like that.

As I was staring at Yuigahama's face, her lips broke into a smile. "Don't be so dramatic. You can go, Hikki. Once I get home, I'll keep an eye on the LINE chat. If something happens, I'll let you know." She adjusted her bag on her shoulder and waved her phone, communicating her intention to go home.

"O-okay. Thanks. Then I'm heading off now. See you tomorrow. Take care on your way home."

"Oh, I live just around the corner anyway," she said, slowly waving her hand, and I started walking off at a similarly slow tempo.

After taking a few steps forward, I felt the urge to look back, but Yuigahama wasn't there anymore.

I let out a big breath and started running as fast as I could.

# Interlude...

It was a good thing I stopped crying.

It came on so quick, it caught me completely off guard. I kinda should've been watching out. Good thing I managed to fool him.

Yeah, it was a good thing I could hide it right away. And that he left right away. And that he didn't come back right away. If I had cried, then he wouldn't have been able to leave.

So it was a good thing the tears stopped.

I won't be that girl he feels sorry for. I mean, then he'd come save me again. Because he's my hero. Because when my friends are in trouble or are worrying about something, I know he'll help out. Because he's my hero. Because he has been from the very, very beginning.

Because he's already saved me.

My "someday" is already over. He doesn't have to be a hero—I just wanted him with me.

Because I know he's not a hero, I actually wanted him to hurt me.

I couldn't ask him not to go. I couldn't ask, *Why are you saving her?*

I didn't want to tell him not to be nice to me anymore.

I understood what she was thinking and feeling, but I couldn't give up, give in, and deny it like her. It should have been really simple, but I couldn't do anything. I made everything her fault instead.

Just like she was dependent on him, I was dependent on her.

I'm the one who's been forcing everything on someone else.

This should be for the best, but I still can't stop crying now.

I wish I hadn't been able to stop those tears.

# Translation Notes

**Chapter 1** ⋯ Eventually, **the seasons** change, and the **snow** melts away.

**P. 6**  "It was the day the world called Valentine's Day, or Dried Sardine Day…" February 14 was designated "Dried Sardine Day" in 1994 by the National Dried Sardine Association, as a play on the word *niboshi* (dried sardine), which sounds like the numbers two, one, and four. It's sometimes used cheekily to suggest that "Valentine's Day is canceled."

**P. 10**  "Somebody said that—Peter or Cheater or Carrousel or whatever." Peter is the stage name of Shinnosuke Ikehata, a singer, actor, and TV celebrity. Maki Carrousel is another actress and TV personality. *Cheater* is just Hachiman coming up with a similar-sounding English word.

**P. 10**  "*Chii is learning.*" This is a *Chobits* reference—a quote from Chii the robot—that Hachiman has made many times before.

**P. 14**  "…I suppose you would call that sort of thing a waste of effort." The original wordplay here uses the idiom meaning "a waste of bone-breaking effort," to which Hachiman corrects her, "I didn't break any bones, I just hurt my back," and Yukinoshita says, "It's a figure of speech. And what's the point of interrupting me?" She uses the idiom "break the back of the conversation," which means "to interrupt."

## Chapter 2 ⋯ Despite appearances, **Haruno Yukinoshita** is not drunk.

P. 33      **"This was way too 'final dungeon' for me, and I think it's wrong to pick up girls in a place like that."** This is a reference to the light-novel series *Is It Wrong to Try to Pick Up Girls in a Dungeon?*

P. 33      **"If I were Basho, I'd even be seeping into stone. What's with this guy Basho—is he Angelo or what?"** Matsuo Basho is a famous poet from the seventeenth century, and this is a reference to the poem "Hushed serenity / and the cries of cicadas / seeping into stone." Angelo is a character from *JoJo's Bizarre Adventure* who gets turned into a weird-looking rock.

P. 48      **"…*Muh-heh!* like the protagonist from a Mitsuru Adachi manga…"** This refers to a scene from *H2* where the protagonist is holding up a pair of panties and smiling while making the lewd chuckle *mufu*.

P. 48      **"…then I'll wind up with the same face as Tatsuya and Hiro!"** Hiro is the protagonist of *H2*. Tatsuya is the protagonist of *Touch*. They both have very similar faces…

P. 51      **"Even if both count as 'waiting,' they're as different as Aming and Yuming."** Aming is the name of a pop-folk duo—their debut song in 1982 is titled "I'll Wait." Yuming is the stage name for Yumi Matsutouya, a singer with a long career stretching back to the 1970s. This is a reference to her 1996 single "Ambush." "I'll Wait" is a straightforward "even if you love another, I'll wait for you" song, while "Ambush" is about a woman who plays at waiting while she's manipulating the situation to get a man to turn her way.

| | |
|---|---|
| P. 52 | **"I have to go lie down. And then I'll even lie about. And then I'll even lie down on the job."** The Japanese gag here is a fairly nonsensical one on "lie down" (lit: become horizontal) moving next to "do what you want" (lit: become vertical) and finishing with "freely and as one pleases" (lit: unlimited, horizontally or vertically). |
| P. 52 | **"...she works on sudden fevers, heart palpitations, and shortness of breath— Wait, is she some kind of heart remedy?"** He's specifically referring to Kyushin, the flagship drug of Kyushin Pharmaceutical Co., a natural remedy / Chinese medicine company. It's supposed to be a remedy for the heart. |
| P. 53 | **"I mean, like, I totally thought *Live TV Till Morning!* was a sexy show."** It is not. It's a late-night debate show mostly about politics. |
| P. 53 | *It's Morning! It's Live Travel Salad* is a travel show that runs in the mornings. This title sounds a touch sexier in Japanese, since *nama* (meaning "raw," or "live broadcast") is also slang for "unprotected sex." |
| P. 53 | **"Has the *Weekly Hachiman* dropped another explosive bombshell?!"** The *Weekly Bunshun* is one of the most prominent news magazines in Japan and is known for investigative journalism. When they make a big exposé, people often say "The *Weekly Bunshun*'s cannon has fired again." |
| P. 56 | **"'Oh, you're sooo niiice. Wooow. What a gentleman!' She smacked my shoulder like she was saying, *So you're the Gentleman Friend who's good at being nice to women, huh?!*"** This gag is rather more noticeable in Japanese, but Haruno's drawn-out *sugoooi* here is reminiscent of a line from Serval in *Kemono Friends*, to which Hachiman follows up with a meme line that doesn't actually appear in the anime, "You're the friend who's good at [blank]." |

Chapter 3 ··· **Komachi Hikigaya** takes him by surprise and gets formal.

P. 63 "Moxie energy wakety" (*yaruki genki neoki*) is a quote from Yui Yumekawa, protagonist of *Idol Time PriPara*—her main catchphrase is "dreamy-cute." Not to be confused with the original *Prism Paradise* series with the heroine Laala Manaka. She's the one who says "Capisce!" with a peace sign by her head.

P. 64 "*She's as calm as if she's been told the end of the century's coming. She's so calm, you might even think she's been made into a wax doll. Wait, that was Seikima-II, huh?*" Hachiman has referenced both these songs before—"Nai Nai 16" from the 1980s boy band Shibugaki-tai, which features the line "Don't freak out, the end of the century [*seikimatsu*] is coming," and the song "House of Wax Dolls" by the 1980s metal band Seikima-II.

P. 67 "*...it'll make both Aming and Yuming blanch. I'll pretend to be cute, and I'll do a good job at it.*" This calls back to his earlier joke. "Pretending to be cute—she does a pretty good job of it" is a line from "Matsu wa" (I'll wait) by Aming.

P. 67 "*...lying in wait behind a tree by the school, murmuring her name like Hyuuma Hoshi's older sister...*" Hyuuma Hoshi is the protagonist of the 1960s baseball manga *Star of the Giants*. His sister Akiko's most iconic scenes are of tearfully watching him from behind a telephone pole or other objects.

P. 69 **Jizo** is a bodhisattva who protects children, and these little statues are ubiquitous around temples, in woods, and on roadsides. They're often dressed in red clothing with little hats or hoods as protection from evil.

| | |
|---|---|
| P. 69 | **"It's a push-button quiz, fastest finger first! Get seven answers right, and you win! If you buzz too quickly three times, then you're out!"** *Fastest Finger First* is a manga about a quiz club—this reference is to the Japanese title, *Seven Right, Three Wrong*. |
| P. 70 | **"...I wanted to call for help like the dude from the insurance ads. Someone help...!"** The original is an explicit reference to Shinichi Tsutsumi, an actor who has been in a bunch of ads for the insurance company Axa Direct. A well-known one features him in a broken-down car in the middle of nowhere going, "Someone help...!" |
| P. 70 | **"Here a hi, there a hi, everywhere a hi-hi."** As in Volume 11, this is from a tongue twister about frogs, although it's more about hopping than greeting. *Kaeru pyoko pyoko, mipyoko pyoko. Awasete pyoko pyoko, roppyoko pyoko.* |
| P. 71 | **"Aha! Then she's a 'hot stud,' eh?"** This is based on the Internet meme *Hahan! Sate ha hizokusei da na* (Aha! Then fire element, huh?) over a picture of a swimmer with a silly expression on her face. The meme is pulled up whenever coming up with guesses that are very apparently wrong. Hachiman uses this meme a second time for "Aha! Then she's an eccentric, eh?" |
| P. 74 | **"My special skills include impersonating a lightning rod and also l'Cie heroes. Though I'm not that pretty."** The original gag here (swapped to a *FFXIII* reference) was "impersonating a lightning rod [*hiraishin*] and also Hirai Ken [an actor]. Though my facial features aren't as sharp as his." |
| P. 75 | **"Being that I also have experience with kids, I can recognize such feelings quite clearly. I'm the champion of children."** In Japanese, Hachiman says, "I am an *okosamaister*, so to speak," smooshing together *okosama* (formal/restaurant word for "child") and *meister*. |

**P. 75** "…I'll also emphasize my interest in politics to go after a collab on the next 'vote at eighteen' campaign. Ministry of Internal Affairs and Communications, are you watching?" The light-novel series *Oreimo* ("My Little Sister Can't Be This Cute") did a cross-promotion encouraging young people to vote, distributing the free booklet titled, *My Little Sister Can't Become the Model for a Campaign to Vote at 18-Learning about Voting at Eighteen with Kousaka Kirino.*

**P. 76** "*Does she mean like my own personal Hikaru Genji plan of winning over Keika to try to raise her into a wonderful lady? Right now, I'm making progress to rave reviews like a frantic Columbus. 'Welcome here' or however that song goes…*" Hikaru Genji is the titular character from the classic novel *The Tale of Genji*, in which he raises Lady Murasaki from girlhood to be his wife. Named after him was the 1980/1990s boy band Hikaru Genji. One of their songs, "Paradise Galaxy," features a line that goes, "Welcome here / let's play in paradise / peel the apple of your heart / adults can't see it / a frantic Columbus / they can't find the island of dreams." The "frantic Columbus" line became famous at the time as people speculated what it meant.

**P. 76** "…but if I caused trouble for the neighbors' children, it might be too much to bear. Maybe not for a bear, though." The original gag here is a pun on *shinobinai*, which means "can't bear." He follows it up with "In English, no ninja."

**P. 77** "…not knowing what to do, *bow wow wow woooow…*" This is a line from an NHK *Minna no Uta* children's song called "Inu no Mawarisan" (The dog policeman).

**P. 77** *Yan-mama* (short for both "yanki mama" as well as "young mama") was a slang term that was in for a brief time in the 1990s to describe young mothers (usually teen moms) who dressed in *yanki* fashion while caring for their kids.

P. 79  **"I didn't even have to bother asking one last bombshell question to nail the perp like Mr. Ukyou."** Ukyou is a detective from the drama *Aibou* (Partners). "May I ask just one last thing?" pretty inevitably comes up when he's questioning people and leads to clinching an interrogation.

P. 80  **"Perhaps thinking about something at the edge of a forbidden borderline, Kawasaki had a slightly pained expression."** "Ikenai Borderline" (Forbidden borderline) is an insert song in *Macross Delta*. One line goes, "Love at the edge of a forbidden borderline!"

P. 82  **"While preparing to hear *Is the water good?!* …"** This is a reference to a video that became a meme of a minor idol drinking from a bottle onstage, and guys in the audience start yelling at her, "Is the water good?!"

P. 82  *Run-tatta* is a nonsense word said by Mimi of the RPG *Princess Connect! Re:Dive*.

P. 85  **"And I came up with eel on the grill, with thyme."** The original Japanese pun here is *himatsubushi* (killing time) and *hitsumabushi* (eel fillets on rice).

P. 85  **"With a whistle of *twoo~* ♪ like Cobra…"** Hachiman is referencing the 1979 manga *Cobra*, an action/SF series with a number of anime adaptations, older and more recent.

P. 86  **"…the divine revelation came down on me. *Mikooon!*"** "Mikooon!" is the catchphrase of Tamamo no Mae in *Fate/Grand Order*. She's a *miko* (shrine maiden) / fox spirit.

P. 86  **"It's in the bag, ga-ha-ha!"** is a quote from the heroine of *Girlish Number*, which Wataru Watari also wrote.

P. 87   **A Got Nothing Fairy** (*sappari yousei*) is from *Magical Circle Guru-Guru*. It appears every time someone says the word *sappari* or something like it.

P. 90   **"I've achieved ultimate victory"** (*kanzen shouri shita*) refers to a meme involving a small monkey doing a victory pump in the air while playing the theme from *Gundam Unicorn*. The video is titled this.

**Chapter 4 ··· Until today, he has never once touched that key.**

P. 97   **"Aw, good grief! You teasing master Totsuka!"** This is a reference to the manga *Teasing Master Takagi-san*.

P. 97   **"As I was firing off sixteen shots per second…"** This is a reference to the old-school gaming legend Takahashi Meijin, who was famous for his sixteen shots per second trigger finger in the games *Star Soldier* and *Star Force*.

P. 101  **"Like that comedy duo who…did a hit-and-run that ended up putting them under house arrest."** Hachiman's anecdote is certainly about Yuusuke Inoue of the *manzai* duo Non Style, who got into a hit-and-run in 2016 and made it into a routine.

P. 102  **"Did you know, Raiden…?"** This is a line that comes up repeatedly in the 1980s martial arts manga *Sakigake!! Otokojuku* (Charge, boys' school) whenever the bystanders need to explain things happening in a fight. It was one of the earliest manga that did that a lot, so it was a bit of a trope-setter.

P. 108  **"If I don't say anything and five seconds pass, it'll time out and count as a wrong answer, and I'll get 'bad communication'! …Not that a perfect will help your affection score."** Hachiman is definitely talking about some Idolmaster game here; multiple ones have this dating-sim-style mechanic.

**P. 108** "**I see them about as frequently as the plates you get from the spring bread festival.**" In March, Yamazaki Baking Company has an event where customers can collect stickers to get a free plate called the "white smile dish."

**P. 110** "**…and figurines having a wild party…**" The Japanese line here, *dottan battan oosawagi*, is a reference to the OP of *Kemono Friends*, "Welcome to Japari Park."

**P. 118** "**Jumping abilityyy…I guess…**" is a quote from Shinzaki-oniisan, a real person (a zoo caretaker) who appears in *Kemono Friends*, and in the first episode he explains the appeal of the Serval with some apparent lack of certainty, which became a meme among fans.

**P. 122** "**Also, an unbelievably basic pick.**" The term he uses here in Japanese is *sabukaru kuso onna* (subculture shit woman), which was popularized by *Pop Team Epic*. The meaning hovers somewhere in between "fake geek girl," "basic bitch," and "not like the other girls."

**P. 123** "**…so she could have herself the whole fancy chic-y set. 'Cause, y'know. She's Isshiki…**" The original pun here is on "one set" (*isshiki*) and Isshiki's name.

**124, 125** "**Some *momo* are *sumomo*…so some *momo* and some *sumomo* are *sakuranbo*?**" "**Miss Yuigahama has lost it, huh…? She's gone bananas…or should I say gone peaches and plums?**" What Yuigahama said here was originally *sumomo mo momo…sumomo mo momo mo sakuranbo*, which literally means "plums are peaches, and plums and peaches are both cherries." It's a riff on a well-known tongue twister.

The original pun here was also on *sakuran* (deranged) and *sakuranbo* (cherries).

**P. 125** **"As a guy, I get more excited about Gwazines than limousines, you know…"** Instead of Gundam, this joke was originally about Virtual-On, a series of mecha-based dual-joystick fighting games originating in the arcade in 1995. Unfortunately, while Temujin (the flagship mecha in the series) sounds like *limujin*, Temjin (the English name) does not sound like *limousine*.

**P. 126** **Jooshy polly yey**, a slurred version of *juicy party yeah*, is a greeting coined by Chiaki Takahashi, a voice actor, singer, and gravure model. It has no particular deep meaning.

## Chapter 5 ⋯ Unsurprisingly, **Iroha Isshiki** is the most powerful of underclassmen.

**P. 137** **Kushiya Monogatari** is a chain restaurant that sells skewers. The name of the restaurant literally means "skewer house story."

**P. 139** **"I…tried to twist my cracking, creaking, and popping back. My spine had so much to say, you could call it a backache *monogatari*."** This *Bakemonogatari* pun originally read, "I tried twisting [*gurin gurin*] it around. It was as *gurin gurin* as the day Papa and I talked together" (punning on the word *green* here). This references a children's song—it's actually an adaptation of a song called "Green Green" by the American folk band the New Christy Minstrels, with entirely different lyrics written by Kataoka Akira. The Japanese lyrics are about a kid speaking with their dad on a green hill, who after that day leaves and never comes back.

**P. 140** **"*Whoaaa, where'd you hear that I haven't been getting enough sleep lately, huh? Where'd you hear that?*"** is another Jigoku no Misawa comic about annoying people.

P. 140   **"Fair play, fair duel"** is a catchphrase from the title cards in the original *Yu-Gi-Oh!* anime.

P. 140   **"I'm getting really sleepy... I can even see angels in front of me."** This is a reference to the famous children's anime *Dog of Flanders*, which ends with the boy Nello saying he's very tired as he and his dog Patrasche die together, and then angels spiral down to them.

P. 141   **"...it would carve itself into my memory like a graphic war documentary."** *Eizou no Seiki* is an NHK documentary series that covers a lot of material, but it does have some fairly graphic war footage in it.

P. 145   **"I wasted so many seeds bumping her stats."** Seeds are permanent stat-raising items in the Dragon Quest series. The long-awaited *Dragon Quest XI* came out in early 2017, a few months before the Japanese release of this book.

P. 146   **"No way, that general dies?! I got spoiled for the taiga drama!"** The taiga drama is the annual big-budget year-long historical drama aired on the NHK.

P. 149   **"The god of entrance exams once wrote: 'If the eastern wind blows through / then let your fragrance ride them / O sweet blossoms'..."** *Toufuu fukaba / nioi wo okoseyo / ume no hana* is a *waka* by Sugawara no Michizane, the god of academics Hachiman has mentioned his father has prayed to (at a Tenmangu shrine) for Komachi to pass her exams. The more explicit meaning of the poem is "Dear plum blossoms, if the spring winds blow, send your scent from Kyoto to Dazaifu (where I am). Don't forget spring, even when I'm not at home in Kyoto."

P. 149   **"So the plum trees have blossomed, but no cherry blossoms yet, huh?"** "Cherry blossoms bloom" is old-fashioned telegram shorthand for young students sending word to their parents, telling them they've passed their university entrance exams. The converse message, saying they failed, is "cherry blossoms fall."

**P. 152** **"She was weeping like a heartbroken celebrity…"** This is an explicit reference to an actor named Tatsuya Fujiwara, who bawled while reading the memorial address of the director who had been his mentor. It was big celebrity news about a year before this book was originally published.

**P. 154** **"I almost expected her to cry, S-Straw Hats…"** This is a reference to a 2ch copypasta about *One Piece* that goes, "Luffy: Whooo! Join our crew!! Me: S-Straw Hats… (sob sob)."

**P. 155** **"Dear Mother / Cherry blossoms bloom / regards."** *Zenryaku Ofukuro-sama* is the name of a 1970s TV drama about a young man trying to make it in Tokyo, with the framing device of sending letters back to his mom. This bit is also formatted like an old-timey telegram, including *sakurasaku* (cherry blossoms bloom) written in katakana, an old-fashioned way of letting your parents know you passed your university entrance exams.

**P. 160** **"But as they say, leaving things unsaid is a grace like a lily—er, wait, like a flower."** "Unspoken is a flower" is a Japanese idiom that means that being explicit about things left unsaid is boring. Hachiman misremembers it as "lily" (*yuri*), the cliché symbol of lesbian relationships.

**P. 162** *A Sister's All You Need.* is another light-novel series under the same Japanese imprint as this series (Gagaga).

**P. 163** **"*This report was a shock to Hachiman.*"** This is another reference to Yokoyama's *Three Kingdoms* manga, originally "This report was a shock to Kong Ming." Many panels of this classic manga have been memeified.

P. 172     "...call her Yukino Yukinoshita RX now. I was really starting to think, *I guess we can just let her handle everything on her own, huh? Even Isshiki was nodding like, …Let's leave this to RX.*" This is a reference to a *Kamen Rider: Black RX* meme, "I guess we can just let them handle everything all on their own." It's used whenever some all-powerful character shows up. The original line from the show was "Let's leave this to RX."

P. 172     "**Rare but often happens**" is another quote from the *FF11* player / 2ch anon legend Buront of "With this, I can win" fame. Many quotes from him have become memes.

P. 174     "**Yee!**" is the cry of the Shocker combatants in the Kamen Rider series. They're basically mindless mooks for the villain.

P. 175     "**I want to know defeat**" was a line often said by the professional competitive 2D fighting gamer Daigo Umehara and then popularized to a meme level by 2ch. He may have originally gotten the line from Keisuke Itagaki's martial arts manga *Grappler Baki*, but it's not certain.

P. 191     "**I have a lot of experience foiling other people's fun, after all.**" This was originally a pun on Hikigaya's name, saying, "They don't call me Hikitateyakun for nothing, after all." *Hikitateyaku* is a foil and also a reference back to Volume 6, when Yukinoshita called him that.

## Chapter 6 ⋯ **Yui Yuigahama**'s thoughts happen to turn to the future.

P. 204     "*You could practically live here if you ever got tired of home. Living space runaway Ikeon…*" The original line here was "*Kaguya-sama: Love Is War* was interesting, too, huh," a pun on *kaguya* (furniture store) and the name Kaguya. It was replaced with a *Space Runaway Ideon* reference.

**P. 204** "*...an armchair that won't break, even if you sit on it six million three hundred thousand times...?*" This is a reference to a viral video clip from the variety show *Hirunandesu!* in which they display an IKEA chair that has gone through six million three hundred thousand durability tests...and they immediately break it.

**P. 208** **The legendary Cure Patissière** is a magical girl from the anime *Kira-Kira☆Pretty Cure a la Mode*.

**P. 209** **Du Fu** was a famous poet of the Tang dynasty, often paired with Li Bai (whom Hachiman quoted in Volume 11) as one of the greatest Chinese poets.

**P. 220** "*...once, there was a recruiting ad for a certain company posted at a certain train station.*" This story is probably referring to a fake recruiting ad made by the city of Hachioji in 2016, the year before this book was published in Japanese, which went viral on Twitter. It seemed like a recruitment ad, while in fact its purpose was to let people know that street solicitation was illegal in the city. It included catchy satirical lines like "Requirements: people who want to be arrested, no experience necessary!"

**P. 221** "**I mean, it's a public school, and you've worked at this school enough years.**" Haruno is alluding to the fact that public school teachers are regularly rotated to different schools. Miss Hiratsuka probably will be gone next school year.

**P. 227** "**...A good kid, a bad kid, and a normal kid? Is this the Imo-Kin Trio?**" The Imo-Kin Trio was a group of three boys from a variety show that formed a pop combo, doing comic songs in the mid-1980s. Their theme was that one kid was a nerd/prep type, one was a delinquent, and one was very average.